I0735350

EXTRACURRICULAR

BOOK 1 OF 3 EPISODIC NOVELS

JOSIE BROWN

A BOOK BY

SIGNAL
PRESS

Library of Congress Cataloging-in-Publication Data is available upon request.

Cover Design by Andrew Brown, ClickTwiceDesign.com

Trade Paperback ISBN: 978-1-970093-02-5

V071619

throat world of college admissions is a must-read. As always, Brown's cast of characters are a delicious mix of sweethearts, scoundrels and the just plain morally corrupt. Never predictable, *Extracurricular* is immensely enjoyable."

—Meredith Schorr, author of *The Boyfriend Swap* and the *Blogger Girl* series

"Delicious, hilarious, and addictive, *Extracurricular* has all the hallmarks of a classic Josie Brown book: fleshed-out, juicy characters, a to-die-for plot, and a ripped-from-the headlines premise. I absolutely loved it and must read the entire series!"

—Samantha M. Bailey, author, *Woman on the Edge*

SOMETIME IN THE NEAR FUTURE

Book 2, in fact...

CHAPTER 1

*T*he San Francisco restaurant chosen for the FBI's first sting in the college admissions investigation that went by the name "Operation Sis-Boom-Bah" was renowned for its exceptional wines (including a 2001 Pomerol Bordeaux), and the fact that it had just netted *Food & Wine*'s highest honor, its Grand Award.

None of this would be notated, however, in Transcript No. 1-00351 of the video recording made of that initial meeting between Cooperating Witness Number One and her targets, Suspects Numbers One and Two.

Nor would there be any reference to the fact that Cooperating Witness Number One insisted that the Bureau honor the restaurant reservation, which she had secured a year in advance of the FBI's sting operation. Case in point: her clandestine client meetings only took place in the best restaurants. Those anxious for her services frequented the same renowned boîtes and expected nothing less of her. It was the unwritten rule that she would pay for these meals—or, in this instance, be reimbursed by the Bureau.

One of the two agents in charge of the case, SallyAnne Jagger, winced at this thought. Austerity was embedded in the rulebook of the country's domestic intelligence service. Still, proper consent from their very reluctant division director was given when the operatives in charge—SallyAnne, along with her partner, Lionel Porter Polk VII—made a believable case that the restaurant's mirrored walls would afford them close-range surveillance of the meeting from several angles, especially if they happened to wangle a couple of stools at the bar immediately across from their witness' dining booth.

"Easily doable on a Monday night," their witness had assured them as they made their way to the restaurant in an FBI-issue unmarked van, tricked out with state-of-the-art surveillance equipment that was to be monitored by a third Bureau operative, Riley Kemp.

Unbeknownst to their witness, this was just one of her numerous random acts of entitlement that had earned her the code name "Maleficent." SallyAnne had come up with it after listening to court-sanctioned surveillance audio in which their witness had coerced one desperate mother to participate in her scheme with a cruel lie: "Besides losing out on better jobs and being ostracized by her more successful friends, your daughter is much too pretty to end up in junior college—where surely, she'll be mauled by the gangs who roam the halls there."

SallyAnne, a product of a junior college that fed into the state university that eventually earned her a jurisprudence graduate degree, let loose with a litany of obscenities that would have impressed a prison yard bully.

From then on, the codename stuck.

The restaurant in which the sting was to take place was located in Presidio Heights, a well-heeled neighborhood of stately Edwardian mansions with the occasional Victorian townhouse thrown in for whimsy and a little color. As they made their way down Washington Street, Lionel pulled out something from one of the van's custom shelves: a tiny, soft flesh-toned disk.

"Put it in your left ear," he instructed. "It allows us to talk to you in case we need you to say something specific."

Maleficent shuddered. "How vulgar! It'll look as if I'm wearing a hearing aid."

"You can cover it with your hair," he suggested. To make his point, he loosened the lock she'd just pushed behind her ear. "See? Like that."

For a second, their eyes met. When she smirked, he turned toward the shelf again, but he was smiling.

SallyAnne wasn't. She knew Lionel hadn't meant it as a flirtation, but it was disconcerting that Maleficent took it that way.

Lionel next pulled a small alligator-skin clutch from the shelf and handed it to Maleficent.

She gawked, repulsed, then tossed it back at him. "What's this? Have you been slumming at Ross Dress for Less?"

"No! It's from, um, Macy's." Lionel pointed to the label, which read GIANI BERNINI. "It's a designer bag. We've embedded a camera. Since it matches your dress, I thought you'd—"

"Well, you thought wrong!" Maleficent rolled her eyes. "'Bernini' is a house brand—ergo, a cheap knock off. One look at the logo and I'll be the laughingstock of all my clients!"

"Oh...kay. Well..." Lionel looked over at SallyAnne and winked.

Maybe he was amused, but she wasn't.

Lionel shrugged off SallyAnne's scowl. As another idea struck him, he reached into a different shelf. This time he pulled out a bejeweled spider brooch. "Okay, then, you'll wear this. It's embedded with a state-of-the-art microphone and is somewhat less conspicuous."

He attempted to fasten it on Maleficent's little black dress, but in the moving van, the task was virtually impossible. Although Washington Street was mostly empty of traffic, Lionel was stymied by the periodic Uber pick-ups and drop-offs, not to mention the van's sudden stops at each corner crosswalk.

Suddenly, Riley took a sharp turn. To SallyAnne's horror, to brace himself Lionel's hands went to Maleficent's chest. To Sally-Anne's relief, at the very last second, he dropped his arms to avoid a possible claim of battery.

They fell to the floor. Lionel landed on top.

Maleficent's response was to slap him, but she was smiling.

He leaped up first. Always the gentleman, he held out his hand to help her to her feet, but she smacked it away. Instead, Maleficent steadied herself on the van's built-in shelves. Then, with the regal bearing of a Victorian side-saddle equestrian (apropos, since Maleficent was quite adept at this revived sport), she rose upright —not an easy feat, considering her short, tight dress and four-inch heels.

Snatching the brooch out of Lionel's hand, she snapped, "Must you ruin my dress? My God, man! *It's an Oscar de la Renta!*"

SallyAnne rolled her eyes. Maleficent's disdain disgusted her, but not as much as Lionel's deference to the woman.

As if talking to a four-year-old on the verge of a tantrum, Lionel gently but firmly replied, "Sorry, but it's our best bet for getting clear audio."

"I've topped the *Nob Hill Gazette*'s 'Best Dressed' list three years straight. Just one glance at that cheap piece of tin and the marks won't believe a word I'm saying anyway," Maleficent retorted.

"Can't you just tell them one of your students made it for you?" Lionel replied.

His suggestion was met with a French curse.

Her response startled him. But by the blush creeping up his neck, SallyAnne realized he was aroused too.

Figures, she thought.

They'd been partners for three years and through a baker's dozen cases—all high-profile white-collar crimes. At first glance, one couldn't imagine why their division director had seen fit to pair them. Standing side by side, they made an odd couple. Everything about SallyAnne was short: her height (she was just five-feet-two-inches tall), her hair (jet black and bluntly bobbed), and most definitely her temper. The daughter of a postman and a librarian, she had worked her way out of the Bureau's assistant pool after acquiring a night school degree in Criminology from the University of Virginia.

In contrast, Lionel was tall, fair, and had the stoic bearing that naturally comes from being the most recent of seven consecutive generations of Lionel Porter Polks, all alumni of Harvard Law School.

He wore the mantle of old money well. This invariably gave their more privileged suspects the mistaken impression that he would sympathize with their plight in getting caught. It also encouraged their hopes that, perhaps, he'd bend a rule or two for this wayward Cantab (Harvard), or that complicit Yalie (Yale), or the other imprudent Quaker (University of Pennsylvania).

Lionel encouraged this misnomer by talking their language: of private club memberships, friends they might have in common, and of the need these days to put up with those lucky enough to have gotten a leg up in their world via Affirmative Action (women, people of color, gay, trans, whatever). At this last, their gaze would shift toward SallyAnne, as if to imply, see what I mean?

After warming them up, Lionel questioned them gently on the specifics of their crimes. Viewing him a soft touch, they lied through their teeth, even after being warned that they were under oath.

Lionel's encouraging demeanor never changed. It was up to SallyAnne to bring down the curtain on their devious act. She played the heavy, countering with fact in response to their fiction. Then, in her blunt, unvarnished way, she'd bark away at them, an unrelenting bulldog digging up the bones of their crimes.

When they finally cracked, they'd eye Lionel as if he were a traitor to their class.

Lionel always answered their silent glares with a shrug and the appropriate Latin phrase: *Lux et Veritas* ("Light and Truth") to the Yalie. For the Quaker, it was *Leges Sine Moribus Vanae* ("Laws without Morals are Useless"). Only one word embodied a Harvard man's shame: *Veritas* ("Truth").

When presented with the evidence against her, Maleficent's face never twitched a muscle. And her response when Lionel reminded her of her alma mater's motto—Radcliffe's *Indsyria Didat* ("Industry Enriches")—was to snicker, "It does indeed."

Instead of being angry with her, Lionel chuckled at her audacity.

SallyAnne's knowledge of Latin was limited. Still, intuitively, it struck her that something had gotten lost in Lionel's translation. When Maleficent joined him with a coy giggle of her own, Sally-Anne realized they were speaking the same language after all: attraction.

As with any suspect, Bureau operatives were just as adept at reading even the most trifling inflection in their partners. In Lionel's case, willowy blond ice queens with steely blue eyes and lips that never rose beyond a smirk were his Kryptonite. In SallyAnne's opinion, the fact that a well-heeled crook fleecing some investment firm had a closet filled with Brioni suits—or in Maleficent's case, was helping the parents of spoiled brats steal college admissions slots from hardworking, better deserving students while decked out in Oscar de la Renta—didn't make her any less culpable.

Up until now, she'd never doubted that Lionel felt the same way. She had to shut down his infatuation with Maleficent, and quickly.

"Listen, lady," she growled, "your dinner dates may be 'marks' to you, but to the Bureau, right now they're designated only as 'suspects'—which is a long way off from 'defendants.' *Ergo*"—SallyAnne loved that Maleficent winced upon hearing that word—"if they can't be incriminated, you are royally screwed."

SallyAnne tore the purse out of Lionel's hand and shoved it against Maleficent's taut, possibly Spanx-trussed abdomen. "Now, if you want to shave a few years off what could be a long sentence, I suggest you take your designer phone and your designer makeup and any other designer crap you have in that overpriced designer handbag and stuff it in here. That includes the credit card already approved by the Bureau. Now, when you get to your booth, you're going to place this flat on the table, like this"—by twisting Maleficent's wrist in a painful position, SallyAnne also flipped the small purse horizontally—"so that the clasp is pointed at the suspects. That way, the video camera will pick up your interactions with them."

Maleficent's eyes narrowed to the point where only her long, feathered lashes were visible.

For a while, it seemed as though time stood still.

SallyAnne had had enough. Grabbing the brooch from Maleficent's hand, she added, "If it ruins this overpriced *schmatta*, well too bad. You are wearing this bug, even if we have to stick it up your—"

"What Operative Jagger is trying to say is that any possible reduction in your sentence will be largely predicated on the success of this operation. It's strictly up to you, Ms.—"

"Really? '*Ms.*?' Come now, Lionel! A moment ago we were snuggled together on the filthy floor of this mobile monstrosity. Plainly, that puts us on a more intimate basis—"

"One block out!" Riley shouted.

To make the point that the time for coy innuendos was over, SallyAnne pointedly pinched the bodice of the de la Renta and then pierced it with the brooch.

Maleficent's painful squeal might have been in protest that the lines of her frock were now forever ruined, but more than likely it resulted from the brooch's pin prick. Riley had stopped quickly to avoid running over a nanny wrangling a double baby carriage and a leashed Doberman as she crossed the street.

Maleficent's screech was loud enough to wake the poor woman's charges. But by the time she calmed them down, the van was already a block away.

The sting couldn't start until Maleficent's curses, threats, and tears had subsided. Lionel watched her worriedly as she touched up the make-up smudges. "Why did you have to be so hard on her?" he hissed to SallyAnne.

"Don't you understand what she's doing?" SallyAnne retorted. "If she's lucky enough to shove these suspects and a few other narcissistic parents into the defendant column, sure, maybe some judge will be kind enough to carve a few years off her sentence. But as far as I'm concerned, for what she's already done to all the kids who should have gotten into those colleges but didn't because some over-indulged cheats took up their slots instead—well, hell, Lionel! I hope he throws the book at her. Don't you?"

"Of course I do," he declared.

SallyAnne exhaled, relieved. *Thank God he's not totally smitten.*

"You know, I can hear everything you're saying," Maleficent muttered.

"Good," SallyAnne snapped back. "And I'll bet you don't feel an iota of guilt."

"Of course I do," Maleficent retorted.

She was lying. SallyAnne knew this because her eyes stayed firmly on the mirror.

In fact, through the mirror, she could see Maleficent's sly grin.

"Ladies—please!" Lionel sighed.

SallyAnne couldn't wait to take her down.

THEY DROPPED MALEFICENT ON THE BLOCK BEFORE THE RESTAURANT.

Riley then turned the next corner. At that point, Lionel and Sally-Anne got out of the van and walked back toward the restaurant. In the meantime, Riley had backed the van into a parking space right across the street, informing them and Maleficent via their earbuds of his great luck in finding a spot so close.

As they entered the restaurant, Lionel asked SallyAnne, "Do you think she'll behave herself?"

He got his answer: a snort.

THE HOSTESS WAS ALREADY SEATING MALEFICENT. THROUGH THEIR earbuds, the agents listened as she demanded a booth directly across from the bar, as per Lionel's instructions.

A moment later the hostess was back at the entrance. SallyAnne informed her, "We'd like to sit at the bar."

The young woman smiled. "Sure, follow me."

As Maleficent had predicted, the bar was practically empty. While passing by, they ignored her, but their eyes swept over the booth.

Watching them, Maleficent held up the Bureau-issued clutch purse. Then, with theatrical aplomb, she slapped it onto the table.

"Ouch!" Riley groaned into their earbuds.

Lionel frowned. Like SallyAnne, he was quite aware that surveillance equipment was sensitive.

"Cooperating Witness One, please angle the purse a bit to the right so that I have a fuller view of both you and the empty side of the booth where Suspects One and Two will be seated," Riley commanded.

Maleficent shifted the purse ever so slightly. "You mean, like this?"

"Yeah, something like that," Riley declared. "But without your middle finger blocking the center of the screen."

Lionel and SallyAnne took a closer look at the booth. Yes, Maleficent was indeed shooting Riley a bird, albeit upside down. Feeling their eyes upon her, she ignored their stares but flipped her wrist so that now her middle-finger salute was aimed in their direction.

Lionel groaned. Like her, he finally recognized Maleficent as a hostile asset.

About damn time.

By grabbing the two stools at the closest end of the bar, Lionel and SallyAnne were now directly across from the banquette where Maleficent waited for her clients: a couple named Gretchen and Seamus McCoppin.

The bartender frowned when Lionel ordered a glass of seltzer water with a lime. The goatee'd hipster's scowl deepened when SallyAnne echoed the order. Then, feeling guilty about it, she added, "Oh…and your house red."

She felt redeemed by the bartender's grudging nod.

Maleficent was also ordering. Through their earbuds, her command to her waiter—"Martini. Dirty, with two olives. And bring it fast!"—came in loud, clear, and obnoxiously snide enough to make Lionel wince.

The bartender placed their drinks in front of him. So that Lionel understood that in no way did she expect the Bureau to pick up the cost of her wine, SallyAnne pulled a credit card out of her purse.

"Don't be silly." Lionel patted her wrist, then handed the bartender the card he used for Bureau expenses.

"Oh!… Well, thank you," she murmured. For just a moment his hand lingered over hers. She wished time could stand still.

Sadly, it couldn't. They were on a mission. To get the optimum sight line, the agents twisted their barstools so that they were knee to knee—something SallyAnne didn't mind in the least. That way, they'd each have a partial view of Maleficent's booth while pretending to be a couple in love. One of them was pretending, anyway.

In seemingly no time at all, the restaurant filled up. Even the bar was getting crowded. Many standing there stared longingly at the lucky diners already seated at tables. A few of the bar's patrons were obviously regulars. When they walked in, all they had to do was nod at the bartender, and a minute or two later he'd place their drink in front of them.

The McCoppins came in on the next wave of diners. SallyAnne recognized them from her numerous stakeouts of the couple's grand mansion, which filled a half block on nearby Jackson Street. To exchange air kisses with Gretchen, Maleficent raised up from the banquette. She then offered Seamus a handshake. By the look on his face, she must have squeezed it firmly.

"Was she signaling him?" SallyAnne wondered out loud.

Lionel watched Seamus for a long moment before shaking his head. "Nah. It was a power play on her part. She claims this pair is low-hanging fruit, but the emails Seamus exchanged with her are still too nebulous for our case. If she doesn't nail them on this, she's got to come up with someone else."

He had a point.

Instead of worrying about whether Maleficent could pull it off,

SallyAnne would do what she knew he'd expect of her: play the role of the infatuated date.

This wasn't much of a stretch.

Not that she'd ever let Lionel in on that secret. Should he ever suspect as much, unlike some of the other agents, he would follow the rulebook to the letter and would request another partner.

No, she'd prefer to keep her mouth shut, even if it meant a broken heart.

———

"Shall I order a few hors d'oeuvres?" Maleficent forced her lips into a smile that she hoped looked natural enough. To hide her jitters, she raised her hand and snapped for their waiter. "The amuse-bouche here is to die for! And having seen your wine cellar, Seamus, I know you'll appreciate the Bordeaux I ordered." She pointed to the bottle that the sommelier had already opened.

Seamus glanced around warily. "Well, maybe a glass—but no food. We want to make this short. I'll be damned why we have to do this in public! What if someone overhears us?"

Maleficent's heart skipped a beat when she noticed his eyes lingering on SallyAnne—until she realized he was gazing at her crossed legs.

Men are such pigs, Maleficent thought. And he's sitting with his wife, for God's sake!

Not that it would have mattered to Gretchen. They were two peas in a pod—both vain and covetous for attention from the opposite sex.

For that matter, if one hadn't known they were husband and wife, one might easily assume that they were twins. Together, they had sandblasted the ravages of middle age from their bodies, minds, and souls. Their faces, devoid of all laugh lines, had been stretched into caricatures of their more youthful selves. Not that they could smile naturally anymore. Their lips, plumped with fillers, drove their smiles into unnatural lines that ran beyond the corners of their mouths and into their cheeks, giving them the appearance of crazed clowns. Their bodies were tautly sculpted. Looking at Gretchen's chest, Maleficent wondered how many ribs she'd had surgically removed to get a waist thinner than Fawn, her seventeen-year-old daughter. As for Seamus, his arrogance was a given, but she assumed his flashpoint temper had something to do with the steroid injections that resulted in forearms that would make Popeye envious. No gray strands could be found in the unnatural chestnut hue on either of the McCoppins' lush heads of hair.

Maleficent stifled the urge to slap his face—not for Gretchen's sake, but for her own. She didn't have time to dawdle, what with the Feds breathing down her neck. If she wanted to lighten her rap, she'd have to make the McCoppins ante up—and fast.

"Hey, you called me, remember?" she huffed. "So if you have something on your mind, speak up."

"Yeah, okay, I do!" Seamus' fantasy of being entangled in Sally-Anne's legs dissipated in the heat of his anger. "I want to know why I had to hear about your super-secret college admissions program from one of the other dads—some VC yutz who claims to have been behind Uber's third round of financing—and at a school basketball game, of all places!" He scowled. "Hell, if anyone deserves your personal attention, it's our Fawn! Jesus, when I think of the boatload of money we've given to Ashbury Academy—"

"And time!" Gretchen chimed in. "I've been the chair of every school auction since Fawn's sophomore year—"

"Don't interrupt me," Seamus boomed. Turning back to Maleficent, he added, "I sit on *the goddamned board, for Chrissakes!*"

His shout pierced right through Maleficent's ear. She wondered if it may have blown out the hearing device hidden there.

"Please, Seamus! Keep your voice down!" Glancing around, Gretchen nodded in Lionel and SallyAnne's direction. "You're attracting attention."

Maleficent's eyes shifted toward the FBI agents just in time to see them look away, mollified at being noticed.

Just my luck to have these Keystone Kops assigned to me, she fumed.

She forced an encouraging smile onto her lips. "Not to worry, Seamus. I'm expanding the program to include a couple more students—but fair warning, they will be accepted on a first-come basis only."

"Fawn is a perfect candidate for the program," Gretchen insisted. "If anyone deserves special attention, it's our daughter. Poor thing is always so distracted! Her cell buzzes constantly. Did you know she was diagnosed with ADD when she turned eleven?"

"Bullshit. She's boy crazy," Seamus grunted. "I'm beginning to think we should have signed her up for an all-girls Catholic school. Not that we remember our own experiences with those hard-assed nuns so fondly."

Gretchen blushed at her husband's indiscretion. "Truth be told, I'm at my wits' end! I'm doing everything I can to make Fawn understand how important the right college will be to her future. I've threatened to take away her phone if she doesn't study. And every year since second grade I've made sure she signed up for at least three extracurricular activities. My God, she's taken lessons on every kind of musical instrument known to man!"

"Only to quit them within a week," Seamus barked. "We could outfit a full symphony orchestra with all that noise-making crap in our basement."

"At least she's still cheerleading," Gretchen pointed out.

"Yeah, wow, great. So she shakes her pompoms in a damn uniform that leaves almost nothing to the imagination," Seamus groused.

Only because Fawn ordered her uniforms two sizes too small—on purpose, Maleficent thought. She knew better than to say that out loud.

"It still counts as an extracurricular," Gretchen argued. "It's all that testing that's holding her back! She hates them and refuses to study for them. Not that I blame her. She's taken Pre-SATs since sixth grade!"

"And we all know how well that's gone over." Seamus rolled his eyes. "Every time she takes one, the grade is worse than the last one!" He shook his head. "It's been a damn waste of money."

"The only thing left is—well, prayer." To prove she meant it, Gretchen crossed herself. "Seriously, what else is there?"

Maleficent looked down at her wristwatch. It was a Vacheron Constantin and had set her back about seventeen thousand dollars. She sighed deeply—not because she felt sorry for Fawn or for that matter her parents, but because she'd probably have to put it on eBay if she were to cover her defense attorney's already humongous bill. "Not to worry," she cooed soothingly. "Fawn is a perfect candidate for this college admissions program. You see, it's for students who are—well, to put it delicately, 'at risk.'"

Gretchen blanched. "'At risk?' Fawn is not mentally deficient! Granted, she's not the best test-taker, but that's because—"

"She's lazy," Seamus insisted. "Well, that, and she has the attention span of a gnat—"

"Let me be blunt," Maleficent interrupted. "Fawn is at risk *of not getting into an Ivy league college.* And, frankly, considering her GPA and her study habits, it's unlikely she'll get into any state school either."

Gretchen's face lost all of its color. "Are you telling me that our only option is junior college?"

"Not necessarily." Maleficent leaned in. "As Seamus has already told you, I've initiated an exclusive concierge college counseling program that guarantees acceptance to at least one of three Ivys."

Gretchen nodded. "Yes, he mentioned something about it. But he didn't explain how it works."

Maleficent shifted her gaze to Seamus.

He shrugged.

Why that son of a bitch. He hasn't leveled with her that they're here to sign off on the bottom line! What, was he too afraid to explain it to her, or was she just too stupid to get it?

Not that it mattered. It was parents like the McCoppins that irked Maleficent most. Getting them both on record agreeing to the scheme would be a delight.

Unless Gretchen said no.

Damn it, Maleficent thought. If she balks and talks him out of it, I'm screwed. They have to take the bait…

Maleficent smiled as if she'd just won an Oscar. "Quite simply, I've built a network of decisionmakers within certain colleges who act as—well, let's just call them 'pre-admission advocates' for those students who aren't readily identified as an exact fit."

"Oh…" Mystified, Gretchen murmured, "I didn't know the universities provided such services."

"Frankly, Gretchen, they don't. But rest assured these strategically placed staff members will point us in the direction of least resistance. Just as importantly, they are ready, willing, and able to sign off on students with unique qualifications for, say, certain little-known sports, or specialized academic programs, or clubs where fewer students are competing for the available spots."

Gretchen frowned. "For example?"

"Here's one: I have a contact at Fawn's first-choice school who runs a university-sanctioned club. He calls it 'Best Face Forward.' It actively recruits admissions candidates who are an inspiration to others and have proven this by volunteering for non-profit causes."

The guy she referred to was a teaching assistant who directed several quasi-legitimate clubs that met enough of the university's minimal requirements to be run on campus. Maleficent paid him handsomely to write enthusiastic recommendations on her clients' behalf.

Gretchen shrugged. "What with cheerleading practice and AA's sports events, Fawn won't have time for any volunteer work between now and the end of basketball season. And besides, it's like pulling teeth to get her to do anything that takes her away from her clique of besties."

Maleficent chuckled. "Not to worry! No one is asking her to actually *show up* at these volunteer events. She can get by with a few photo ops. We'll put Fawn in tee-shirts bearing the names of a few little-known non-profits and—*voila!*—we've got all the proof we need. Oh, and she'll write a few paragraphs imagining her experiences at such events. She'll then post them to her social media accounts. You know, Instagram, Snapchat—"

Gretchen shook her head. "We don't allow Fawn onto social media. Every parent knows that colleges troll those entities to find out all the ways our children are getting in trouble!"

"Valid point," Maleficent purred.

Especially in Fawn's case, despite her mother's assumption otherwise. After Seamus contacted her, Maleficent did a deep dive into Fawn's social media presence. The result was eye-opening. Too much so. Unbeknownst to her parents, Fawn was prominently featured on several sugar daddy websites. She'd also created a YouTube video in which she demonstrated a seductive way to eat a banana.

When Maleficent informed Seamus of his daughter's indiscretions, she'd quoted a fee of one hundred thousand dollars "to make Fawn catnip to college admissions directors." She now realized she'd sold herself short.

To offset Gretchen's concern, Maleficent added, "In this case, the photos won't be posted on Fawn's social media accounts but those of the benefiting nonprofits."

Creating websites for fake charities would be no small task, and the black-hat hackers up for the job weren't cheap. The McCoppins' rate just went up exponentially.

Gretchen nodded slowly, but by her pursed lips Maleficent realized she was still unconvinced. "When Fawn gets on campus, what if she's too busy to join this club?"

"Once your daughter is attending the university, going to club meetings are optional."

Gretchen frowned. "Wouldn't that be lying?"

Seamus guffawed. "That's the whole point, Gretch! It'll have to be faked because she's too lazy and too selfish to have done this do-gooder crap in the first place!"

"Oh!..." As if weighted down by this reality, Gretchen dropped her head. When she found the strength to raise it again, it was to fret, "Even so, what about Fawn's grade point average?"

"As part of the program, I will personally coach her on those subjects that seem to be the most challenging," Maleficent vowed.

"That would be all of them," Seamus muttered.

Ignoring him, Maleficent continued, "And I'll also nudge her teachers to do all they can to increase her comprehension of their test material so that we can inch up that meddlesome GPA."

Gretchen's lower lip trembled. "There's still the issue of her Scholastic Aptitude Test. And, from what I've heard, there's only one more scheduled before transcripts are due to the colleges."

"Yes, well that does present a major hurdle." Maleficent shrugged. "However, as part of the program, Fawn's test will be given a leg up at the discretion of the proctor."

"What does that mean?" Gretchen prodded.

"Woman," Seamus huffed, "what she's trying to say is that someone else will be taking Fawn's test for her."

Turning to Maleficent, Gretchen asked, "Is that... is that true?"

"Yes."

Gretchen's eyes grew large. "Then... this cannot be sanctioned by Ashbury Academy!"

So that there would be no mistaking her meaning, Maleficent looked her straight in the eyes. "It isn't."

"And it's got to stay that way," Seamus warned Gretchen. "Do you understand?"

Gretchen's mouth tensed into an anxious moue.

Maleficent froze as Gretchen processed this new reality.

Finally, Gretchen nodded meekly.

First crisis averted.

Maleficent found herself breathing again. She continued: "As I explained to your husband, I am not an employee of the school but an independent contractor whose job is to assess and assist Ashbury Academy's junior and senior students on their college admissions process. As for this specific program, it is of my own creation. But because the methods needed to guarantee success are somewhat unorthodox, the program is run independently of the school." She sighed. "And thanks to Seamus and a few other board members, it was approved so that, at my discretion, I could solicit specific parents whose children I deem are most at-risk."

Gretchen's blank stare seemed to go on interminably.

In Maleficent's ear, Riley murmured, "Did the mic go dead?"

That was Maleficent's cue to bring it home. Steeling herself, she added, "At this point, if you're not interested, no need to continue. Shall I?"

The McCoppins exchanged glances. Finally, Gretchen whispered, "Yes."

Maleficent stifled the urge to leap up for a victory dance.

Now, time to close this deal…

She smiled grandly. "Which brings us to a very delicate topic…"

SALLYANNE WAS SO ENGROSSED IN MALEFICENT'S DECEIT THAT, AT first, she didn't feel the tap on her shoulder. When it dawned on her that someone was trying to get her attention, she looked up and found herself gazing into the eyes of a man who seemed vaguely familiar.

Her mind raced through the possibilities. An old acquaintance? Maybe a former colleague? Perhaps a prior conviction now out on parole?

It couldn't be the latter. Otherwise, his playful smile would not be lifting her spirits, making her heart race, and sending a thrill through her.

"Is this seat taken?" The man was pointing to the now empty stool on the other side of her.

That voice…

SallyAnne had an uncanny ability to hear a voice just once and remember it forever. In this case, she'd listened to his years ago: when he'd been interviewed on the radio.

By the way he now slurred his words, she was surprised she'd recognized it at all.

She had explicitly listened to the show because he was her favorite author. He'd earned that honor with his debut effort, a coming-of-age novel entitled *Extracurricular*.

The face on the back of that oft-read book's well-worn jacket cover now stared down at her.

When his author photo was taken, he'd been two decades younger. His hair had been thicker and longer, his physique thinner, and his life hadn't yet suffered the gravitational pull between great success and some catastrophic fall from grace noted so nonchalantly in the press.

She was so stunned that she murmured, "No, not at all—*Mr. Gable!*"

Her apparent interest in the stranger earned her a scowl from Lionel, who expected her undivided attention for the task at hand.

Intrigued by her recognition, Egan Gable plopped down hard on the stool. "Do we know each other?" He leaned in closer.

Too close. He exhaled enough Scotch to make her eyes water. Taken aback, she stammered, "I read your book—*Extracurricular*. In fact"—the words came out of her mouth before she could stop them —"it's my favorite."

Egan's eyes softened. "Thank you for that. In fact, *THANK GOD* for that! I thought you were another infernal AA parent!" Without pretense, he scanned her head to toe. "But of course, you're much too young to have children of your own."

When their eyes met again, she blushed.

Suddenly, SallyAnne noticed that Lionel was staring at her too. But unlike Egan, he wasn't smiling. "Um…AA?" she stammered. "You… you mean Alcoholics Anonymous?"

"In this case, no," he chuckled. "Albeit, many of AA's—that is, Ashbury Academy's—teaching staff are chip-carrying members." Egan's last word was accompanied by a burp. Noting her dismay, he quickly added, "Not me, mind you."

Her anxiety had nothing to do with his sobriety and everything to do with the mention of Maleficent's school. Was he here to meet with their cooperating witness?

Egan Gable waved at the bartender. "Speaking of which, may I buy you another"—he looked down at her barely touched glass—"wine? Or, perhaps something a bit more adventurous? I can vouch for the fact that the barkeep makes a mean Sneaky Pete: whiskey, coffee liqueur, and just a splash of milk—"

Lionel leaned over SallyAnne and proclaimed, "Sir, do you mind? The lady is on a date!"

SallyAnne gasped. She never thought she'd hear those words come out of Lionel's mouth, let alone so—*so fervently*. She turned to face him, only to realize he was staring back—

As if he were seeing her for the very first time.

It was the same look he'd shared with Maleficent when she'd teased him about her alma mater.

SallyAnne's cheeks felt as if they were on fire.

A deep blush was creeping up Lionel's neck as well.

Egan, obviously too drunk to notice, chortled, "Well, you've got an odd way of showing it, sir! Not only are you ignoring this, this"—a second burp came out loud enough to turn a few heads—"this beautiful young woman, the whole time I've been chatting her up you've been staring over there, at that over-inflated Barbie doll!"

Swaying precariously, he swung his arm toward Maleficent—

At which point he took a closer look at her.

Suddenly, his eyes opened wide, as if they were no longer hazed. "Well, well! It seems I know Barbie—and for that matter, her plasticine friends too—Ken and Midge." As if attempting some semblance of sobriety, he straightened his tie, and then patted it flat against his shirt. "If you kind gentlefolk will excuse me, I think I'll mosey on over and pay my respects."

He walked off quickly but seemed to be listing to port.

Like Lionel, SallyAnne's fear that Egan Gable might ruin their sting operation had them ready to grab him and yank him back. It didn't help that Riley was yelling something at them through their earbuds. From what they could make out he seemed to be saying: "Let him go! She just said she's expecting him!"

Maleficent knows Egan Gable? SallyAnne's jaw dropped at the thought.

For some reason, she found this new bit of information disconcerting.

In truth, it was downright depressing:

My favorite author of all time is not only a lush but he also has awful taste in women.

A Few Minutes Earlier...

"...Which brings us to a very delicate topic"—Maleficent was saying—"the cost of Fawn's participation in the program. As you can imagine, such guarantees aren't cheap." She faced Seamus. "In fact, after hearing some of the hurdles Gretchen just pointed out, to do Fawn justice I must reassess my previously stated fee."

Seamus's glare left Gretchen cowering. When he turned back to Maleficent, he snarled, "How much now?"

She thought for a moment, then declared with a shrug: "Two hundred and fifty thousand."

"You've got to be out of your mind!" Seamus sputtered.

"On the contrary," Maleficent assured him. "It took a lot of work to set up a network that assures your daughter will end up in a college worthy of your investment in her." She glanced at her watch. "Time for you to decide if she's worth it. If not, no harm no foul. However, in an hour I'm meeting another set of parents who were disappointed you'd beat them to this appointment slot."

The color went out of Seamus's face. "You didn't mention our names to them, did you?"

Maleficent frowned. "Of course not! When it comes to this program, I'm the soul of discretion—for obvious reasons."

Seamus muttered something indistinguishable.

Hell, if I can't understand him, Lord knows the Feds can't, either!

Irritably, she asked, "Can I take that as a yes?"

"Yeah, okay," he grumbled.

"Alright then." She handed him a business card. "When you return home, wire a donation in the correct amount to this charitable organization. In fact, it's the recipient of Fawn's new extracurricular activities. In return—*huzzah!* Automatically, you'll receive a tax-deductible receipt."

"Well, that's something anyway..." Her husband, who silenced her with a scowl, did not share Gretchen's relief.

"Tomorrow I'll begin Fawn's transformation into the student we all know she should be," Maleficent promised.

Unsaid was obvious: should be—*but isn't.*

Not that the McCoppins needed their noses rubbed into this unflattering reality.

Gretchen leaned in so close that Maleficent thought she was going to kiss her.

Why? For being some sort of lifeline for Fawn? Ha! If only she knew!

Maleficent's instinct was to recoil. Instead, she steeled herself, only to realize Gretchen was whispering in her ear: "Please... Fawn mustn't know anything about this!"

Maleficent shrugged. "Mum's the word."

The vow was barely out of her mouth when she heard her name followed by the exclamation, "Well, I'll be damned! Small world, isn't it?"

The McCoppins blanched at the man approaching them.

Maleficent stifled a curse—one that she might have shouted out loud, and in English, no less.

Egan Gable...?

What the hell was he doing here?

She forced her lips into a smile before declaring, "Ah, well, look who's here too—AA's illustrious literature professor, Egan Gable!"

Noting how Gretchen's eyes lit up, she then lowered her voice so that only the McCoppins could hear her say, "By the way, Mr. Gable is my top candidate for SAT proctor. I know how much Fawn dotes on him."

"Oh? Well, …that's great, I guess." For some reason, Gretchen seemed both elated and upset by this bit of news.

Has he… and she…

Ha! She is such a harlot!

Maleficent wasn't surprised in the least. Like daughter, like mother.

Egan's appearance gave the McCoppins the perfect excuse to skedaddle. No one was more pleased about this than Maleficent. She had nothing but disdain for her marks.

OPERATION SIS-BOOM-BAH

[Transcript #1-00351(A) between Cooperating Witness Number One (CW-1) and Person of Interest Number One (POI-1)]

CW-1

Fancy seeing you here.
(Stares back at Agents Polk and Jagger)
Slumming?

POI-1

What, with that pretty little damsel at the bar? Are you jealous?
Surprise, surprise! Not that I blame you. She struck me as smart and beautiful—and kind.

CW-1

She is also a…
(Pauses)
Jesus! Never mind! Enough of this bullshit—and enough of your little head games, Egan Gable! Oh, and as far as I'm concerned, our little deal is off.

POI-1

No... *NO!* You can't renege on what you promised!

CW-1
Says who?

POI-1
But—but... Please... don't!

CW-1
Well... Since you're begging. Perhaps we can work something out.

POI-1
(Sighs)
I told you twice already. I'm just not that into you—

CW-1
Don't be a fool! I don't mean sex, you imbecile! I'm giving you back
what you so desperately want—
(Pauses. Then:)
If you'll agree to be the proctor for Ashbury Academy's SAT test.

POI-1:
(Suspiciously)
Are you joking?

CW-1:
Not at all... But you must do everything the job entails—to the
letter.

POI-1:
(Shrugging)
How hard can it be?

CW-1:
Just the usual. Of course, the most challenging task concerns the

seven special needs students. Their math portions must be substituted. Will you have a problem with that?

POI-1:
Why should I? Like you say, they're special needs, and all that implies.

CW-1:
I thought not.
(Sighs:)
There's something I hadn't mentioned before. It is a necessary evil. It involves the essay portion.
(Pauses:)
You're also to provide substitute essays for those students.

POI-1:
(Frowning:)
How is that even possible?

CW-1:
It probably means pulling an all-nighter, but, unfortunately, it goes with the job.

POI-1:
Wait... I'll be staying up all night with the kids?

CW-1:
Don't play stupid, Egan. It doesn't suit you.

POI-1:
(Frowning:)
You've got to be kidding me!

CW-1:
Suddenly, you have a conscience?

(Clicks her tongue:)
I assure you, the pay will make it worth your while.

POI-1:
(Pauses. Then:)
Oh yeah? How much?

CW-1:
Fifteen thousand.

POI-1:
(Snorting:)
Knowing you, you're pocketing at least a hundred thou.

CW-1
You arrogant bastard!
(After a long pause:)
Alright then! Thirty-five thousand. Take it or leave it.

POI-1:
(Pauses. Finally:)
So, how does this little scheme of yours work?

CW-1:
A week from Friday I'm to get the SAT answer keys for both math
and reading, as well as the essay questions. That night, I'll drop
them by your place along with the names of the students involved.
After they take their tests, you're to substitute the math and reading
portions with ones that you've already filled in correctly—especially
the math portion, although, so that the tests look valid, you're to
miss one or two answers in the reading questions. And Egan, just
make sure they are different mistakes on each student's test, okay?

POI-1:
Yeah, yeah, okay, whatever. And what about the essays?

CW-1

The way the SAT board weights things, a well-written essay is merely icing on the cake. I know you well enough to appreciate your bullshitting skillset. I'm sure elevating the students into the literary stratosphere should be child's play for you. And since you already teach these students, matching the essay topics to their voices shouldn't be that difficult for you.

POI-1:

If you say so.

(Sighs)

One caveat, babe: I'll want my money a week before the test, or it's no go.

CW-1:

(Seductively)

That's the easy part. In fact, I can stop by later tonight with the cash and a receipt for—let's call it "services rendered."

POI-1:

(After a pause, then a resigned shrug:)

Sure, why not?

———

REALIZING THAT EGAN AND MALEFICENT WOULD BE PARTING WAYS ANY moment now, Lionel directed SallyAnne to make her way to the van first. "That way, Romeo doesn't have a reason to stick around."

She nodded but said nothing. Still, she was flattered that Lionel would assume as much. She was out the door in a flash.

A moment later, Egan left the table too. By then, SallyAnne had joined Riley in the back of the van, where he was watching Maleficent on the monitor. Pointing to her, he muttered, "She's one cool bitch."

SallyAnne hoped he didn't mean that as a compliment.

As directed, Maleficent paid her bill with the credit card in the purse. When she rose to leave, she noticed that Lionel was now sitting alone at the bar. She'd been given strict instructions to ignore the agents, but she could not resist the urge to saunter over. She even dared to take SallyAnne's stool.

She waited until the bartender went off to make her signature martini when she murmured to Lionel, "I'm scared. I hope you know that. And I'm doing my best to help you—"

"Cut the bullshit," he muttered. His lips barely moved as he stared straight ahead, but his words came out clearly and firmly. "We're the ones helping you—*to save yourself*. And lady, from what I can tell you actually enjoy taking the others down with you. So if you want sympathy, look elsewhere. In the meantime, head for the van so that you can turn in your gear."

Maleficent stared at him but knew better than to say anything. Instead, she tossed a twenty on the bar, then did as she was told.

Between the time Lionel put Maleficent in her place and she arrived at the van, Riley had finally stopped laughing at Lionel's putdown.

Although SallyAnne was also impressed, to hide it from Riley she merely shrugged.

Maleficent entered the van. Without a word, she pulled out the ear mic and tossed it along with the clutch purse to SallyAnne. As for the brooch, she practically ripped it off her dress. When Sally-Anne offered to help, she snarled, "Don't you dare touch me."

A few minutes later, Lionel showed up. He sat up front with Riley.

When they dropped Maleficent in front of her home—a high-rise building on Russian Hill with a straight-on bay view—it was up to SallyAnne to tell her: "You did a great job in covering your tracks.

Too good, in fact. Unless you figure out a way to get evidence on the other six families, we'll have a difficult time convincing the judge that you're doing your best to cooperate. In these few weeks before the SAT test, I suggest you call to set up meetings with the other suspects to go over the process again with them. That way we can record their corroborations."

Maleficent purred, "My, my! Aren't you the little taskmistress! Silly me—I thought naming names would be sufficient." She stuck out her hand in a Nazi salute. "I'm on it, *mein Führer*." She slammed the van door on her way out.

<hr>

RATHER THAN HEADING BACK DOWNTOWN TO THE OFFICE TO TRANSCRIBE the video, Lionel suggested they tackle it at SallyAnne's place, which was just a few blocks away in San Francisco's Cow Hollow neighborhood. The idea seemed reasonable enough. Despite the look of longing he'd let slip in the restaurant, SallyAnne had no illusions that he'd breach protocol over it.

After she typed it up, they read it over. When Lionel got to the part where Maleficent was left alone with Egan, Lionel suddenly declared, "You need to change something." He pointed to the first time in the transcript that SallyAnne labeled Egan Person of Interest Number One.

"But...why?" she asked "He isn't yet a suspect or a defendant—"

"You're right, he wasn't—that is, up until the moment he agreed to participate in Maleficent's scheme. Ergo"—Lionel smirked as he said the word—"in keeping with Bureau policy since we'll soon be arresting him for conspiracy to commit fraud, we can go ahead and use 'Defendant Number Three' as his descriptive."

"Granted, he conspired. But how do we know if he committed the overt act of actually accepting the money?"

"Maleficent doesn't know it, but we're still recording her through her cell. Remember? In fact, Riley is still on surveillance. He followed her over to Gable's apartment and texted a confirmation ten minutes ago—along with a few jealous comments about your crush's staying power."

"Oh." The impact of this revelation was heard in her soft delivery.

Lionel clicked his tongue in mock dismay. "Agent Jagger, I'm beginning to think you're sweet on Defendant Number Three."

To deflect the heat she felt in her cheeks, she retorted, "Don't worry. I'm not. For that matter, if it were true, would the thought of it make you jealous?"

"Heck, yeah, it would." He shrugged. "But... Just... Never mind." To avoid her gaze, he looked at his watch. "I should take off."

She nodded.

SallyAnne followed him to the door. When he opened it, he stood there just long enough for her to give in to her impulse to do the unthinkable: she raised up on tiptoes to kiss him.

She'd aimed for his cheek but he turned his head, and their lips met instead.

He didn't pull away. In fact, he took her in his arms.

When they finally parted, neither said a word. But there was longing and shame in his eyes. She had no doubt hers reflected the same spectrum of emotions.

After locking the door behind him, she leaned against it and cried.

As SallyAnne's head hit her pillow, her feelings were still thrumming from Lionel's kiss. She didn't dare guess what would become of their friendship. But if their professional association were to survive, she'd have to keep her feelings for him at bay.

To put him out of her mind, she thought of Egan Gable.

From his writing, she'd always imagined he had a great strength of character. Frankly, now knowing what depths he was willing to sink to—and for so little money at that—made her want to cry.

How does that happen, she wondered. How could someone who writes so eloquently—and with such passion—be so callous, so unfeeling?

But then she remembered that she was judging him on a book he'd written two decades ago; and a work of fiction at that.

She teared up at her own naïveté.

People change over time, she realized. Really, it's tiny twists of fate that change us.

The proof was Lionel.

She smiled at the thought of him.

Suddenly, she pitied Egan. He's like Icarus, she reasoned. He flew too close to the sun, only to fall into a sea of despair.

And now he's drowning…

TWENTY-TWO YEARS AGO

Here's where the story really begins...

CHAPTER 2

If Audrey Thorpe hadn't caught Jeremy Blake, her boyfriend of two years, nailing some cheerleader who, rumor had it, could tie a knot in a cherry stem with her tongue, it's just possible that she might not have been so susceptible to Egan Gable's charms.

The break-up happened during an SAT testing session hosted by a rival school, Saint Ignatius Prep. Both Audrey and Jeremy had taken the test once already, in the spring. And although they'd both scored over 1500, each was competitive enough to want another go at it. For Audrey, it was the math segment that tripped her up the first time, whereas Jeremy had gotten a perfect score there. He was, after all, San Francisco's Mathlete champ.

They'd gone over to St. Ignatius together, in Jeremy's father's car. But because their last names were at the opposite ends of the alphabet, they were put in separate auditoriums. Unlike their school, Ashbury Academy—which was relatively new and crammed all of its 120 students into a timeworn Victorian mansion on the outskirts of San Francisco's Haight-Ashbury neighborhood—S.I.'s campus was humongous, boasting two ball fields and two theaters, as well as the two auditoriums. In fact, the private school's coffers were so full that it was in the process of building a second gymnasium.

During the first hour of testing, Audrey and Jeremy tackled different sections of the test. For Audrey, it was Evidence-Based Reading and Writing. For Jeremy, it was Math, so it was no surprise that he whipped through it with at least twenty-three minutes to spare, giving Audrey a thumbs-up through the auditorium's exterior window, indicating that he'd wait for her outside until the break period.

Although creative writing was Audrey's strength, the essay question was stumping her:

According to Winston Churchill, "In wartime, truth is so precious that she should always be attended by a bodyguard of lies." Is there any personal situation in which a lie would be validated? Explain why or why not.

Hmmm, thought Audrey. Is there only one right answer to this question? And if so, what if I choose the wrong one?

Or, is this one of those times in which there is no one right answer, and therefore I'll be judged on not what I write, but how I make my case?

Audrey's dilemma was, in a nutshell, the Achilles' heel on her high school's academic philosophy. Although Ashbury Academy was known for its focus on its students' critical thinking skills, in some cases (at least, in Audrey's case) too much of it went on.

And on. And on.

Inevitably, emotional paralysis set in.

Twenty minutes later, Audrey was still in a panic. *This essay counts for a quarter of my total score! I can't afford to screw it up!*

The reason for her hesitation was personal: the notion of deceit was foreign to Audrey.

Unlike the majority of her peers, she had never lied to her mother, Lavinia. Granted there had been numerous opportunities, but Audrey just didn't see the point in it. During the few times they'd disagreed on something, Lavinia had never pulled rank. None of that "It's my way or the highway" crap, and certainly no guilt trips.

Instead, they'd talk things through and usually came to a compromise.

They even agreed on how Audrey should handle her relationship with Jeremy.

"Are you having sex?" Lavinia had asked her one day very nonchalantly.

Audrey shook her head slowly. "No… Not *yet*. But he'd like to."

"Would you like that, too?"

"I've thought about it, yes."

She would have felt guilty admitting this if it weren't for Lavinia's wistful smile. "Your first time making love is a special moment. But even more important than the desire or passion you feel now is the issue of trust. When the person you love has earned your trust, then the time will be right."

Audrey let that sink in. Did she trust Jeremy? For the most part, yes. At least she wanted to believe that, but it wasn't always easy to do. For one thing, he liked to flirt with other girls. For another, she'd heard him make several bald-faced lies to his parents. In fact, the whole reason they had driven over in his father's car—a brand spanking new Ferrari F355 Spider—was because he'd told his dad that his own car had a faulty brake line.

"Why don't you just tell him the truth," she teased him, "that what you really want is to make the other guys jealous when they see you drive up in it?"

Jeremy graced her with a smug grin. "Because that would piss him off. Besides, what he doesn't know won't hurt him."

"I hope you don't say that about me, behind my back."

He said nothing but gave her the same tightlipped smile he'd just given his father as they'd waved off.

That, and then he kissed her hard as if that would relieve her of any doubts.

Love means never having to tell a lie, thought Audrey.

Oh my God! That's it!

From that point on, the essay flowed out of her:

It's easy to tell a lie. You can validate doing so by telling yourself that those you lie to can't handle the truth, or that what they don't know won't hurt them, or that in fact, you're saving them a lot of pain.

But the reality is that, yes, your loved ones can handle it. You have to trust them to do so, just like they trust you not to lie to them. Wouldn't it hurt them much more should they discover that you didn't give them the benefit of your doubt?

If you're really worried about their pain, first think about the devastated looks on their faces when they realize that you didn't trust them to understand the truth.

Trust needs truth.

So does love.

Audrey fairly tossed her paper at the test monitor. She couldn't wait to tell Jeremy how well she'd done.

JEREMY WASN'T IN THE AUDITORIUM'S LOBBY WAITING FOR HER, OR even out in front of it. Finally, she found him: in his father's Ferrari—or, more accurately, rocking the car with some big-breasted harlot.

Audrey recognized the girl because she'd sighed throughout the essay test when she wasn't sucking on her Number 2 pencil. She had also cut out early from the English test. The frown on the girl's face indicated she'd be retaking it at a later date.

It suddenly dawned on Audrey that she'd seen the girl a week before, on SI's cheering squad during a home game with AA. The girl was easy to remember because, invariably, the timing on her jumps was off.

In hindsight, Audrey reasoned, that might have been deliberate. It got the crowd to notice her.

The players saw her, too. The very first thing they noticed was that she wasn't wearing a bra.

Like now.

Or for that matter, panties.

As Audrey watched Jeremy's ass cheeks rise and fall in unison with his paramour's squeaky yelps of orgasmic pleasure, she stumbled through all five stages of heartbreak:

- Denial, (Maybe that wasn't Jeremy, but some other guy who'd stolen his keys… But no, she'd recognize his Ashbury Academy letter jacket over that bare ass anywhere!)
- Anger. (How DARE he do it—and with a pea-brained tart, no less!)
- Bargaining. (Obviously, it was a hormonal lapse of judgment! And, besides, Audrey had already allowed him to get only as far as third base. Granted, whenever he'd attempted to go for a home run she'd slapped his hand away, or worse yet murmured some seemingly offhanded teen pregnancy statistic—but still!)
- Depression: Had her prudishness pushed him away? If only he'd give her a second chance, she'd... she'd what? Give in to his begging? Why do so when her love obviously meant so little to him? Was this how it was to be with her future relationships with men?
- Finally, there was acceptance: Jeremy wasn't hers anymore. He now belonged to some double-jointed cheerleader who would use him to tutor her for her next shot at the SATs.

And he'd enjoy every minute of it.

Audrey wondered how long Jeremy had known the girl. Not that he'd tell her the truth if she were to ask him. Even if he did, what would it matter? The bottom line was that her relationship with him was a joke; a total sham.

No, worse: it was a lie.

I guess the testers will laugh when they read my essay, thought Audrey. They'll think I'm just a stupid, naïve little girl.

Well, I guess I am.

She felt like running all the way home, but she knew that if she left now, she'd be forfeiting the second and third portions of the test, and that would ruin her score.

Nothing was more important than that. *Certainly not some horny boy.*

At least none of this had happened in front of Lavinia. Her mother would have insisted that addressing her heartache was more important than anything, including the test.

Considering her role as founder and Head of School at Ashbury Academy, it was an odd stance, but that was Lavinia for you. Feelings mattered most.

***

WHEN AUDREY TOLD HER FRIEND, TALLULAH WISHART, ABOUT Jeremy's desertion—more to the point, with whom Jeremy had two-timed her—her friend had laughed so hard that she spewed her latte.

"Ha," said Tallulah, "I guess that proves the adage, 'Abstinence makes the heart grow fonder—*of someone willing to give it up.*'"

Audrey shifted uncomfortably on her stool. "The saying is 'absence makes the heart grow fonder,' and it has nothing to do with sex."

Tallulah snorted. "Trust me, little virgin, abstinence has everything to do with sex."

"No, what I mean is… Just never mind." It was useless to argue semantics with Tallulah, or anything else, for that matter.

Lavinia called Tallulah "an old soul," which, to Audrey's way of thinking, was just a polite way of saying that she spoke her mind on anything and everything, whether she knew what she was talking about or not.

Jeremy had always called Tallulah a blowhard. Audrey was too loyal to her dear girlfriend to let him know she agreed with him.

Thinking about Jeremy, Audrey teared up again.

Seeing this, Tallulah growled, "He's lucky I wasn't there. I would have tossed a brick through that Ferrari's windshield."

Audrey had no doubt about that. Tallulah had a horrible temper. She'd gotten away with a lot of crap because of her mother's fame. Maggie Wishart was the sultry lead singer for Chameleon, one of the legendary rock bands that had gotten its start during San Francisco's infamous Summer of Love.

At that very moment, Audrey vowed to stay a virgin forever.

Or to at least date grown rational men, as opposed to horny pubescent boys who wore their pants belted below their hips as if showing the top half of their boxer briefs was sexy or something.

By, say, twenty-five, she reasoned, any hormone-induced frenzy would have subsided, along with the urge to drop trou in public, let alone to lie to the woman he loved.

As fate would have it, the very next day Egan Gable, with his crisply creased khaki pants belted at his waist, came into her life.

The opening day of Ashbury Academy's fall term was still two weeks away, but Audrey, who was to be a senior that year, had made up her mind that she wasn't going to stay home and mope. Better to keep busy by helping out around the school. Since Lavinia was AA's headmistress, Audrey was well aware that there was always some task in need of someone's immediate attention. And because Clare, Lavinia's assistant, had extended her Mexico vacation through tomorrow, she knew Lavinia would welcome her help.

Egan had arrived early for his interview with Lavinia. He was applying for a position as the instructor of AA's Advanced Placement course called *Shakespeare's Influence on World Literature*. Unbeknownst to him, he was the one and only candidate for the position, and that made him a shoo-in—if he lived up to the *curricula vitae* he'd faxed over just the day before.

Audrey, who had just finished conducting a tour of the school with a prospective student and his parents, saw by the lit button on Clare's phone console that Lavinia was still fielding calls from parents preparing for the new school year. She smiled apologetically to Egan and then pointed toward the chairs backed against the administration office's large bay window.

Egan took the hint: prospective students and their parents came first.

Noting that the coffeemaker on the sideboard was still on, he poured himself a cup. But before settling into one of the reception room's folding chairs, he grabbed an old and well-thumbed copy of *Utne Reader* from the large coffee table, which was, in fact, the stump of a Redwood tree.

"'Magic circles are mandatory.' What the hell does that mean?" The applicant's father, Mr. Siler, who had been reading the admissions brochure, hadn't even realized he'd muttered his question out loud until his wife nonchalantly took his hand in hers and proceeded to pierce his palm with a French-tipped nail. Audrey knew this by the man's pained wince.

Nevertheless, he took the hint: *Shut your yap! Don't blow this for Seth. And keep it that way. At least until he is officially accepted into the school.*

To Audrey's mind, that was certainly still up in the air, considering that Seth—tatted up high above the collar of his Mötley Crüe tee shirt and sporting a nose ring to boot—had been a total pain in the ass throughout the tour. For his parents's sake, Audrey had pretended not to notice.

"A magic circle is how students here at the academy resolve conflicts," she explained. "You see, a river stone is passed around. Whoever has it is allowed to express their concerns or feelings. We find it quite effective in inspiring open debate amongst the students." Audrey's tone was gentle enough to use on a five-year-old, let alone a master of the universe such as Mr. Siler.

By his suspicious grimace, she knew he wasn't the type to appreciate the historical relevance of the custom. Understandable. Truth be told, it had more to do with Lavinia's misspent youth on a commune in Mendocino County and the potency of the psychedelic mushrooms that grew under the mammoth Sequoias. But had this been divulged, Mrs. Siler might not have been so pushy about Seth's acceptance.

"They told us on the phone that AA does have an opening for another senior in this year's class. Is that right?" Mrs. Siler asked anxiously. Noting Audrey's nonchalant nod, her quivering smile finally steadied itself. "That's good to know."

"Not to look a gift horse in the mouth, but what gives?" asked Mr. Siler. "I mean, it seems as if every other school has a wait list. And the tuition at the others runs a third higher than Ashbury's."

He had every right to be suspicious. According to their application, the Silers were recent transplants from Seattle, where he'd been one of The Chosen Ones: a Microsoft senior tech executive. From Seth's snarky comments about his previous school, Audrey gleaned that his teachers hadn't appreciated his study habits. Surely the corporate largess that came with his father's connections more than compensated for that.

But the Silers were in Apple country now. In fact, the city was rife with deep-pocketed corporate donors: not just Apple, but also Gap, Pacific Telesis, Hewlett-Packard, Bank of America, and Wells Fargo. The rosters of other schools were already filled with the progeny of their management staffs. This hot list included Charles Schwab, where Mr. Siler had just been hired to head up its fast-growing tech support division. If by some quirk of fate a student slot suddenly opened up, the first call would go to a corporate wonk whose company was underrepresented at that school. Why not bring one more industrial titan into the fold and help spread the wealth?

So yes, Ashbury Academy might just be the Silers's last hope, even if they didn't yet realize this.

What they couldn't know was that the school needed Seth just as badly as he needed it.

Ashbury Academy was only three years old. Despite this, Lavinia had worked hard to keep the school more affordable than the city's other private schools. Her vision was that the school would appeal to parents much like herself: those who, for whatever reason, were disappointed with the public schools but felt that the privates were too structured or unduly influenced by the whims of the parents as opposed to the needs of the students.

In fact, half the students at Ashbury were on either full or partial scholarships.

AA's great weakness was that it had yet to build its reputation among those whose corporate connections or old family money might fund its mission. Knowing this, Audrey's sales pitch played to the school's strengths: its school's class sizes and academic philosophy.

"Ashbury Academy has a few select openings because Lavinia and her staff have devised a curriculum model that is grounded in the essentials while remaining fluid," Audrey explained. "For example, we have several students who excel in the performing arts or have a unique facility for science and math. As such, they are often presented with learning opportunities outside the realm of the typical classroom environment. So, should a particularly promising student cross the school's threshold, AA's fluid student body model allows for him to be accommodated."

Her choice of pronoun was deliberate.

Audrey immediately segued into a usually well-received selling point: the respect she had for the school's instructors. "Lavinia only hires those who've had actual hands-on applied experience in their subjects," she explained. "That way, students are taught by someone with innate knowledge and a genuine passion for it."

"You mean, the sex-ed teacher was once a porn star?" Seth smirked. "Awesome! Does she tutor on the side?"

Hearing this, Egan choked on his coffee.

Audrey's smile suddenly set into a grimace. She hated the boy for making her sound silly.

No way will Lavinia let him into our school—

Oh, who am I kidding, Audrey thought. Schwab just hired this Neanderthal's daddy, and he's offering to pay full tuition. Provided the jerk isn't an arsonist, she'll let him in, if only to cover the new teacher's salary.

Seth's jibe was rude enough to make Mr. Siler look up from the school brochure and give his son a warning glance.

Little good that did. Seth smirked and rolled his eyes.

If Audrey had to guess, she was willing to bet that the sealed envelope holding his transcripts would reflect eleven years of mediocre grades. So why should the boy give a damn if he were accepted or not?

Seth may have given up, but obviously, his parents hadn't. It was natural to assume they'd already heard the horror stories about the San Francisco public schools from Mr. Siler's new co-workers. The scuttlebutt: if you couldn't get your child into the public school's crown jewel, Lowell (and no one could; not with a waiting list that was, perpetually, four years long) you had no choice but to cough up the bucks for private school.

San Francisco's more prestigious non-sectarian private high schools–University, Lick-Wilderming, the Lycée Francais, not to mention Urban just a few blocks away—had numerous students waitlisted for each class. Even without the tattoos, nose stud, and bad attitude, Seth Siler would have a hard time finding a slot.

That is, unless it turned out that Seth was a legacy or a sibling.

And the Silers were willing to donate a new wing.

No, the Silers were just as desperate to get into Ashbury as Lavinia should be to have them.

Resigned to this reality, Audrey glided toward the large double door marked HEAD OF SCHOOL. "Lavinia is off the phone now. Why don't I knock and see if she's available?"

BECAUSE IT WAS HIS FIRST TIME AT ASHBURY ACADEMY, EGAN WASN'T aware that the pretty young brunette with the big gray eyes and dimples on both sides of her mouth wasn't named Clare, despite the placard that sat front and center on the school's reception desk.

Nor had it occurred to him that she was only seventeen years old.

And why should it? AA's receptionist was emboldened with a solemn maturity that belied her years.

Her sad luminous eyes didn't dart away with the giddiness found in most teenaged girls. No Madonna-esque corset peeked out from under a sheer blouse or denim jacket, no short flouncy skirt over fishnet stockings, no Doc Martens. Instead, she wore a long fitted black cashmere sweater over black slacks and ballet slippers: sensible for a traditionally chilly August day in San Francisco. Her hair wasn't big and frowsy, but straight and angled with the sides cut bluntly even below her chin line, and bangs that stopped just above her naturally arched brows.

"Zelda," Egan murmured, just loud enough for her to hear him.

She looked up to find him gazing at her.

"I'm sorry. I was admiring your, er, hair," he explained.

Obviously, she knew the reference to F. Scott Fitzgerald's wife because her dimples deepened again.

He had accomplished his goal.

He could see that she was struggling with a comeback, but before she could get it out the phone rang, giving her the perfect excuse to ignore him again.

What she didn't know was that he enjoyed eavesdropping on her because it gave him an inkling of what he was getting himself into. By the lecture she delivered, he assumed it was a parent new to the school's procedures: "No, students do not wear uniforms here, because Lavinia feels that how we choose to dress on any given day is part of a student's creative process." After a pause, she rolled her eyes in disgust, adding, "No, upper class-persons will not be allowed to go off campus for lunch. The food choices are less than desirable here in the Haight—"

Albeit the drug choices on every street corner of the 'hood are second to none, Egan thought to himself. This bit of public knowledge brought a slight smile to his lips.

Seeing it, Audrey smiled too and then held the phone away from her ear so that he also could hear the concern in the parent's petulant voice. When it finally broke off, she responded, "No, you've been misinformed. The traditional senior trip is not Lake Como, but *Mono* Lake... Yes, well again, the whole point isn't 'culture,' but self-discovery. The students separate and live on their own for three days... Accommodations? They take sleeping bags and camp under the stars! No, sorry, Lavinia would never consider Rome, Paris, or Madrid instead... Why? Because if you can't find yourself in the middle of nowhere, what are the chances of finding yourself anywhere else?" She moved to slam down the phone, but at the very last moment, she resisted the impulse. She murmured goodbye and gently placed the receiver in its cradle.

Egan waited until their eyes met, then smiled. "I for one found myself in Paris. If you'd allow me, I'd show you where."

My God... He's flirting with me!

Egan Gable's offer left Audrey speechless. Perhaps this was for the best because just then Lavinia opened her door to usher the Silers back into the reception area.

Noting the frowns on all their faces, Audrey closed her eyes, relieved.

Good, she thought. Ashbury may be poor, but it's pure, too. That's what makes us so different. So special. That, and the fact that the school only exists because Lavinia created it for me.

As if reading her mind, Lavinia met her gaze with a wide smile.

In that singular moment, Audrey vowed to live her life just as her mother had.

No lies. No secrets.

And I'll always put my children first.

EGAN'S POLITE COUGH BROKE THE TRANCE BETWEEN THEM.

Lavinia looked over. "Oh, there you are," she exclaimed. "Egan Gable, am I right?"

Her smile now embraced him like a warm ray of sunshine. He'd already recognized her from the photo collages that adorned the students' lockers flanking the wide hallway leading to her office. She'd been front and center in many of the pictures. That same grin, shared with the students who embraced her in the photos, was also reflected on their faces.

Noting Lavinia's obvious delight in his presence, Egan relaxed a bit. "And you must be Ms. Thorpe!" He stood and shook her extended hand. "A pleasure to meet you."

"Call me Lavinia. Everyone does, even the students. Even my daughter. In fact, Audrey is one of our seniors this year." Lavinia glanced over at the woman behind the desk.

No—*the girl.*

Egan couldn't help but stare. He was embarrassed for having missed the resemblance between the two. In his defense, there were enough variations–in their physical looks, their mannerisms—to throw him off. For example, the daughter was more slender, the mother taller. There were also the slight nuances that came with an age difference of thirty years or more. Although not yet fifty, already the skin had pillowed out around Lavinia's chin line, and a delicate web of wrinkles had formed at the corners of her eyes. But what had thrown him off even more than Lavinia's long prematurely graying curls or her colorful mode of dress was her ecstatically cheerful demeanor.

It was the antithesis of her daughter's quiet reserve.

She's Mary Poppins for the Brat Pack, he marveled. Okay, yeah, I can dig it.

Noting his surprise, Lavinia said to Audrey, "Dear, do you think you'll finish inputting those new class schedules into the computer before Clare returns tomorrow?"

Audrey glanced at the clock on the wall. "Oh, I'd say I'll be done by the end of the day, no problem." She shuffled the pink phone messages into a neat stack and handed them to Lavinia. "By the way, thus far five parents have called begging that we reconsider the senior trip to Mono Lake." She was looking at her mother, but her sly smile was meant for Egan. "The overwhelming consensus is Paris."

Egan could feel the blood draining from his face. Great, he thought. I almost got caught coming on to Lavinia Thorpe's underage daughter! Talk about blowing a pretty decent meal ticket...

But she is adorable.

Lavinia sighed. "For many of the seniors, that would be their second or third trip to the City of Light. They'd be bored! The parents never seem to understand that the sole purpose of the senior trip is to—"

"Find yourself," Audrey and Egan said it in unison.

"Yes—exactly!" Lavinia looked from one to the other before scrutinizing Egan carefully.

He stared back innocently. He hoped she took it to mean that, instinctively, he understood their mission; that he got what they were all about, there at the academy.

At least, what she was all about. After all, Lavinia Thorpe was AA.

As he followed her into the office, she shut the door behind him.

CHAPTER 3

August 2

Phone tree message left for all parents via Ashbury Academy Parent Auxiliary:

"Hi, Regina, sorry I missed you! I hope your summer has been fab! Hey, are you guys still in Tahoe?… Oh, darn it, hope you're checking your messages! Listen, I'm calling because Lavinia asked the Auxiliary to call and remind all parents that Ashbury is breaking tradition this year. We are not—repeat, NOT starting the fall session on the day of this month's full moon, as in the past. Instead, we're starting on the day of the Lunar eclipse, which is August 17th. Isn't that cool? I think the significance of that will stay with our kids for a lifetime—"

"Tell me about yourself." Lavinia eased herself into one of her office's five comfortable armchairs that circled the perfectly round redwood stump sawed knee-high. She then motioned for Egan to do the same.

"Well…" he took a deep breath. "I got my undergrad at Berkeley

51

—Lit major. I speak French and German. And I'm working on my thesis—"

"No, no…what I mean is—well, tell me about you. Where did you grow up? What was the most fun thing you did as a kid? What are the most important lessons your parents taught you? Why did you become a literature major? Is there anything you'd change about your academic journey?" Lavinia leaned back, as if in anticipation of some mystical revelations. "And lastly, why did you answer the ad for this job?"

Egan's mouth opened, but no words came out. He didn't dare tell her the truth: the whole truth, and nothing but. Instead, he massaged his life's sore realities into soft, pliable fibs.

For example, he was honest when he told her he'd grown up just north of the Golden Gate Bridge: in the lily-white suburban neighborhood of Greenbrae, where some seven hundred mid-century ranch homes were grubstaked on several hills. From Greenbrae's rocky peaks, San Francisco twinkled through the bay's pearlescent mist, like Emerald City before being swathed in Technicolor.

When Egan remembered his childhood, the word "fun" never came to mind. Boring was more like it. And yet, he told Lavinia that he'd spent "many joyous hours" making up adventurous tales that transported him to faraway places.

It was partially true. His real goal was to get away from his dull, disillusioned parents. Even going no farther than one of the larger cities across the bay—San Francisco, Berkeley, wherever—was far enough. His parents never crossed any of the bay's bridges. Why should they? Marin County was safe. The rest of the world was not.

As for any lessons he may have learned from his parents, one had indeed left an indelible mark. He saw firsthand how inertia killed everything in its wake—motivation, careers, dreams, and most importantly, love.

Egan doubted his parents still loved each other. At the very least their unity was a habit. Worse yet, it was an obligation.

He likened his father, a life insurance salesman, to a modern-day Willy Loman: stuck in a deep rut of boredom, but not imaginative enough to catapult himself beyond a mundane but comfortable life financed by automatically-renewing commissions and sweetened by the occasional bonus of a free company trip.

As for his mother, to Egan's mind she was her generation's Madame Bovary: dismayed at how her life had turned out, yet in denial of her role in its outcome. But unlike Flaubert's heroine, lust wasn't what she craved. The next Nordstrom Half-Off Sale would do just fine, along with a noontime shaker's worth of Negronis.

Regarding Lavinia's question as to why he chose literature as his calling, he answered, "Quite simply, because those I admire most were novelists."

He explained that he appreciated Hemingway's spare words and wanderlust; how he admired Fitzgerald's way to heighten his characters' emotions, but sympathized with his desperate yearnings for recognition and financial success. He marveled at Greene's aptitude for weaving intricate plots from his character's misguided motives.

At the same time, he prayed he'd never experience the depth of pain and depression that gave this celebrated British author the ability to create such complex characters. Not that he could admit that to Lavinia.

As for her next question—"Is there anything he'd change about his academic journey?"—he assumed she was asking about high school. In that regard, his answer would have been one word: EVERYTHING. His public high school was the largest in Marin County. Sports ruled, and the academic faculty was on rote. He'd felt invisible in the school's continually milling throng of a thousand students.

So instead, Egan answered as if Lavinia had asked about his years at Berkeley: "I had teachers who inspired me, and opportunities that challenged me. Everyone should be so lucky."

Wasn't a half-truth better than no truth?

In this case, yes. Otherwise, he'd have to admit that, as far as Berkeley was concerned, he was a failure.

Egan had just turned twenty-six. He hadn't exactly rushed to get out of college, tacking on the university's six-year Ph.D. track behind his major, Comparative Literature. It was understood that as long as he stayed enrolled, his father would pick up his school tuition and living expenses, which included a studio apartment in the basement of a small cottage elbowed between two old Victorians just north of the campus.

He'd worked tirelessly at his craft, inspired by his creative writing instructors, many of whom were renowned novelists. At the same time, he'd analyzed the English, French, German, Russian, and Scandinavian classics.

To his credit, he'd done his best to keep the requisite allotment of sex, drugs, and political activism in moderation. He didn't want it getting in the way of his creativity. And yet, at times it did—

At least, regarding sex.

Was it his fault he was a good-looking guy? Women responded eagerly to the lazy scratch in his voice and to the all too obvious invitation offered through the unflinching gaze of his deep-set pale green eyes.

It was to be expected, particularly on a campus that was known for its hot-blooded activists and frustrated intellectuals. Merely letting it slip that he was working on a novel was catnip to the girls he met in the many coffee shops that dotted Shattuck Avenue.

So yeah, sex got in the way.

After Egan's first year in the program, his faculty chair—the much-revered Pulitzer Prize-winning novelist, Clive Munt-Luckin-bill—had encouraged him to submit his novel as his senior project.

By the program's third year, Gable Senior's pleas that Egan get a job—*any job*—to help out with his expenses were coupled with a threat: "Or else it's time you drop out."

Although worried that any sort of job would distract him from his writing, as a compromise Egan charmed the head of the Lit department into awarding him one of the coveted teaching assistant positions. It consisted of slogging through the lifeless term papers of undergrads.

But Egan's hard work was for naught. He turned in his novel halfway through his fifth year in the program. It earned a passing grade, but as a literary endeavor, it garnered only spare encouragement from the dissertation committee.

Even his faculty chair had gone so far as to declare that it "Lacks a soul. The voice is tentative, the narrative half-hearted, and the plot pedestrian. The author falters in developing an honest tone. Perhaps a different POV would have given it the needed gravitas…"

Fuck you and your gravitas, Egan thought at the time. I'll give you a different point of view, alright.

To get back at the man, he had seduced Clive's wife, Clementine, then added a scene in his novel that memorialized the pathetic experience, including the woman's inclination for naughty talk.

It gave Egan great pleasure to think that, were the book to be published ("No," he chided himself, "*when* it's published") his nemesis would read it and her oft-shouted command—"Show me that big, thick joystick, lover boy!"—would ring a bell with the old fool.

A recent sideways urinal glance had him doubting it.

In the meantime, Egan queried twenty-two literary agents. Unfortunately, the final rejection came the day before his lover's tearful confession to her husband.

Egan's teaching assistant position was immediately terminated.

That evening, Egan invited his father to Marin Joe's, one of the old man's favorite haunts. Three bites into their medium-rare prime ribs, Egan begged for an extension on his financial support.

"That way I can focus strictly on my writing for a year—in New York," Egan explained.

Gable Senior almost choked on a forkful of creamed spinach. His insurance commissions were hard won. Egan's undergraduate tuition payments had been a stretch, even with Egan taking out a student loan—which, having co-signed for it, turned out to be the nightmare about debt that kept Gable Senior up nights.

Gable Senior frowned. "Why New York, of all places?"

"It's the center of the book publishing industry. If I'm there, I can meet with literary agents and editors about my novel—"

"So, you've finished it?"

"Sort of." Egan shrugged.

"In other words, no." Gable Senior swiped his napkin over his mouth. Aggravated, he declared, "Seriously, Egan, why the rush to move away—and to one of the most expensive places on Earth—when you've still got your position at the college? That should impress them, right? When you're ready to show the damn thing around, you can set up a few appointments from here and then fly to the Big Apple, drop off the book, and fly out again–"

"About my job"—Egan winced—"I've…I've been let go."

Egan Senior deflated in front of his eyes.

"Look, if it puts your mind at rest, I won't even live in Manhattan," Egan promised. "To offset costs, I'll find a place in, say, Brooklyn. It's cheaper there, but still a great place for writers—"

Egan babbled on, but Gable Senior heard none of it.

Finally, the steam ran out of Egan's dream. The whole time his father hadn't said a word. Instead, he pushed back his plate, stood up, and walked out.

Gable Senior hated the thought of telling the boy's mother of their son's request. Should she then have the audacity to suggest that he cash in his 401(k), he'd give her an earful. He'd been saving that little pot of gold to build a cabin on the Tahoe lakeside plot he'd purchased years ago—which, thankfully, was more than a hundred miles from the nearest Nordstrom.

Egan came home to find his mother's shaking voice on his answering machine, imploring him to forgive her for standing firm with his father on the rejection of his request.

"I think we may have made life too easy for you, Egie." She sighed fretfully. "I'm not saying that your writing isn't good. Maybe it has potential…Oh, *I don't know!* All I'm trying to say is that real life isn't like baseball camp, where you're allowed to play all day, and everyone gets a trophy at the end of the summer. We can't all be Barry Bonds, sweetie—"

Egan threw the machine up against the wall.

He'd hated baseball camp.

The lid cracked off and one of the audiocassette tapes—he

couldn't tell whether it was the one with his outgoing message or the other—popped out onto the floor. His black lab, Casanova, couldn't resist what he took to be an unexpected treat. The dog was gagging on it before Egan could wade through all the clothes and books on the floor to get to it. But he knew better than to wrestle it from Casanova's slobbery jowls. He'd just wait until the damn dog spat it out.

Maybe it was for the best. He had no desire to talk to anyone anyway, least of all his parents.

I'm doing this for all of us, Egan reasoned. When my novel is a bestseller, I'll insist that Dad retire. Maybe then he'll take Mom on a real vacation, not another Winnebago road trip to Tahoe.

It was their loss, he reasoned.

But Egan was a realist. His dream of being a bestselling author would have to wait,—for now, anyway.

That afternoon, he pocketed a discarded copy of the *San Francisco Chronicle*'s help wanted section he'd found on a chair in the Peet's across from the Claremont Hotel, where he'd just applied for a job as a waiter. Lavinia's ad sounded like a good match for him. "Seeking an instructor for three courses: *Beginning English (two classes)*, *Creative Writing*, and *Shakespeare's Influence on World Literature*. For the latter, you must be versed as well in Shakespeare as you are in classic Western literature, and adept at articulating your love of both to inquisitive high school students in a creative setting…"

It would do.

At least, for the time being.

AND SO, IN ANSWER TO LAVINIA'S FINAL QUESTION—WHY HE'D answered Ashbury Academy's ad for the position—Egan explained, "I feel it's a good fit. Shakespeare's plots and characters have inspired generations of writers. I look forward to giving your students a different perspective of the Bard through their works. Who knows? Perhaps the next great author will come from AA."

"Anything is possible," Lavinia replied. Leaning over, she held out her hand and declared, "Welcome to the Ashbury Academy family."

Egan was elated.

More importantly, he felt redeemed.

And then, because it bugged the shit out of him that the cuckolded Clive might just be right about his book, he tried to impress Lavinia by mentioning that he was working on a novel.

"An admirable and challenging endeavor, but certainly within reach for one with your passion for literature." She then added, albeit hesitantly: "By the way, the potential benefactor I met with—he's the senior partner in a law firm—he was curious as to whether or not Ashbury had a debate team. Seems he excelled in debate in college, and was hoping to inspire high schoolers to pick it up." Her lips bowed into a wicked smile. "So I told a little white lie: that we'd just established our own debate club. Of course, he offered to sponsor it." She put her hand on Egan's sleeve. "Would it be too much of an imposition on your time to mentor our newly established debate team, too? Of course, I'd raise your compensation to include this additional responsibility."

"Sounds great." What else could he say? To keep writing, he needed the money, so yes.

Even with that, Egan's new position didn't pay much. But it would undoubtedly sound better to say, "I teach at a private prep school" than "I currently work in the foodservice industry."

To hold onto the job, he knew he'd have to live up to Lavinia's expectations as well as his own.

In other words, Audrey was off limits.

Audrey waited until Lavinia ushered Egan into her office and closed the door behind them before rummaging through Clare's desk. Finally, she found the folder she sought in Clare's inbox:

The curricula vitae of one Egan Gable.

It told Audrey what she needed to know: that he was twenty-six and a Ph.D. candidate in Comparative Literature from UC Berkeley.

The university was Lavinia's alma mater. It was also Audrey's first choice.

So yes, Mr. Egan Gable was a shoo-in, in more ways than one.

For the first time since Jeremy's defection, Audrey didn't feel bereft.

She felt euphoric.

Audrey clicked onto Clare's computer and scrolled through its files until she found the Fall Term curriculum database. The new teacher's position was slotted for three courses.

Introduction to English Literature was a required course for ninth graders. Creative Writing was part of the tenth grade's curriculum. Thankfully, the third course, *Shakespeare's Influence on World Literature*, was something she hadn't yet taken. And because it was an AP course, she could drop an elective for it.

It only took a few seconds for Audrey to find her class schedule. By eliminating Glee, she could accommodate her Physics class in fourth period, freeing up her seventh period for Egan's class—

Except that the course was already filled: mostly with seniors, who would cry foul if they were bumped. It was one of the few APs offered, and their transcripts needed as many 5-plus GPAs as they could cram onto it…

But wait—there were four juniors on the class roster too. As AP candidates, they'd had the choice of Egan's seventh period class or one entitled *The Influence of 19th Century Female Authors on Current Fiction*. It was the only course still taught by Lavinia, who, until Egan's hire, had been AA's sole English Studies instructor.

Audrey wrote each junior's name on a slip of paper. After folding and placing the strips in Clare's empty coffee cup, she closed her eyes and plucked one of the names:

Mandy Blackwell

Audrey couldn't picture the girl. She must be new to the school, she realized.

Mandy's sixth period class was PE. When the change went through, she'd be taking it as her last class of the day. To Audrey's mind she'd be doing the girl a favor. At least now she wouldn't have to shower before her final class, right?

With a flick of a button, the change was made.

A thrill raced through Audrey. For some unknown reason, she just knew it was going to be a memorable year.

CHAPTER 4

About Your Interaction with Your Students:

Rule #1: No one is asking you to love every student. However, you should do your best to like them: if not as friends, then for the simple reason that they too are human beings.

Rule #2: Treat each student with the same respect you'd hope to receive in return.

Rule #3: When it comes to your students' feelings toward you, use the judgment of a parent. You are the adult, and he or she is the child. Never forget that.

—Excerpted from *The Ashbury Academy Teachers' Handbook*

"Well, well, well! Indiana Jones is back." Cornell, the prissy Chemistry and Biology teacher, patted a napkin to his thin lips but not in time to hide his smirk.

He shifted his glance from Egan to Berney, the tall, tanned man on the other side of the teacher's lounge. Berney taught Geography, World History, and Workshop, a required course where AA's students, both male and female, learned to use all sorts of tools. "Scrumptious, isn't he? All summer long he digs up dinosaur fossils somewhere in Wyoming. I wonder what he does to keep warm on those cold starry nights?"

Egan noticed that Cornell's vest was an original Harris Tweed. He'd seen a similar one in the latest issue of Esquire, so he imagined it had cost his co-worker a pretty penny. It bugged him the way Cornell held his coffee cup, with his pinky finger arched. The cup and its saucer were almost precisely the same shade of powder blue as the cashmere sweater draped casually over Cornell's shoulders.

Egan wondered if he accessorized this way every day. Did he have a rainbow hue of cups stashed in his desk?

If Egan were to guess, he'd say yes. And as the newest member of AA's illustrious staff, he'd soon find out.

Odette Pettigrew, who taught French and Spanish, giggled, "*Merde*! Berney is happily married, you little harlot—so back off! However, if he were to ever leave that sweet wife of his, remember the golden rule: share and share alike." She'd been hovering near Egan's elbow and touched it gently.

It's unfortunate that Odette looks like one of Notre Dame's gargoyles in drag, Egan thought. Still, he found her sense of humor somewhat attractive. Besides, she'd brought chocolate croissants for everyone, which she'd made herself. Paired with the freshly ground Peet's brewing in the faculty lounge's coffeemaker, Egan felt his new job was off to a great start.

Shrugging off Odette's admonishment, Cornell turned to Egan. "How about you, New Kid on the Block? Got any interesting hobbies?"

Both gave him such hungry looks that Egan almost burst out laughing.

Before he could answer, Lavinia, who seemed to hear every conversation at once even while standing halfway across the room, proclaimed, "I anticipate we will all be impressed with what Egan offers this school, its students, and the world of literature."

Egan blushed slightly at her declaration.

It was seven-thirty on the morning of the first day of the fall term. The school's main building took up one square block at the base of Ashbury Street, just across the street from the park greenbelt known as the Panhandle. Having endured 1967's Summer of Love, its most recent reincarnation as a progressive prep school for almost two-hundred precocious teenagers with overly indulgent parents should be a cakewalk for the grand old dame.

Or so you'd think.

Listening to his new colleagues' chatter, Egan realized Audrey had been right to boast about them. How had she put it? Oh yes— they had hands-on applied experience in their subjects.

Larry Tabke, a nuclear physicist who had retired from Lawrence Livermore Labs, taught Physics. Hardy, who had once been a researcher on the staff of the California Academy of Sciences, taught Earth Sciences and Astronomy. The head of the Math department, Robert Brownstein, had resigned ("on principle," he declared to Egan) from the IRS, where he'd worked as an accountant. ("I also count cards," he offered in a fervent whisper. "But don't leak that to the Feds.")

Paulo, a union activist who had worked the lettuce fields and marched in Sacramento and Washington with Cesar Chavez, helmed government and Political Science classes.

History—United States and World—was Nicholas Lavinsky's domain. Tweedy and softened with age, "History Nick" had written books on both subjects now used in the curricula of several state universities.

Even the part-time staff members were the real things. Nick McGregor, or "PE Nick," was also a personal trainer. The demure Art instructor, Osprey Talbot, had metal sculpture installations all over the world; and the honey-toned Music teacher, Andrée Conley, spent her weekends fronting a jazz band made up of A-list studio musicians.

I'm the imposter here, thought Egan. I've done nothing.

At least not yet.

Until he'd demonstrated he was the real thing, he'd do his best to make this his new home.

To prove it, when Lavinia asked the staff to consider ways in which they could use that day's anticipated lunar eclipse as an overriding theme across all academic disciplines, he quickly answered, "I'll walk the students through the relevance of the lunar calendar on the plot of King Lear."

"Ah, perfect!" Lavinia's approval swept over him like a warm, welcoming breeze. "Hardy, yours is somewhat obvious: perhaps a student field trip to California Academy of Science's planetarium? The eclipse isn't until eight o'clock tonight. Maybe the students can take in the show at, say, around five or so? We can order pizza for them afterward. What are your thoughts about that?"

Hardy's frown caused his bushy brows to arch downward. "Doable, for sure. I'll call over there and leave a message for a group showing tonight." He paused, embarrassed, he added, "But I'll need volunteers for this field trip."

Berney blinked. "Why? It is, quite literally, just a walk through Golden Gate Park. It's not like there's any carpooling involved."

Two pink spots appeared on Hardy's cheeks, the only part of his face that wasn't covered by hair. "Yeah, well, the last time I took a group over there I was the only one of a few looking up at the stars. Half of the kids were counting each other's molars with their tongues."

This drew resigned shrugs from many of the staff.

"Biology in its most primitive human form. Should be a piece of cake for you and your volunteers, Hardy," murmured Lavinia with a grin. "Any takers? I'd join you, but tonight I'm hosting the school's trustee dinner right before the eclipse."

There was a collective groan. Other than that, no one moved a muscle.

All Egan could think of was the long ride back to Berkeley via the Transbay Tube. Stuffed with commuters on the way into San Francisco earlier that morning, the ride in had been claustrophobic enough. Granted, it would be emptier by the time he came home from the field trip. Still, the thought of shooting through a tube 135 feet below San Francisco Bay with a bunch of hungry potheads heading to Gordo for burritos kept his hands at his side.

But then, glancing at Lavinia, he found himself mesmerized by the one feature she shared with her daughter: those luminous gray eyes.

Slowly his hand went up.

As if shamed by him, some of the others followed suit. Odette waved hers gaily and gave him a sly wink. Seeing Berney's hand go up, Cornell sighed loudly but lifted a hand as well.

Egan knew instinctively that they didn't resent him. Why should they? It was apparent to him that they all revered Lavinia; that she would have gotten what she wanted anyway.

In fact, she now had more volunteers than she needed.

"Super! Thank you all! We'll cap it at eight. The rest of you get the next go-round, right?" She laughed along with the others.

What followed was a lively, albeit friendly, debate among the teaching staff as to the mating traits of bonobos compared to that of human teenagers.

"At least with bonobos, there is less drama and more action," Cornell muttered.

As he looked around, it struck Egan that Lavinia's staff was a lot like the furniture that crowded the room: overstuffed and worn down, but comfortable and welcoming.

It's not like Berkeley at all: no infighting, none of the smugness or the petty politics, he thought. She's chosen well. They like her, and buy into her cockeyed mission. She'll never find herself amid a mutiny with this group.

As if reading Egan's mind, Lavinia murmured just loud enough for him to hear, "Welcome to my ship of fools."

***

AUDREY WAS NOT AT ALL SURPRISED THAT, BY THE END OF ASHBURY'S opening day assembly, Egan had been declared the school's top hunk.

After all, he was the youngest and the cutest of the teachers. This was all too obvious when Lavinia introduced him along with the school's other instructors.

The immediate shuffling of schedule cards could be heard throughout the assembly hall (not to mention a few delighted squeals and disappointed moans) as the female students in the school checked to see if, in fact, they'd somehow won the scheduling lottery that put them in one of Egan's four classes. Audrey could only imagine that the angry cry of "WHAT THE HELL—" she heard emanating from one of the back rows was the overachieving junior by the name of Mandy Blackwell, who realized she'd somehow been bumped from Egan's *Shakespeare's Influence on World Literature* class.

Validation of Egan's newfound status could be heard in the gossip being murmured all day through the hallways. But where it really hit home to Audrey was in the Senior Girls' restroom, where she'd gone to check her makeup before seventh-period.

"—And that Gable dude! My God, he is *bitchin'*! But I thought he'd never call on me! And when he finally did, I stuttered like some stupid airhead! What do you think, was it that noticeable? Did I make a total fool of myself?"

Audrey had been touching up in front of the mirror by the far window. Hearing this declaration, her lipstick stopped mid-stroke over her upper lip.

She couldn't see the restroom's two other occupants because they were in the toilet stalls.

"Honestly?… Okay, yeah. In Creative Writing, you sounded like an absolute dweeb," her friend said in all seriousness. The girl seemed to take joy in telling her so. "But don't worry. I don't think he was paying attention. That was the exact moment Lanie Henderson did that thing—you know when she yawns and arches her back so that her boobs practically fall out of her blouse? Like, how obvious is that?"

Audrey shuddered. She had seen Lanie do that exact move countless times. But Egan was too mature to fall for that, she reasoned. He'd graduated from Berkeley, where they burned bras, not stuffed them. That alone proved he was a serious guy who would never fall for petty flirtatiousness—

"And I love that whole 'intellectual vibe' he's got going. I mean, he quotes Voltaire as if he's the fifth Beatle! Isn't that totally righteous?" The girl in the first stall was on a roll. "I am, like, *so* ready to be teacher's pet!"

In the mirror, Audrey noticed her cheeks had turned the same candy apple red as the shade of her lipstick. As much as she wanted to believe that she was embarrassed for the girl who had admitted her lust so candidly, in truth she was ashamed that they were so similar to her own feelings for Egan.

What makes me so different from her? Audrey wondered.

The answer was all too obvious: Nothing.

No, that's not true. My feelings for him are more profound than just sex...

Hearing the toilets flush, Audrey tossed her lipstick in her purse and scrambled out the door. She was late for class anyway.

Egan's class.

CHAPTER 5

*A*ny presumptions Audrey had left about her connection with Egan were stomped into the ground (along with her heart) as she saw, first hand, the pull he had over her classmates.

All a student had to do was look into those deep-set green eyes, and immediately she—or he, for that matter—was drawn to the young instructor.

Davis Wong, Audrey's closest guy pal, slipped her a note that summed it up succinctly:

It's like watching a Klingon tractor beam lock onto a clusterfuck of Federation starships!

He's right, Audrey thought. You can't help but feel completely sucked in. You feel as if you're the only two people in the world—

But then he lets you go, only to aim his charm at someone else.

When that happened to Cherry Conover, the girl seemed to deflate physically. In her case, that was not easy to do considering, as Audrey's friend, Bliss Thackeray, had pointed out on numerous occasions: "Those breasts of hers are natural floatation devices!"

But by the end of class it seemed as if Audrey was the only one who didn't get to mind meld with Egan. Instead, he called on everyone around her, tossing out backhanded compliments that had the chosen ones blushing or giggling at their own expense.

Worse yet, whenever his eyes swept over Audrey at all, he seemed to look right through her.

Hurt and confused, she wondered, Why not me? Am I not pretty enough?

Or is it because I look too desperate?

Even her friends were fighting for Egan's attention. When he casually mentioned to Davis that he thought his vintage bomber jacket was cool, Davis puffed up with pride.

Audrey had been with Davis when he'd bought it off of some old queen who claimed he flew with Jimmy Stewart during World War II. Hearing that, Davis didn't argue. The damn thing cost him all of ten bucks anyway: a great find at that price, for sure, so why quell the deal? But as they walked away from the man, Davis muttered, "Yeah, sister, we're all waiting for some flyboy to sweep us off our feet. Mine is Tom Cruise in *Top Gun.*"

Now Davis was acting as if it had come off a runway in Milan.

Tallulah let it drop to Egan that her mother was Maggie Wishart. When Egan mentioned that Chameleon's debut album, *Make Lust Not Love*, had been his favorite album as a teen, and that he'd played it so many times that he'd worn out the grooves, she offered to bring him another copy—autographed of course, by her mother.

Watching Egan's eyes open wide in gratitude, Audrey felt as if her heart had just broken into a million tiny shards.

Traitor, she thought.

Not of Egan, but of Tallulah.

Well, yes, of Egan, too.

Finally, the chimes in AA's bell tower rang out, heralding the end of the school day. Like the other students, Audrey gathered up her books and bags, only to find Egan standing next to her, scrutinizing her intently.

He was looking into her soul. Or so it felt.

But she was mistaken. She realized this when he gently tapped his bottom lip with his finger. "Um…Did you forget something?"

"I'm sorry... what?" Her mind raced to the obvious. Was he asking for a kiss?

He leaned in and murmured, "Your lipstick. I think you'd better look in a mirror."

Suddenly Audrey remembered she'd completely forgotten to apply it to her bottom lip before leaving the restroom.

Well, isn't that just perfect! All this time I've looked like a clown. No wonder he ignored me!

She only saw pity in his grin.

"Have a nice day," he said, as he sauntered back toward his desk. "Oh, and do tell Lavinia I had fun today in class. Better yet, tell her you did too."

Fun. Yeah, right.

That's when it hit her: He ignored me because I'm the Head of School's daughter.

The realization that she'd never connect with Egan on any other level—not even as a student—brought angry tears to her eyes.

Thank goodness he didn't see them. But that was only because he was too busy chatting up Tallulah.

Davis saw them. He pulled a folded kerchief from the breast pocket of his jacket. "Aw, hell, baby cakes! You look like a *raccoon*."

She stared down at the crisp white square of linen. It was monogrammed with his three initials: DXW. No doubt he had special-ordered it from Wilkes Bashford.

Only Davis had the style to match up an old bomber jacket with an expensive snot rag, she thought.

His life was certainly a study in contrast. A first-generation Chinese American, his parents had kicked him out onto the street for admitting to them that he was gay. Lavinia, who had seen him soliciting in the Panhandle, had offered him a full scholarship to the school.

Because he always seemed so sleepy in the morning, Audrey wondered if he was still hooking on the side for quick cash. He had promised Lavinia that he wouldn't do that anymore. It was the one and only prerequisite for him staying at the school.

Davis winced as Audrey blew her nose into his kerchief. A few of the other students turned to stare and snicker.

Well, too bad, Audrey thought. I'm still Lavinia Thorpe's daughter. I can get away with a lot of things, but walking out of class with snot hanging out of my nose is not one of them.

Neither is flirting with my teachers.

"LET ME SEE YOUR BINOCULARS." AUDREY POKED BLISS, WHO SEEMED fixated on something on the other side of the starlit planetarium's auditorium.

To avoid the other students, Audrey, Bliss, Davis, and Tallulah had set up camp in the balcony of the planetarium so that they could observe everyone else while pretending to listen to Hardy's lecture.

"Keep your mitts off," Bliss muttered as she slapped Audrey's hand away. "I'm watching Kyle Moody go at it with some little junior. Man, his technique is so *whacked!*" She shook her head sadly. "You'd think he was milking a cow or something! I guess some girls are just so desperate that they'll put up with anything."

Obviously disgusted, she sighed and handed the binoculars to Audrey, who immediately lifted them to her eyes. "Wow," Audrey exclaimed. "You didn't tell me these were night vision binoculars."

"Let me see," begged Davis, but Audrey held on tight to them and leaned forward over the balcony's banister so that he couldn't reach them. He had a fear of heights, so she knew he wouldn't try again.

He gave her the finger then turned back to Bliss. "Where the hell did you get these, anyway?"

"They're my dad's. Cool, huh? Really, they belong to our store. He's put them on all the shop window mannequins. This week's theme is *The Matrix.*"

Bliss's parents, Maude and Reggie, owned the hottest boutique on

Union Street, which meant that she was the school's unofficial fashion diva. Like many of the parents who sent their children to Ashbury, they'd known Lavinia forever—or at least since the '60s, when, like she, they'd come to the Haight to turn on, tune in and drop out, only to eventually come to the conclusion that life was a participatory event.

Parenting, especially, had a way of doing that to you.

Creating Utopia was still the goal, only this time creating it for the whole family became the new mission. Maude and Reggie were a perfect example of this. From the pictures Audrey had seen in Lavinia's photo album, the store the Thackerays had opened in the Haight before Bliss was born, called Over the Rainbow, was no more than a hole in the wall where they sold long gauzy skirts, tie-dyed halter tops, jeans with the widest bell-bottoms imaginable, granny gowns, and velvet Sergeant Pepper jackets, along with incense, scented candles, and bongs.

After Bliss's birth, the store mirrored the personal changes in the Thackerays' lives. The sweet musky smells stayed, but the drug paraphernalia went out, as did the second-hand clothes. Instead, they displayed cutting-edge fashions created by many of San Francisco's up-and-coming designers, all made from fibers that were organically grown. One section of the store was even devoted to children's clothing.

By the time Bliss was six, ecstatic write-ups of the store were regularly appearing in the *San Francisco Chronicle* and the alternative weekly, the *Bay Guardian*. But a rave review from the tony *Nob Hill Gazette* put them on the radar of the town's socialites.

This gave the Thackerays the incentive to open a second store in the posh Union Street shopping district, right down the hill from San Francisco's most exclusive neighborhood, Pacific Heights. When the new store tripled the Thackerays' income, they realized that they had at last outgrown the Haight.

The year Bliss started high school, the Thackerays took their company public. In the three years since, they'd opened Over the Rainbow retail outlets in six other cities, and moved into their own

Pacific Heights mansion, near their wealthiest San Francisco patrons.

But they weren't Lavinia's only friends who, with whatever fame and fortune they'd made for themselves, had moved from the Haight to one of San Francisco's more prestigious neighborhoods— Sea Cliff, Presidio Heights, St. Francis Wood, Pacific Heights, Russian Hill—or even out to Marin County; or to one of booming Silicon Valley's exclusive communities like Atherton, Burlingame, or Portola Valley.

Tallulah's mom, Maggie, was another example. After her second album went platinum, she'd moved over the Golden Gate Bridge to Mill Valley, the rustic little village that sat at the base of Mount Tamalpais. With baby Tallulah and her latest boyfriend in tow, she held court to a myriad of musicians, singers, songwriters, and hangers-on in a rambling six-acre estate with picture-book views of the whole bay, accessed only by a tiny road that zigzagged halfway up the mountain.

It was a long way from the old Victorian that now housed Ashbury Academy, which had been a communal crash pad for Maggie, Lavinia, and the Thackerays among others.

It seemed to Audrey that sending their kids to the academy gave them a perfect excuse to reconnect with the youthful ideals that had brought them to San Francisco in the first place. She could just imagine the many crazy hazy memories sparking and flaring once more in full psychedelic color as they walked the hallways of the academy during the school's monthly family potluck nights.

The only light coming into the planetarium was from the simulation of a lunar eclipse. Audrey could barely make out her friends' faces. That was okay, because Audrey knew them by heart: blond wan Bliss would be smiling widely, despite her braces. And except for her perpetually naughty smirk, redheaded Tallulah had the face of a Botticellian angel. Davis's cheekbones were angled high, although pocked deeply with acne. He never smiled or frowned. In the three years she had known him, she had learned to read his thoughts in his almond-shaped eyes, not his mouth.

I wonder if the school will mean half as much to us as it does to Lavinia and the other parents, she thought. Probably not. High school is just—well, it's high school. Everyone wants to forget about it. It's too painful to hang onto.

Her feelings for Egan were proof of that.

"Oh my God, just think: In another twenty years, we'll all need night vision goggles because the sun will have been blocked out by pollution and all that other crap! Won't that be, like, so sad?" Bliss proclaimed this loud enough that Hardy's pontificating stopped cold.

Audrey and her friends ducked as he searched the room for his heckler. As Tallulah's head bobbed out of sight, the colorful Lobro Swatch, which she'd used to tie back her wildly coiling hair, glowed ominously, giving away their location.

Hardy sighed. "Once the balcony trolls will cease their declarations, I shall continue."

Silence.

Audrey lifted her head in time to see him shake his head in resignation.

Finally, his monotone drone picked up where he'd left off. "As I was saying, people: what makes this eclipse unique is that the moon is passing through the center of the earth's shadow—"

Tallulah went back to what she'd been doing before Bliss's outburst: flicking M&Ms off the balcony railing onto the students below. "Audrey, seriously, if you're looking for Jeremy, he's sulking in the far-right corner, under Orion." Then, with a knowing smirk, she added: "You know he's dying to make up with you."

Audrey frowned. "That's too bad. He's made his bed—his Ferrari, anyway—and now he can lie in it with his stupid new girlfriend."

"He was never your type in the first place," declared Bliss.

Audrey shrugged. True, her relationship with Jeremy was dead and buried, but her pride was alive and well. At least her friends had held off a few days before doing the postmortem on what they assumed was a broken heart.

"I don't have 'a type,'" Audrey insisted.

Davis lowered his sunglasses so that he could look her in the eye. "Sure you do. We all do."

"Speaking of heartbreakers, who's got the skinny on Egan?" Tallulah tossed an M&M at Audrey. "Your mama done good, picking *that* boy."

Audrey shrugged. "Don't look at me. I know nothing about him. Fair Master Gable is an enigma wrapped in a conundrum."

"I beg to differ." Bliss arched a brow. "That young man is an open book."

Audrey shifted uncomfortably in her seat. "I don't know what you mean."

"Well, I do." Tallulah declared. "He loves being big man on campus. Did you see the group of students on his heels as he walked here through the park? It looked like that old fable—what's it called again?"

"The Pied Piper." Davis shivered. "Frankly, I think that says more about us than it does about him. If he's really all that great, why is he teaching at AA? No offense to Lavinia or anything, but Ashbury isn't exactly Stanford or Harvard. And it's certainly not University High."

The others took that in silently. Audrey bristled at the inference: that Ashbury wasn't good enough for Egan.

She wondered if he thought that too.

The realization that he might made her hand shake slightly, but she kept her eyes focused through the binoculars, scanning each row slowly, left to right. She'd never tell her friends who she was really looking for:

Egan Gable.

But he was nowhere in sight.

To find him, Audrey had only to look up. Egan was watching

her and her friends from the security catwalk that circled the top of the planetarium.

He couldn't hear them, but even their slightest moves were animated, their murmurs rising and falling in the currents of their capricious emotions.

He was jealous of them. If only he were as connected to his life as they were to theirs.

If only he could somehow be connected to Audrey.

So, this is what it's like to be in love, he thought.

Since puberty, lust had been his constant companion. A beautiful face never failed to put a smile on his lips. And somehow he always seemed to find the right words to entice its owner.

But Egan's attraction didn't come from his looks. He was more self-assured than handsome. His confidence intrigued women. His penetrating gaze dared them to ignore him.

Most didn't.

Should a potential conquest proffer a blush instead of an instant acquiescence, even better. Granted, he'd have to work harder to get her into his bed, but he'd relish the conquest all the more.

Egan loved a challenge. But Audrey was more than that. In every way, she was forbidden fruit: the daughter of his boss, and underage at that.

More to the point, Egan would hate himself if he broke her heart.

He had never felt that way about another girl.

Woman.

Person.

He held no illusions: in the mere twenty-six years since his birth, he'd disappointed more people than he could count on both hands. Hell, he'd upset his dad more times than he'd even admit to himself. He had friends whose girlfriends he'd bedded without a second thought. One guy's iron fist left Egan with a souvenir of the misadventure: a fake front tooth.

Egan could tell that Audrey was attracted to him, but so what? All kids her age were fickle. He'd been at AA for only a day and already he'd witnessed six romantic summer-love break-ups and three crying jags induced by unrequited love.

Life won't always be this way, he reasoned. This is just a singular moment in time. The obstacles standing between us won't always be here.

She'll grow up—

And so will I.

All the more reason to play it cool; to just wait it out.

If, somewhere in the future, the stars aligned, then so be it. Some things were just meant to be.

Perhaps this was one of those times.

CHAPTER 6

Debate Terminology

Ad hominem fallacy: Attacking a person rather than the argument.

Ad populum fallacy: Claiming that something is true because of popular belief.

Burden of Proof: The affirmative's responsibility to prove that the resolution is true. If the affirmative fails to prove the resolution, he/she/they ought to lose the debate.

—*National Forensics League Coaching Guide*

"*L*isten up, mam'selles and gents!" Egan's declaration cut through the classroom chatter like a buzz saw. At the same time, all heads turned in his direction. The sort of fidgeting that was usually found in a room filled with twenty high-achieving and highly hormonal teenagers stopped suddenly as if they were merely images caught in a camera's flash photo.

Satisfied, Egan honored them with his thousand-watt smile.

It was a month into the school year. Thus far, from what Audrey could tell, Egan was retaining his crown as Teacher with the Most Pets. It sickened her how anxiously her classmates vied for his attention. He rewarded them by doling out praise like fairy dust.

At least, it was better than the students who were quite literally throwing themselves at him.

Every day for the past four weeks she sat in his classroom while he conversed, cajoled, inspired—and yes, flirted—with her classmates. Sure, every now and then he called on her, too. But on these rare occasions, his tone was always serious, completely deferential.

She hated that.

He treats me with kid gloves, like I'm—oh, I don't know, Princess Di or something.

No, worse… Oh my God, it's like I'm *the First Lady!*

Just the thought of that made her shudder.

From then on, she left her pearls at home.

Instead, she tried to break him.

She thought having the best grades in class would do it. Apparently, he expected that, so other than writing EXCELLENT on her papers, she got no other response.

For a whole week, she tried answering every question he broached to the students. But if he called on her at all, it was at the very end of the hour, just in time for the class chimes to cut her off.

The following week she asked countless questions in class, sometimes about the most obvious things. She could tell he was annoyed with her, but he answered patiently. But he never gave her the response she sought and would have been the most obvious: "Why don't you see me after class and I'll answer your questions at that time?"

Because he'd rather not see me after school.

He'd rather not see me at all.

Well, too bad.

Today, in desperation, Audrey decided it was time she lower herself to the ploy generations of women had used before her. Right before entering Egan's class, she freed the first two buttons on her blouse so that he couldn't miss the obvious: her generous cleavage, the result of a recently purchased purple push-up bra.

Her scheme backfired. Egan's sole glance in her direction was to chide her for being late, which brought her to the attention of every other male in the room.

Jeremy was practically panting. But when Egan intercepted the note Jeremy had scribbled to reaffirm his love for her, Audrey was mortified.

Holding it up to the class, Egan declared, "Seriously, Mr. Blake, if one is to profess one's love, one should skip the use of the term 'blue balls.'"

Everyone laughed uproariously—except for the writer, his subject, and their torturer.

Audrey didn't know if she was angrier with Jeremy for caring so much for her that he made a fool of himself, or at Egan for caring so little that he made her the butt of his joke.

I should give up, she thought.

But no, I can't. Because if I'm right and he likes me but is afraid to show it, he'll never know I love him too.

And eventually, he'll give up on me.

He'll forget about me.

If he really cares for me, he's doing the right thing: he'll let me know, even if there's nothing we can do about it.

At least not now.

From then on, she'd have to accept that he talked to the other girls in the class. She'd have to pretend not to care when he teased them. She'd ignore it when he flattered them with off-handed compliments.

And when he was the subject of the other students' personal musings or coy remarks, she'd act bored, feign nonchalance, or completely ignore them.

Anything to keep from crying.

Like now. She watched as Egan opened his bottom desk drawer, pulled out a stack of small pamphlets, and moved to the front of his desk. As he leaned against it, he scanned the students. Periodically, he paused while making eye contact: honoring one recipient with a wink, another with a nod, and yet another with the shadow of a smile.

When, finally, his glance shifted in Audrey's direction, her heart skipped a beat—

Until she realized he was actually grinning at Tallulah.

Audrey turned in time to see Tallulah's response: she stuck out her tongue at him.

Impressed at her audacity, Egan guffawed.

Tallulah winked at Audrey.

Thank you, my friend.

Egan smirked as he shrugged off the slight. "Great news, people! Lavinia has given me the honor of coaching Ashbury Academy's newest team: *Debate.*"

The announcement drew an awed murmur.

"Tryouts will be held this Thursday. It'll be heralded in tomorrow's student bulletin. But because you're my favorite students, I'm giving you a head start."

"I bet you say that to all your classes," Davis declared.

Everyone laughed.

Even Egan, proving the jibe had hit its mark. "Despite my propensity toward universal favoritism, if you're serious about making the team I suggest you prepare accordingly. It will be small: only eight students, and made up of seniors and juniors." He held up one of the pamphlets. "This handy little booklet outlines the National Debate Society's rules and regs. You'll also find four debate questions on page sixteen. Be prepared to debate two of them—and, in debate parlance, both for and against. You must also be ready to debate a third question. Please write it down now: 'Should Ashbury Academy students be drug tested?'"

Snickers accompanied the scratch of pencils on paper. Egan waited a moment until all scribbling ceased.

"Got it?… Good," he said. "I'll be judging you along with Nick and Cornell."

"History Nick, or PE Nick?" Jeremy shouted out.

"You're in luck," Egan replied. "It's PE Nick. History Nick has a dental appointment that afternoon."

Everyone chuckled at Jeremy's expense. They knew that because Jeremy was a jock PE Nick might be more generous in his scoring.

"You'll be judged on four criteria." Egan counted them off with his fingers: "First, we'll grade you on your argument's organization and clarity. Then, we'll consider the reasons that support your argument. Next, we'll assess your cross-examination and rebuttal. A perfect score is sixteen. Times the three judges, that means you can earn as many as forty-eight points. Got it?"

The students nodded.

"The judges will be using a four-point rubric for each criterion," Egan added. "A full four points is granted for complete clarity and an orderly presentation, three points for being less than perfect of that, two points if you are not up to speed overall, and one point if you screw up miserably."

This time, the laughter was half-hearted: sour and unpleasant, like a fart which left both the culprit and the victims ill at ease.

Egan added, "Remember, making the team gives you what you desire most—another leg up on your college applications. May the best debaters win." Egan sighed. "Which brings me to another significant announcement. I've graded last week's essays, and I have to tell you"—he paused, as if seeing how high he could ratchet up the suspense—"I'm duly impressed. Almost everyone did their very best to draw an analogy between the Bard and the contemporary author of their choice." Egan's eyes rested on Bliss. "In particular, I want to give a shout-out to Ms. Thackeray's creative comparison of *Much Ado about Nothing* to Ms. Bushnell's sure-to-be-a-classic"—he rolled his eyes—"*Sex and the City.*"

"Wow! I'm glad you thought so!" Bliss preened at what she deemed was a compliment. "Frankly, I felt it was a stretch!"

"Ditto. And just so we're clear, 'creativity' doesn't necessarily translate to an A grade."

She frowned at this reality.

Bliss's most exceptional charm was her naïveté —or, so it was assumed by everyone *but* her three closest friends. Ashbury's clock tower chimes weren't going to stop her from making some cocka-mamie argument as to why Egan should reconsider her paper's grade.

And Audrey knew he'd enjoy every minute of it.

Until he's free to be with me.

Eight months from now, I'll have graduated from high school, she reasoned. The fact that I'm Lavinia's daughter will no longer stand in our way.

By that time, he'll finally realize I'm worth waiting for.

In the meantime, Audrey would make her way to the school library. She was determined to spend more time with Egan. If it meant making Debate Team, so be it.

She grabbed one of the pamphlets on her way out.

***

As the other students took off, Bliss went into her pitch for a higher grade.

Egan sat silently. Every now and then he'd nod slightly, but his mind was elsewhere.

He was thinking of Audrey.

Since the first day of school, it had hurt him to glance in her direction. It was too tempting to let his eyes linger on her.

He knew she was frustrated with him too. Still, he'd hoped ignoring her would discourage the apparent attraction they shared.

Boy, was he wrong. If anything, she'd come on even stronger.

He'd almost lost it today when he noticed her blouse was partially unbuttoned. He'd only succeeded in making things worse when he called attention to her tardiness. Every other guy in the room turned to gawk at her—especially that Neanderthal, Jeremy Blake. Egan had heard the rumors of their recent breakup, but watching Jeremy's note on its journey to Audrey had him thinking the worst:

That they'd gotten back together again.

That Audrey's plunging neckline hadn't been a wardrobe malfunction at all but a seductive ploy—

Not for Egan's benefit, but for Jeremy's.

Out of jealousy, Egan had taken the note and read its silliest part out loud to embarrass the boy. But in doing so, Egan had embarrassed Audrey too.

She hates me because I shamed her, he reasoned. I can't say I blame her. It was a childish and despicable thing to do.

It dawned on him that she might ask to be transferred out of his class. And after his callousness, she certainly wouldn't dare try out for Debate Team.

The thought saddened him. Having read her essays and listened to the ease with which she made her points in class discussions, he knew she'd be a natural debater.

Maybe it's for the best, Egan thought.

It would certainly make it easier for him to hold to his mantra:

Don't lead her on. Hold onto my job... Don't lead her on. Hold onto my job...

"So, what do you think, Egan?" Bliss's voice roused him from his worst nightmare: losing Audrey.

"Huh?... I think... I..." He tried to remember a single word she may have said, but nothing came to mind. The hope in Bliss's eyes only made him feel worse; not about tuning her out, but about hurting her dearest friend.

It's why he muttered, "Yeah, okay. Whatever."

Delighted, Bliss squealed. "Alright! Wow! If I can get a C minus changed to an A, maybe I should try out for Debate Team after all!"

Egan held his groan until she was too far down the hall to hear it.

FOR AUDREY'S DEBATE TEAM TRYOUT, SHE CHOSE THE TWO TOPICS least likely to appeal to her competitors because of the amount of research involved: allowing the Internet to stay free, and eliminating the position of the vice president.

Because the former topic's merits were continually being debated, a myriad of information could be found online. As for the latter, Audrey knew the perfect reference source. One of the more arcane tomes in AA's library was a book on the lives of United States vice presidents. The book, no longer in print, chronicled every vice presidency up until Richard M. Nixon.

That alone is a perfect rationale for why the vice presidency should be eliminated, Audrey reasoned.

As the librarian, Eloise, stamped Audrey's selection with the return date, she exclaimed, "Well what do you know? This book has never been checked out! Ah, well, the VP is always the bridesmaid and never the bride, isn't he?"

Audrey thought for a moment. "Wouldn't that make him the best man?"

Eloise laughed. "Right you are."

Audrey took the book to her favorite corner: a small alcove tucked into the bookcase right behind Eloise's desk.

"Excuse me, I'm looking for the book called *They Were Our Vice Presidents*. Do you know where I might find it?"

Audrey's ears perked up. For the past hour, she'd been making notes from that very book.

The student's voice, a girl's, wasn't one she recognized.

"I'm sorry," Eloise's clucked sympathetically. "It was just checked out."

"May I ask by whom?"

"Well..." Eloise's hesitation turned her one-syllable response into three.

"I just want to see if... Well, maybe this other student would consider sharing it with me."

Indignation stiffened Audrey's spine. *The audacity of this person!*

Eloise sighed. "It was one of the seniors—Audrey Thorpe."

"Oh." The student's reply was more like the plaintive wail of a wounded animal.

"I guess you'd have to ask her yourself—"

"Oh! You mean she's still here?" The girl's whine was replaced by a menacing wheedle—one that might have easily been growled by a Gestapo commissar.

"I...I don't know! I don't think so." The doubt in Eloise's tone was too tepid to hide the truth. Audrey wondered if, at the same time, the librarian's eyes had shifted to the alcove behind her, and thus betraying her.

"Oh. I see. Well, I'll just have a look around."

I'm trapped, Audrey thought.

Her ears followed the girl's slow, deliberate footsteps.

Audrey imagined her making her way through each row of bookshelves, peeking into every nook and cranny on the hunt for her prey.

As the footfalls receded, Audrey relaxed—

But not for long. Suddenly it seemed the footsteps were right next to her.

The alcove's desk was solid wood on three sides. Audrey ducked under it and pulled her chair in as far as it would go in the hope that the girl would walk right on by.

She did—

But then retraced her steps. She must have turned down Audrey's aisle because now the *clump-clump-clump* was slow but steady.

Audrey froze.

Finally, it stopped right in front of Audrey's desk.

Audrey held her breath. Only her eyes moved: downward, taking in the girl's shoes—Dr. Martens, an AirWairs style she'd never seen before. They were pale pink and illustrated with double-decker buses, telephone booths, the Queen's horsemen with their big furry hats...

Finally, the girl moved away—and fast. She was running.

Clumping, really, what with those boots—

Audrey crawled out from under the desk. A quick glance at her workspace and she realized why the girl had taken off so quickly:

She'd stolen the book.

Damn it! Damn it! How could I have been so stupid?

As quickly as she could, Audrey stuffed the rest of her things in her backpack and ran from the library—

But it was too late. The hall was empty.

"WHERE HAVE YOU BEEN?" TALLULAH ASKED. SHE, BLISS, AND DAVIS were sitting on AA's front stoop.

"Isn't it obvious?" Audrey retorted. She stared down at her arms, which were loaded down with library books on politics and constitutional law.

The missing book was the one she'd needed most.

She'd asked Eloise about the girl. Eloise claimed she'd never seen her before—doubly troubling since the librarian knew every student in the school.

"If for any reason she doesn't return it, I won't charge you for it," Eloise vowed.

"I should hope not," Audrey grumbled under her breath. She'd have to make do with biographies of the presidents and pray that the vice presidents were mentioned too.

Bliss, who had been perusing a recent issue of *Vogue,* was mimicking the come-hither pout on Cindy Crawford's face. "Whoa, wait! Those books are about the government. Aren't you debating about killers?"

Both Audrey and Davis gave her a blank stare.

Annoyed, Bliss added, "It's about *forensics,* silly gooses! You know, murder and stuff like that!"

Tallulah rolled her eyes. "All by your lonesome you're perpetuating the 'dumb blonde' myth for the rest of your kind." She thumped Audrey's books so hard that they almost dropped. "By the way, in this case, 'forensics' means extensive research."

"Oh." Bliss's eyes glazed over as she stared at Audrey's haul. "Well, that leaves me out. I'd rather be shopping."

"Same here," Davis replied. "And besides, the kind of guy who tries out for Debate Team isn't exactly man candy."

Tallulah shrugged. "You're right. You'd be better off as the football team's towel boy."

Davis sighed. "If only!"

Audrey nudged Tallulah with her foot. "What about you?"

Tallulah snorted. "Who needs Debate Team? Hell, if I want an argument, all I have to do is go home. Every day, Maggie and I fight over some bullshit." Her tightly coiled curls bounced as she shook her head angrily. "And I win because I'm not the one who's always drunk and living with some gross creep."

Maggie's latest boyfriend had been coming on to Tallulah. For just that reason, the girl had taken to staying over in the spare twin beds in either Audrey's or Bliss's bedrooms. "We've got enough homework as it is. Aren't you going a tad too far to get Egan to notice you?"

"Oh, he noticed her today, alright." Davis slipped his finger around the top button on Audrey's blouse, releasing it from its hole.

Audrey's face turned bright red. "You've got it all wrong. It's a great extracurricular for college applications—"

Bliss giggled. "The lady doth protest too much, methinks."

"Jesus! Egan even has her talking in tongues!" Davis slapped his forehead. "Other than Tallulah and me, is there anyone who hasn't joined the Nefarious Cult of Egan?"

Audrey shivered. "Nefarious is right! And some of its members are willing to steal to be in it."

"What?" Suddenly Audrey's friends were all ears.

"I'd checked out a book to use as research for my debate study. I overheard some girl ask about the same book. Next thing I know, she stole it off my library desk."

Tallulah's eyes opened wide. "Who was she?"

Audrey shrugged. "I wish I knew. She was gone in a flash. The only thing I can remember is her boots. They were Doc Martens, but a style I'd never seen before. Pinkish with what looked like a cartoon map of London—"

Bliss squealed. "Oh my God! I'll bet they're these boots!" Furiously, she flipped through her magazine until she found the page: a Dr. Martens ad displaying the exact same boots.

Davis frowned. "I've never seen those before."

Bliss rolled her eyes. "You wouldn't have because this is British *Vogue*." She flipped back to the cover so that he could read the magazine's issue title. "Maude leaves them around the shop—along with the French and Italian issues so that customers can see that what they're buying is sometimes straight off the fashion runways."

"Or great knockoffs," Davis retorted.

Bliss stuck out her tongue at him. "So what? Someday we'll carry the real thing—"

"Well, now that we know something about Audrey's thief, we can find her"—Tallulah cracked her knuckles menacingly—"Even if we have to look under every girl's bathroom stall. Considering what she did, she shouldn't be able to just waltz into the tryouts and run rings around our champ here!" She stuck a thumb in Audrey's direction.

"She won't, I promise you that," Audrey vowed. "Even if I have to memorize the rest of this stuff just to play catch-up." She heaved the books. "Listen, Nancy Drew, if I'm to make up for lost time, I've got to get cracking. But don't let that stop you, Bess, and Ned Nickerson here from finding the culprit."

"Why can't I be George Fayne?" Davis asked.

Bliss snickered. "Despite her name, she's really a *tomgirl*, silly!"

Davis sighed. "That's my point, genius."

Tallulah swept her arm over Bliss's head.

Bliss cringed. "What's wrong? Did you see a bee?"

Apparently, the point was made to everyone but Bliss.

CHAPTER 7

he hunt for the book thief went on all week. Although
Audrey and her friends scrutinized the feet of every
junior and senior in Ashbury Academy, by Thursday afternoon they
had yet to identify the girl.

Audrey was just about to enter Ashbury's assembly hall for
Debate Team tryouts when her friends fell into lockstep beside her.

Surprised, Audrey murmured, "What are you doing here? I
thought you'd decided to sit this one out."

"We are—sort of." Tallulah nodded toward Davis and Bliss.
"We're here to find the thief. That bitch has no right to make the
team"—she lowered her voice to a snarl—"and to make sure she
doesn't, we *will* expose her."

Audrey was startled by her friend's ominous tone. "How? And
to whom?"

Tallulah threw up her hands, perplexed that Audrey couldn't
grasp the obvious. "To Egan, of course! She's given us all the clues
we need to trap her at the scene of the crime. So, if she's chosen for
the team, we'll storm the stage and let her know she gave herself
away by her choice in stylishly unique footwear, and demand to see
the stolen book!" She put one arm around Bliss's shoulder and the
other on Davis. "Am I right?"

Davis pumped a fist in the air. "Right on!"

"Power to the people!" Bliss shouted.

Audrey understood their frustration. Hell, she was madder than anyone. Still, the thought of a revolt made her cringe. If her friends stood up and made a fuss because somehow the mystery girl had gotten on the team and Audrey hadn't, it might look as if Audrey was jealous and had put them up to it.

And Egan would side with her against the girl—not because she'd won her way onto the team fair and square but because she was his boss's daughter.

He'd then think she was petty. And Egan Gable could never love someone who would sink so low.

Worse yet, Lavinia would suggest they resolve the issue with a Magic Circle.

Audrey shook her head. "No, Tal! You can't do it! I mean…So she absconded with the book. So what? I'm smart. I didn't really need it to make a few debate points."

Frustration darkened Tallulah's face. "But—it's the principle of the thing!"

Audrey took Tallulah's face in her hands. When she had her dear friend's eyes focused only on her, she whispered, "That's my point exactly."

Time seemed to stand still.

Finally, Tallulah shrugged. "Okay, have it your way. We won't make a scene." She nodded toward the others. "But we're still going in."

Audrey frowned. "Promise me."

Tallulah smirked. "What, now you want to pinky swear?"

"Yep. Exactly. The last thing I want is for you to wrestle the culprit to the floor while I'm making my closing argument." Audrey held up her hand, pinky extended.

Tallulah rolled her eyes but held up her hand anyway.

When the girls' fingers entwined, Audrey nodded her thanks but turned her head before the others could notice her eyes were glistening with tears.

Twenty-one other students were there to debate.

Audrey knew all but three girls and two boys. From what she knew about the sixteen students she recognized, at least nine of them would make worthy teammates. Like her, they studied hard, excelled at their classes, and readily took part in class discussions.

Jeremy was there too. Seeing him, Audrey almost groaned out loud.

Based on her assessment of the competition, there was no way Jeremy would make the cut. Not that he knew the rules of debate anyway. His way of winning any argument was to toss out a few snarky jibes or parry with a couple of stupid jokes. If neither method got him what he wanted, he'd close with some ominous sulking.

She doubted he'd get beyond the first competitive round.

If I'm going to make the cut, I can't let his silly attempt to woo me back get in my way, Audrey reasoned. I need to focus!

She'd created a mantra and repeated it now in her head:

CONTENT: know what you're going to say, backward and forwards... MAKE YOUR CASE: Summarize it succinctly; then break it down using logic, statistics, examples, and quotes...REBUTTAL: undermine the other side's contentions; then summarize the flaws of their case.

And do it all with a blend of persuasion and conviction.

Above all else, she'd make eye contact with those who count most:

The judges.

Cornell, Nick, and of course, Egan.

Smiling brightly with her head held high, she walked in and sat down.

She has the grace of a queen, Egan marveled.

He had fully expected her to disappear from his course; to

transfer out without saying anything. Instead, she came to class each day, turned in her work, but did not participate or vie for his attention in any way.

Although it was contrary to what Egan knew was right, he greatly missed her attempts to garner his attention.

He was annoyed that Jeremy felt the need to use the debate team's tryouts as a chance to woo Audrey back. If the gossip Egan heard was true, Audrey wouldn't fall for Jeremy's malarkey.

At least, Egan didn't think she would...

Unless she's trying to get back at me for snubbing her, he suddenly realized.

In that case, she might consider making up with him just to make me jealous.

Cornell waved his hand in front of Egan's face. "Why the long face, buttercup?"

Egan shrugged. "No reason."

"Well, then, time to turn that frown upside down and get this show started," Cornell cooed.

"Sorry," Egan grumbled. He grabbed a stack of blank index cards. As he rose, he chided himself for having created the scenario in which Audrey was once again vulnerable to Jeremy's attentions.

It suddenly dawned on him how he could nip that disaster in the bud.

Forcing his lips into a smile, he faced the contestants and exclaimed, "I'm happy to see so many of you here for Ashbury Academy's debate team tryouts. As you already know, to make the team, you'll be playing by National Speech & Debate Tournament rules. PE Nick and Cornell have graciously agreed to act as my co-judges. So let's get started." He held up the index cards. "First and foremost, put your name on these index cards and turn them back in to me."

He passed the cards to the first person on each row, who in turn passed it to the next person, and so on.

Within minutes the students had turned in their cards—except for Davis, Bliss, and Tallulah, who ducked out of sight.

Egan collected them. As he walked back to the judges' table, he seemed to shuffle the cards.

As a child, he'd had an interest in magic tricks. This served him well now. With sleight of hand, he palmed the cards with two names —those of Audrey and Jeremy—and moved them to the bottom of the pile.

"To choose who debates whom, I'll pull two cards at a time from the stack," Egan continued. "Those two students will debate the question chosen for everyone: 'Should students be drug tested?' The first name called will be 'for' first, and then 'against.' The debates will take place in front of judges only. We'll be in the anteroom, there." He pointed to a set of double doors that belonged to a smaller room. "The eight students who win their matches with the highest scores will make up our team."

Egan watched as the students silently calculated their odds. They'd have to beat fourteen others.

For a moment, his eyes shifted toward Audrey. Her face looked as if it were carved from stone.

Unfathomable.

"Good," Egan declared. "Now, continuing: On Monday, those who have made the team will then get the chance to compete for team captain. Competitors will be sorted and matched by the two alternate questions they've chosen to debate." He scanned the competitors. "Any questions?"

No hands went up.

"Great," he finally declared. "Then the first two debaters are"— he turned over the first two cards—"Adrienne and Monica. Good luck to you, ladies."

THERE WERE TO BE ELEVEN MATCHES.

The first debate took all of ten minutes. Waiting for it to end was agony for Audrey. She just wanted to get hers over with. From the silence in the auditorium, the others must have felt the same way.

When the door to the judges' chambers finally opened, Adrienne came out. She smiled broadly and gave a thumbs-up to the others.

Monica was stoically silent.

Two more names were called. None were Audrey's.

Then two more. And another two. And yet two more names. Too antsy to sit alone, Audrey moved next to her friends. Two debates later, she was regretting it. Bliss was holding tight to her arm. Every time the doors opened, her friend's nails dug into her wrists.

"It's worse than waiting for the electric chair," someone muttered loudly.

Another student guffawed. "If that were our debate question, I'd gladly take the 'for' position."

That elicited a few nervous giggles.

But everyone went silent again as the door opened. The victor moonwalked out. His defeated opponent shot him a bird.

Egan could be heard calling out: "'Audrey Thorpe…"

She sighed, relieved. When she stood up, she smoothed her skirt before picking up her debate notes—

"…and Jeremy Blake."

"Shit!" Tallulah squeaked. She slapped her hand over her mouth.

Audrey glanced over at Jeremy. She'd been so caught up in reviewing her debate points that she hadn't noticed he hadn't been called yet either.

Jeremy stared back at her. His tan from his many afternoons on the football field seemed to fade by several shades.

For a second, she felt sorry for him.

Just not sorry enough.

She smiled sweetly but made it a point to stroll into the judge's room before him.

JEREMY AND AUDREY EACH TOOK A PODIUM AND THEN WAITED FOR Egan's signal to start.

Audrey noticed Jeremy wince when she began her opening argument in support of student drug testing. She wasn't surprised he was ruffled.

She was on fire; hitting all the bases.

She was annihilating him.

Audrey began by stating the school's mission: to enhance the health and wellbeing of its students and to create an environment in which critical thinking skills were learned, developed, and allowed to flourish.

She then pointed out that the school's mandatory rules forbidding the use of street drugs was the outgrowth of this stated mission. She followed with hard statistics about the effects of drug use on teens, their subsequent health issues, school dropout rates, and the financial and emotional cost to those who were early drug users.

Finally, despite fears it may cost her a few points, she ended with an emotional appeal: "The choices we make in our teens affect us for the rest of our lives. During these years, we are at our maximum potential—physically and mentally. We can't let social pressure dictate our actions. We have to think for ourselves. As Albert Camus said, 'Life is the sum of all our choices.'"

As she spoke, she stared straight at Egan. She hoped he'd deduce her message: *WAIT FOR ME.*

Egan gazed back. Then he winked at her.

Yes, he'd heard her.

JEREMY ISN'T YET OUT OF THE BARN AND ALREADY SHE'S SLAUGHTERED him, Egan thought.

Damn, she'd make a good lawyer.

He noticed the tremble in Jeremy's hands as the boy positioned his note cards on the podium. If the quiver in his voice wasn't bad enough, he stumbled over his opening argument: that if thirteen is old enough to be a man in the eyes of a religious faith five thousand years old, it should be the age in which students can make decisions for themselves—including what drugs to use, when, and where.

From there, his presentation went downhill.

Egan just sat back and let nature take its course.

He almost snickered when Jeremy quoted from the Torah. He then moved on to other societies in which a male's rite of passage began as a teen or younger: the Mardudjara Aborigines of Australia, the Satere-Mawe tribe in Brazil, the Maasai of Kenya, "…and even the Pacific Islander tribe, the Vanuatus, are considered men as young as age five."

In her rebuttal, Audrey countered that if every society used the cutting of a male's foreskin as a sign of manhood, toddlers could then be recruited into the U.S. Army. "And I suppose, by that standard, a girl is a woman on the day of her first menstruation."

Jeremy blanched at her statement. The men winced, but by their nods, they were duly impressed with this rebuttal.

The highest rating allowed was sixteen. Thus far, he'd only given that score to four students. Audrey's argument had been much better than theirs, but he'd figured he should shave it—but only by a point, so that it wouldn't look as if he were playing favorites.

He gave Jeremy a score of 10. Despite his personal animosity, in his opinion even that was generous.

"OKAY, GENTLEMAN," EGAN SAID. "LET'S HAVE YOUR VERDICTS."

Cornell and PE Nick handed him their scoring cards.

Audrey: 14 +15 + 10 = 39
Jeremy: 10 + 16 + 13 = 39

What the hell? THEY TIED?

Cornell had given Audrey the score of fourteen, which meant Nick had graded her a lowly ten.

"Students, will you wait in the hallway?" Egan hoped the anger didn't come through in his request.

Startled, Audrey and Jeremy rose. From their pace, you'd think they were being sent to the gallows.

Still, Egan waited until the door was firmly shut before growling, "Did we see different debates?"

Nick shrugged. "Frankly, I thought Audrey overplayed her hand."

"Oh yeah? Does that mean you preferred the way Jeremy underplayed his?"

Nick snickered. "Let's just say I rewarded him for giving it the old college try."

"If that's the case, he won't do better than junior college."

Nick guffawed. "Jeremy will end up in an Ivy. Hell, if he doesn't get there on a football scholarship, he'll make it based on his math scores."

"If he's such a shoo-in, why is he even trying out for Debate? And for that matter, why are you helping him?"

"Because the kid wants it badly," Nick insisted.

"No—he wants *her* badly," Cornell sighed. "Anyone can see that. Ah, *l'amour, l'amour!*"

Egan shook his head. "That's not what Debate Team is about."

"I'm sticking to my score," Nick insisted. "When Jeremy is happy, he carries the team with him."

Egan turned to Cornell. "How about you? Didn't you feel Audrey's argument merited more than a score of fourteen?"

"Well, yes, I did—up until she brought up that thing about lady bits." Cornell shuddered. "TMI, to say the least!"

"And yet Jeremy's mention of foreskin was okay in your book?" Egan smirked.

"Everything Jeremy says and does is okay by me," Cornell purred. "Hey, cut me some slack! I took off three points—legitimately. And I did it even though he ditches my class whenever he can."

"You're both very generous," Egan muttered. "To a fault, which could negatively affect everything I'm trying to do here."

Nick sighed. "Give it a break Egan! So what if Audrey and Jeremy are tied? They now both have a shot at making the team. Why is that a bad thing?"

If only you knew, Egan thought.

Not that he'd say that out loud. He shrugged. "Okay, I'll let them know they tied."

As Egan announced the tie, Audrey was able to keep the shock off her face that somehow Jeremy's score had matched hers.

How could that be, she fumed. My God, his presentation was all over the place! And his opening statement was so lame! I mean, seriously: *the Vanuatus?*

A realization hit her: Egan would have preferred having Jeremy on the team. He didn't want to show her any favoritism, so he scored her low on purpose—but not low enough to offset the other judges' scores.

The thought angered her.

He's decided he can't be himself around me. Well, that's too bad! Because at the same time he's stifling any attempt I make to live my life; to be myself.

Well, she wasn't going to let him.

There were still three sets of competitors left to debate. She prayed the winners' scores wouldn't beat hers. She deserved to be on the team.

Egan knew it too. She wasn't going to let him steal her chance to make it.

At least if my score is too low to make the team, Jeremy can't be on it either.

The thought gave her enough relief that she could smile again. In fact, she felt generous enough to thank Jeremy for holding the door for her on their way out.

He must have been shocked that she wasn't angry with him because he blushed. And then, feeling emboldened, he placed his hand on the small of her back.

She turned in time to see Egan flinch and took some solace that his misguided plan hadn't worked.

CHAPTER 8

"That's the girl!" Bliss's frantic whisper was followed by a nod toward the row behind them on the right.

Tallulah flipped around to see their suspect. The girl, sitting by herself, was plump and wore square small-framed glasses. The frizzy shorthairs near the nape of her neck had escaped the tight topknot that held the rest of her dishwater blond mane.

It looked as if she were talking to herself too.

Probably memorizing her opening argument, Tallulah figured. "Bliss, are you sure it's her?"

Her friend nodded. "Heck yeah! She's wearing the Docs!" Now that the scouting expedition was over, Bliss stood up and waved Davis over. When she got his attention, he trotted their way.

Tallulah snickered. "If she wore them today then I guess she thinks those boots are lucky for her."

"Or comfortable," Bliss countered, "which they are. Our shop sells a ton of Martens." She nodded toward the girl. "So, what do you want to do about her?"

"She's yet to be called into the judges' chambers," Tallulah reminded her. "By then I'll have figured something out."

They didn't have to wait long. Just as Audrey and Jeremy were walking out, Egan shouted, "Mandy Blackwell and Franklin Zorn!"

Startled, Top Knot leaped up, spilling the note cards that she must have placed in her lap. Furiously, she gathered them, took a couple of deep breaths, and then made her way to the judges' room on the heels of her competitor.

"I've got a great idea!" Tallulah nudged Davis. "She left her backpack by her seat. Find her locker keys. Make duplicates. The workshop room should be open." Berney left it that way so that the students could work on their projects at all hours.

"On it." Davis sauntered up the aisle. When he got to Top Knot's row, he lifted her bag and walked off with it without anyone noticing.

"I'M SORRY, AUDREY. YOU SHOULD HAVE WON, FAIR AND SQUARE." Jeremy's apology was too guileless to be anything but sincere.

"Thanks for that," she murmured. "It means a lot to me."

"And I want you to know...I mean, about us." He pursed his lips. "I know I screwed up—big time. If we could...I mean, if there were any way you could find it in your heart to—"

Jeremy—*groveling*? Audrey was so embarrassed for him that she shifted her eyes away—

To the students passing them on the way into the judges' room.

The boots...

That girl is wearing THE BOOTS!

Audrey's eyes moved up toward the girl's face: round, pitted with zits, pocked with anxiety.

And she had the misfortune to debate Franklin, a senior with one of the highest GPAs in the school. Everyone liked Franklin. He was quick with a quip. A real charmer.

At that moment, Audrey felt sorry for the girl—

Until their eyes met.

Until Audrey saw the girl's lips curdle into a smirk.

She then dared to wink at Audrey.

Audrey was too upset to do anything but watch as the girl walked around her.

By the time the fog of her anger had subsided, she had realized Jeremy was saying something: "So, you're okay with that?"

"Huh?... Yeah, sure." She shrugged helplessly. At that moment she noticed Bliss waving her over. "Look, Jeremy, I've got to go." Her legs seemed to turn to jelly as she stumbled down the aisle.

***

"The boots—"

Before Audrey could finish her sentence, Tallulah replied, "We know. On the girl who just went inside." She opened the girl's bag and held up an Ashbury Academy student ID card. "She's Mandy Blackwell. A junior. Lives in Pacific Heights."

Blackwell—Mandy…

For some reason, the name sounded familiar to Audrey, but she couldn't place it.

She reached for the girl's bag and opened it. As she'd hoped, the book was inside. "Bingo!"

Tallulah nudged the bag with her foot so that it was beyond Audrey's reach. "And it's got to stay in there—for now, anyway." She nodded to the students milling around them. "Think about it! She can always claim she found the book somewhere, and that you —we— had no right to open her bag, let alone rummage through it."

Audrey sighed. "Okay, alright! But what if she loses it?"

"You immediately reported it stolen to Eloise. Now that we have the name of the girl, Eloise can confirm she asked about the book right after you signed for it. In the meantime…" She shifted her glance to Davis, who was making his way toward them.

He landed in the seat beside Audrey. He was palming something, which he handed to her:

A set of keys.

"What's this for?" she asked.

Bliss hissed, "They open the Blackwell girl's lockers."

Audrey frowned. "What am I supposed to do with them?"

Tallulah arched a brow. "It's your chance to take back what's yours—when the time is right."

Davis opened Mandy's notebook. He rifled through the papers on the inside pocket until he found what he was looking for. "According to little Ms. Blackwell's class schedule, she has PE during seventh period."

PE?...

Audrey groaned.

Oh my God! Mandy Blackwell was the junior I bumped to get into Egan's class. Talk about bad karma...

"What's wrong with you? Tallulah asked.

"It's ...nothing." Audrey shivered at this turn of events. "Debate Team's first practice is on Monday. We'll be debating to see who makes captain. If she makes the team, she'll hang onto it through the weekend."

"Tomorrow is Friday," Davis pointed out. "She'll probably stash her bag in the girl's PE locker room while they're playing on Kezar Field." This historic ball field was located just a few blocks from the school.

Tallulah grinned wickedly. "She'll freak out when she realizes it's disappeared."

"Hey, how are we getting out of Egan's class?" Bliss asked.

"We'll figure something out." Tallulah shrugged. "But if we all disappear, he'll suspect something. It's not like there's an outbreak of measles or something."

"Fine with me. I wouldn't be caught dead in the girl's locker room anyway," Davis assured her. "Tell you what—while you're B and E'ing, I'll create a diversion.

"Can I help too?" Bliss asked hopefully.

"No," the others declared.

She pouted for a moment. Finally, she groused, "What's 'B and E'ing'?"

"In police lingo, it stands for 'breaking and entering,'" Davis explained.

Bliss's eyes opened wide. "How would you know that?"

Davis shrugged. "Don't ask, because you don't really want to know."

"It's part of his dark, deadly past," Tallulah scoffed.

"Bottom line—if you get caught, it's not fun," Davis retorted.

Tallulah chucked his cheek. "Then be sure we don't." She pointed to the bag. "Speaking of which, maybe you should put this back by Mandy's chair before she returns."

Davis nodded. Holding the bag low, he walked away as if he hadn't a care in the world.

Noting Audrey's frown, Tallulah asked, "You're up for this, right?"

Audrey shrugged. "I'd feel bad if I embarrassed Lavinia."

Tallulah put her arm around her friend. "I'd feel bad about that too. But Audrey, be honest: what's worse, scaring that lunatic by stealing back the book she stole from you, or informing Lavinia about Light-Fingered Mandy's odious theft, whom she'd then have to suspend? The girl is new at AA. She'd take a public shaming pretty hard."

She's got a point, Audrey reasoned. If this Mandy person felt disgraced, she'd leave the school for good, Audrey reasoned. And AA would lose her tuition money.

No, Tallulah's way is much better. And besides, maybe Mandy won't make the team. If not, she'll return the book on her own, and we won't have to go through with the theft.

The thought was barely out of Audrey's mind when the doors to the judges' room opened. Mandy waltzed out as if she'd just danced with Prince Charming.

She beat Franklin? But… how?

Egan stood at the door behind them. He was smiling too.

Why? What has this Mandy person done? What has she said to make him so happy?

Audrey turned to Tallulah. "How long do we make her sweat

before we tell her we returned the book to the library, safe and sound?"

Tallulah laughed. "If it were up to me, at least a month. But you're a much nicer person."

Not this time, Audrey vowed.

THE REST OF THE TRYOUTS TOOK UP THE NEXT HOUR.

When the last competitors emerged from the judges' room, they told the rest of the students: "If you won your match, you're to stick around while the judges pull the eight highest scorers."

While those who lost their matches shuffled out, the winners stayed seated, but barely. Skittishness came through in nervous giggles, ponderous pacing, and hands that wouldn't stay still. Anxiety seemed to suck all the air from the room.

Audrey spent that time staring at her feet and wondering if the quest to get Egan to admit his love for her was futile.

What if I imagined what happened? Worse yet, what if he was just flirting like he does with everyone else?

What if he doesn't love me at all?

She had to find out.

FINALLY, THE DOORS OPENED AGAIN. EGAN CAME OUT. CORNELL AND PE Nick were at his side. "Okay, gang. I want to just say that all of you gave spectacular debates. You left me in awe. I'm proud of each and every one of you." He sighed. "If I could, I'd put all of you on the team. But, unfortunately, I can't." He lowered his head as if their apprehension weighed heavily on him as well. "Okay, so, here we go."

Egan read each name deliberately.

He read Audrey's somewhere in the middle so that it wouldn't seem so obvious.

He hoped he'd kept the pride out of his voice—

And the guilt that he'd had to bump two students with higher scores to slip Audrey and Jeremy onto the team instead.

That Jeremy kid has no place on the team, he fumed. And not just because he loves Audrey…

No, he doesn't love her. He just wants to fuck her. To be her first.

As he watched Audrey's joy in hearing her name, he was ashamed to admit it to himself:

And so do I.

It was just a few seconds after the final bell announcing the start of seventh period that Egan noticed Audrey's absence.

Jeremy's chair was empty too.

Egan felt his heart drop into the pit of his gut.

Damn it! They skipped my class—together?

If Audrey and Jeremy wanted to be alone, Audrey would know where to go to make that happen. She knew every nook and cranny of the school.

Egan was overcome with the desire to find them—now.

I've got to stop her from doing…something stupid.

In the meantime, he had to take care of his students. He stood up. "Okay, class, it's time for a pop essay based on your homework assignment last night on *Macbeth*. Today's assignment: compare that power couple to another found in either nineteenth or twentieth-century literature." He looked down at his watch. "I'll give you a half hour. Afterward, you can regale me with your thoughts."

He waited until the groans gave way to the scratching of pencils on paper before making his way down the aisle in front of Bliss's desk. Reaching it, he murmured, "Bliss, may I see you for a moment?"

The girl raised her head. Her eyes widened in surprise. Instinctively, her eyes went to Audrey's empty seat.

She knows something.

"Would you mind following me out into the hall?" he asked.

By the time she stood up, her lip was trembling, but she did as she was told.

"WHERE IS AUDREY?" EGAN DIDN'T SEE THE NEED IN BEATING AROUND the bush.

"She isn't feeling well." The words came out thick as if they were sticking in Bliss' throat.

"I see." Egan hoped his nod came off as sympathetic. "So, if I were to go to the reception office, I'd find her there with Clare?"

"No!" As soon as the word was out of her mouth, Bliss pursed her lips. "I mean, I'm sure she'll be back before class ends."

"Oh? What makes you so sure?"

"Because… she wasn't feeling *that* sick." Bliss had a nervous habit: twirling the ends of her hair. Egan watched as she did so now.

Egan nodded. "I see. So, where is she right now?"

Bliss gulped but stayed silent.

"Whatever she's doing, it's wrong, and you know it. Please, Bliss, tell me where she is so that I can stop her from making the biggest mistake of her life."

Bliss dropped her head. "The PE locker room…"

He nodded. It makes sense, he thought. This period's PE class would be out on the field. No one could bother them there.

"Go back to class," he commanded. "Don't mention what we've discussed to anyone."

Nodding, she scurried back into the room.

As Egan made his way through AA's halls, he tried to keep his thoughts from what he might witness as he entered the locker room:

Audrey and Jeremy's clothes piled haphazardly on the tile floor;

The two teens, naked and damp with the sweat of their desires; grunting from the high of their ecstatic union; groaning in the throes of climax…

He pushed these heartbreaking thoughts from his mind.

He wondered how Audrey might feel when she finally realized he was there. Surprised? Shamed?

Maybe triumphant.

What better way to thumb her nose at him, to make him realize what he could have had if only he'd asked?

But I care too much to ask it of her. Not now, anyway.

And after today, maybe not ever.

<hr>

AUDREY WATCHED FROM ASHBURY ACADEMY'S CLOCK TOWER AS THE seventh period PE class made its way down Haight Street toward Kezar Field. When they were out of sight, she murmured, "We can go in now."

Tallulah's emphatic nod sent her tightly coiled curls into a frenzied dance. "Okay, let's do this thing!" She beckoned for Audrey to follow as she made her way down the tower's staircase, to the school's basement level.

As they'd hoped, the basement hallway was empty.

The changing rooms were never locked. They entered the one designated GIRLS and scanned the rows of lockers, which were stacked in columns of two.

"There it is!" Tallulah pointed to a bottom locker numbered 415.

Audrey followed her over. Her hands shook as she inserted one of the two tiny locker keys. The first one didn't work, so it must have belonged to Mandy's book locker, somewhere outside the Junior Class' homerooms.

The second key opened the shiny new lock.

"Eureka!" Tallulah squealed.

"Shhhh!" Audrey looked around. Satisfied no one had heard her friend, she pulled the lock from the door.

Mandy's bag was there, as were her clothes.

So were the boots.

As Audrey unzipped the bag and took out the book, Tallulah pulled the boots from the bottom of the locker too.

Audrey frowned. "What are you doing?"

"To the victor go the spoils." Tallulah shoved the boots into Audrey's arms. "Oh, and you're in luck! They're exactly your size."

"I can't wear these! She'll know we stole them," Audrey argued. "Or that *I* stole them."

"So? What of it? She wouldn't be able to prove it. You heard Bliss. Her parents' store sells all kinds of Doc Martens. Maybe they sold you this pair."

"Tallulah, I told you: we can't get caught!"

Ignoring Audrey, Tallulah shut the locker door, snapped the lock into place, and pocketed the key. As she slipped the boots and the book into her backpack, she argued, "And we won't—because Mandy won't dare tell anyone. Otherwise, she'd have to admit she stole your book."

Audrey shook her head. "I don't know..."

The sound of footsteps shut her up.

Tallulah must have heard them too because she shoved Audrey toward the locker room's back door. It was designated as the basement's fire exit and it led out onto Haight Street.

To avoid being seen by anyone who might be looking out the school's windows, the girls hugged the building's brick wall as they made their way back to the school's main doors. When Clare looked up from the receptionist desk, they ducked behind a wall. Then, when her back was turned, they flew up the grand staircase to the second floor and Egan's classroom.

THEY WERE SURPRISED TO SEE THAT EGAN WASN'T THERE. EXCEPT FOR A few whispering cliques, their classmates were in the midst of a writing assignment.

Bliss waved frantically to her friends. When they took their seats, she leaned over and hissed, "Egan went looking for you. Did he catch you?"

Perplexed Audrey shook her head adamantly. "You told him where we went?"

Bliss didn't have to say anything. Her answer was given by twirling a lock of her hair furiously with her index finger.

Tallulah slapped her forehead. "Damn it, Bliss!"

Audrey was about to scold her when she felt a tap on her shoulder:

Jeremy.

"Where were you?" he hissed.

"What's it to you?" she muttered.

"Everything—since you promised to go with me to PE Nick and ask about our scores."

"Wait...*what?* I don't remember..."

Jeremy glared back. "Yesterday, when we walked out of the judges' room, I told you I was sorry we'd tied. Audrey, I'm no fool. You wiped the floor with me! If PE Nick scored you low on purpose, I wanted him to admit it—and make good on it."

Audrey couldn't believe her ears. "You were willing to do that for me?"

He nodded. "Audrey, I'd do anything for you."

"Jeremy, please... What we had—*that's over.*"

"That's what PE Nick said too." Jeremy's face hardened at the memory. "He said the fact that you stood me up was proof I'm wasting my time trying to get you to forgive me."

"Gee, he's a regular relationship counselor," Audrey retorted. "So, tell me: did he also admit he graded me lower on purpose?"

"Of course not. But... I know in my gut he did."

Don't be so sure, Audrey thought wryly. Her bet was still on Egan.

Jeremy continued: "He's worried I'm losing my edge on the field because I'm still hung up on you. He thinks I'm killing my chances for a sports scholarship. And he's right." He put his hand over hers. "But that's no reason to take away something you badly wanted and deserved. Audrey, if you ask me, I'll leave Debate Team."

For the first time since the day of the SATs, Audrey felt grief-stricken: not for her loss but Jeremy's pain. "Jeremy, I would never—"

"Ms. Thorpe and Mr. Blake, I'm so glad you finally found your way to class!" Egan's voice came from the front of the room.

Startled, they looked up in unison.

Egan tapped the blackboard. "Since you missed the class assignment, I'll expect you to stay after the bell and make it up."

Jeremy gawked. "But, I've got football practice—"

"I'm sure PE Nick will understand." Egan's tone sent a shiver through Audrey.

Jeremy nodded meekly.

They stayed silent as Egan called on some of the others to read their essays.

When the last bell of the day chimed, they stayed put while the others rose to leave. As Tallulah followed Davis and Bliss out the door, she nudged Audrey with her backpack. The outline of the book and the boots were easy to make out.

Egan waited until the last students trickled out before closing the door. When he turned around, he pointed to Jeremy. "You go first. What was so important that you had to skip my class for it?"

SAY IT. SAY YOU WANTED ANOTHER CONQUEST—THE ONE WHO GOT AWAY: Audrey.

Boast about it to me, just like you'll do to your jock buddies.

Give me a reason to knock that smirk off your face.

Despite Egan's silent wishes, Jeremy merely shrugged. Still, he kept some semblance of a casual grin on his face as he replied, "I stayed after sixth period PE to talk with Nick."

Egan rolled his eyes. "I see." No doubt Nick would vouch for Jeremy. Hell, he'd do anything for his star quarterback. To prove it, he'd almost ruined Audrey's chance to make Debate Team.

In fact, Egan wouldn't have been surprised to learn that Nick suggested that the couple use the locker room for their tryst.

He gave Audrey a sidelong gaze. "And where were you?"

Audrey opened her mouth, but nothing came out.

Hell, she's traumatized, Egan thought. That son of a bitch sullied her—and now she's in shock! I'll kill that little asshole—

"Audrey was…with me."

Egan seethed at Jeremy's admission. Not that he could show it. He cocked a brow. "With you, talking to PE Nick?"

Jeremy nodded.

"Why did you both feel the need to talk to him during my class?" Egan asked.

Jeremy sighed. "Because it was about Debate Team tryouts. I felt I didn't deserve my score. I wanted his assurance—in front of Audrey—that he hadn't been too generous on my behalf at the expense of her place on the team."

"How chivalrous," Egan snapped. He turned to Audrey. "Is what he says true?"

All the color left her face. Still, she nodded. "Yes. I was with him."

Egan flinched. *So she admits it. They were together.*

But where?

Egan knew he'd scared Bliss into telling him the truth. And yet, when he'd checked both the boys' and girls' locker rooms, Jeremy and Audrey were nowhere to be found—

Unless…

Unless Jeremy blew his wad too quickly.

Or, worse yet, he couldn't get it up.

Ha! Egan swallowed his urge to scoff at the irony of that. Maybe Audrey's long face had something to do with her disappointment in missing the big moment…

With the wrong guy.

Or maybe she just couldn't go through with it.

Hope surged through him. He looked at Audrey, praying he'd read this theory in her face.

She was staring back at him. There was no triumph in her eyes:

Just longing.

Egan hated himself for having thought the worst of her.

He felt ashamed for wanting her as badly as he did.

I care too much for her.

"I'll expect your assignments on Monday," he muttered. "And by the way, Jeremy, don't blame your coach for doing his best to save you from yourself. Every great teacher has the same instinct."

By Audrey's blush, he knew she realized the message was for her.

CHAPTER 9

$\mathcal{L}$avinia knocked on Audrey's bedroom door. "Darling, you've been in there all weekend! Why don't you come out and spend some time with me in the garden?"

Audrey sighed. Her mother was right. Since leaving school on Friday, Audrey had holed up in her room, preparing for the first Debate Team meeting. In that regard, the library book on the vice presidents was providing a font of information for Audrey's for-and-against arguments.

She was determined to be the team captain. It was the best way to force Egan to see her as a competent person.

And maybe more.

Hopefully, much more.

Audrey knew why her mother was concerned. Lavinia's rule about homework was simple: there should never be too much of it —and none on the weekends.

AA's teachers were comfortable with that philosophy and managed their class time for new information and the open discussion of it. Any homework assignment was, at best, an item to read for discussion the next day, or an essay to write. Tests were short, and usually required an essay answer. The process was geared toward nurturing critical thinking as opposed to rote test taking.

Few nights or weekends went uninterrupted by some school event. Realizing this, Audrey cherished time alone with her mother. She knew Lavinia felt the same way.

This would have been such a time of joint solitude.

Audrey usually studied in their cottage's sunroom, so she felt doubly guilty for hiding out in her bedroom. Or, if it were a warm day, she'd sit on the chaise out in the yard, so that she and her mother could talk and laugh and gossip as Lavinia nurtured the flowerbeds. It was a futile attempt, but Lavinia never gave up hope that they'd flourish despite San Francisco's foggy nights, chilly summers, and a peek-a-boo sun that ducked and dodged the city's tall buildings and even taller hills.

Lavinia was right. This was *their* time.

"I'll be down in a second," Audrey exclaimed.

She was about to tuck the library book under her pillow when something fell out from between its pages. It was a contact sheet containing miniature black-and-white photos of—

Egan?

She could tell immediately that it had been taken by the professional photographer hired by the school for the formally posed headshots of teachers and students displayed in AA's yearbook.

One of the photos had a heart drawn around it in red ink.

Admittedly, it was the best one of Egan. He was gazing directly into the camera. His brow was arched as if he were about to say something intriguing.

His grin was an open invitation to come closer and listen.

So, Mandy has a crush on him.

And because of Audrey, Mandy had been bumped from the one opportunity she had to get close to him.

Until she made Debate Team.

Such irony.

But how did Mandy get ahold of these photos? Only the students who worked on the yearbook staff would have access to the school's photo archives.

Lavinia would know if Mandy was on it.

For that matter, maybe she just walked into the yearbook production room and stole it. Heaven knows she isn't above taking what isn't hers.

Audrey wondered what she should do with the contact sheet. There was no way she'd return it to the school, what with the red heart drawn around Egan.

I should burn it, she thought. But she knew she couldn't do it.

Instead, she put it in her keepsake box—antique, carved out of burlwood, and lacquered. She'd found it at a garage sale a couple of years ago.

After Monday's meeting, Audrey planned on placing the book in the library's overnight box. She could then ask Eloise if it ever showed up. Once Eloise confirmed it had, she'd be off the hook for it.

And Mandy would too.

———

"I can't believe Egan assigned homework for the weekend." Lavinia's swipe at the bead of sweat hanging at the end of her nose only replaced it with a smudge of mud. "The teachers know how I feel about that."

"Officially, it's not homework," Audrey assured her. "Monday's debate practice will determine who will be the team's captain. I want to take a shot at it."

"Ah! Well, then. I can't be angry with him, can I?" Lavinia was all smiles again. "And I certainly can't stifle your admirable desire to lead your team." Lavinia shoved her hand spade into the flowerbed's rich, dark soil, enlarging the hole by several more inches. "What with Debate Team and four classes, I hope I didn't burden Egan with too much responsibility."

"He seems to be enjoying himself—in my class, anyway." Audrey kept her eyes on her notes.

Lavinia stopped digging in order to look up at her daughter. "Is he a good teacher?"

"Everyone loves his class." *No lie there.*

Lavinia laughed. "Something tells me his popularity isn't just based on his teaching skills."

"You're right," Audrey admitted. "But he has a passion for teaching, and it shows. My class is also a lot of fun. He encourages us to think about what influenced the writers who came after Shakespeare, and why. And he makes everyone feel...well, I guess the right word is *special*." She turned her head so that her mother couldn't see her cheeks pinking up.

"That's good to know." Gently, Lavinia tapped the base of a plastic pot holding a small lavender plant. When she determined it had loosened the soil around the plant's roots, she lifted it out and placed it in the hole in front of her. "I was surprised to see your name on his Comparative Lit roster. I thought you'd decided on Glee instead."

Audrey shrugged. "I figured it wouldn't hurt to have one more AP course on my transcript."

"It was a full class," Lavinia reminded her. "Another student was bumped: Mandy Blackwell. She was very upset. Her mother called me about it."

What a cry baby!

It was on the tip of Audrey's tongue to divulge the lengths Mandy had gone to get close to Egan. But then she thought better of it. Her own actions toward him would seem questionable to a stranger.

For that matter, Lavinia would question them too.

But I'm not some lovesick schoolgirl. My God, I'm a year away from college!

"No class schedule is set in stone until the first day of school," Audrey argued. "And besides, seniors have always had first dibs on courses."

"All I'm saying is that you should have discussed it with me before going into the computer and making the change yourself," Lavinia continued.

Audrey muttered. "Isn't she on the yearbook staff?"

Lavinia nodded absently.

So, I was right. She stole Egan's photos from there!

"Mandy's mother didn't threaten to pull her out of the school, did she?" Audrey wondered if she'd sounded too hopeful. She and the girl had yet to exchange a single word and already she found her incredibly irritating.

"No," Lavinia replied. "Slowly but surely, Mandy is finding her sea legs at the school. It helped that she made Debate Team."

"Well, then, that should keep her busy," Audrey muttered. "And yearbook looks great on college transcripts. Frankly, I don't know why she's making such a big deal over getting bumped, and in her junior year, no less!"

Lavinia sighed. "I wish it weren't a big deal either. But when parents are paying for school tuition, they look at educators through a different lens. Everything is magnified—especially perceived slights. They feel their children deserve special treatment in all matters."

The memory of Egan laughing with Mandy as he walked her out of the judges' room came to mind.

I know what kind of "special treatment" Mandy is hoping for…

Audrey had a horrible thought. "Had you mentioned her disappointment in missing out on Comparative Lit to Egan?"

"No…" Lavinia paused from planting to think for a moment. "At least, I don't think so. Why do you ask?"

Audrey shrugged. "A lot of students tried out for debate. I'd hate for anyone to think he was playing favorites."

Lavinia frowned. "I wouldn't stand for it."

"I know that, and so does everyone on the staff. But you're Egan's boss. He's new and he wants to please you." *It's why he won't look twice at me.*

The thought of his disregard for her feelings made her even angrier about Mandy's crush.

"The Blackwell girl is a junior," Audrey huffed. "She can take Egan's class next year."

Lavinia patted the loose dirt around the plant's stem. "If he's still around."

That got Audrey's attention. "What do you mean? Where do you think he'll go? To another school?"

Lavinia smacked the dirt from her hands. "Doubtful. In his mind, teaching anywhere is just a temporary situation. He's young, and he has goals. He wants to be a novelist."

"He's not all *that* young," Audrey protested. "He's twenty-six."

"Twenty-six may seem old to someone in their teens, but in the scope of a lifetime, he's still young. Think about it: he's only eight years older than you. When he's forty, you'll be thirty-two."

Audrey enjoyed the thought that, in just a few years, no one would question their attraction, let alone their dating.

And certainly not their marriage.

She rewarded her mother's wisdom with a laugh. "You've got an excellent point."

At that moment, she decided to give Mandy Blackwell a very clear message:

Stay away from me.

And stay away from Egan.

She'd start by winning Monday's debate.

And so that Mandy understood just who she was messing with, she'd wear Mandy's boots.

CHAPTER 10

Only four students from Egan's seventh period class made it onto Debate Team. Jeremy and Audrey were two of them. The others were Gemma Sisley, whose father had been one of Berkeley's renowned Black Panther activists; and Johnny Ruiz, whose mother ran a free clinic in San Francisco's Mission district. They stayed behind when their classmates filed out as AA's clock tower rang Monday's end-of-day chimes.

Within minutes, the rest of the team filtered in. Two were the auburn-haired Kennedy twins—Caleb and Jeb, each whip-smart in some arcane form of trivia. Another was a junior girl: Portia Rosenberg, a pixie in stature who spoke rarely, but always eloquently.

Mandy Blackwell was the last to enter. She held her head high, but by her frown, it was obvious she wasn't happy.

Audrey could guess why.

<hr>

Tallulah was still lingering in the doorway when the junior made her entrance. As Mandy walked past her, Tallulah declared, "Wow, nice sneakers! They make quite a fashion statement."

Mandy's face darkened with anger. She was wearing shoes her stepfather, Simon, had insisted on buying her: Women's Air Jordans.

The sneakers were a name-brand cliché. Trimmed in black and sporting the red logo of a player palming a ball while leaping high in the air, the shoes were white and puffy, like marshmallows inflated by the heat of a campfire flame.

Mandy didn't play basketball. In fact, she despised sports in general. It showed in her doughy figure. Still, her mother had insisted she wear them, if only for PE class.

Mother will do anything to please that jerk, Mandy thought furiously.

She knew this from the disgusting sounds that emanated from the master bedroom on the far end of the third-floor hallway on any given night.

Mandy had no choice but to wear the sneakers home on Friday, after the discovery that the coveted library book and her Doc Martens had been stolen from her PE locker. The theft of the book upset her only because she'd hoped to spend the weekend making notes from it, whereas the boots were her pride and joy.

She cringed when her stepfather saw the sneakers on her. He puffed up with pride, under the assumption that he'd finally won her over.

As if!

Unlike her mother, his money didn't impress her. She refused to fawn over him, let alone coo and grovel like she'd seen her mother do for him.

And for what, a couple of hundred dollars in tip money?

Mandy wondered if Simon stuffed the bills in her mother's panties and then made her strip down. She wouldn't doubt it in the least. Her mother was just the most recent of Simon's three wives and she was hell-bent on being his last.

Maybe that's the reason Mom spends several hours a day working out, she reasoned.

Mandy's goal was much bigger: to make sure she'd never have to rely on a Simon of her own.

Besides, she preferred stealing from the wad of cash he left in his bureau drawer; not any of the numerous Benjamins crammed between the old fart's tighty-whities but a twenty or two, every couple of days.

Simon never even noticed.

The best thing about Simon was that he was willing to fork over the money for AA's tuition. Getting into a decent school with a reputation for strong academics was her ticket into an Ivy League school–preferably far away from the Simons of the world.

She knew AP courses were a great shortcut. It was why Mandy had made her mother scream bloody murder when she'd been cut from Egan's class.

Although Mandy had somehow gotten bounced from Comparative Lit, she'd accomplished the next best thing: making it onto Debate Team.

That's where Egan came in. Her goal: to be teacher's pet, one way or another.

Doing so would make her school of choice, Berkeley, very probable. She'd heard he was well connected with the Lit Department. It was an easy major, so why not make that her next academic perch?

Mandy wasn't a virgin and Egan was a hottie. If getting a recommendation to Berkeley meant sleeping with him, she'd do it, and willingly. If she sucked up properly, no doubt he'd write a recommendation for her.

She rolled her eyes at the thought that, in this case, "sucking up" would prove to be more than a double entendre. Granted, had he looked like a troll—like, say, Hardy or History Nick—the task would be harder to swallow—literally.

Mandy knew all too well that close personal connections were also key to her future success. Her goal: to get as close as possible to those who could do her the most favors.

Since the first day of school Mandy had made note of the kids, both the girls and the guys, who were deemed popular by their peers. Audrey Thorpe topped the list—not just because she was the Head of School's daughter or because she'd proven to be one of

AA's smartest students. She had a reputation for kindness. She never had a bad word to say about anyone. She inspired others and was respected for doing so.

In other words, she was her mother's daughter.

At that moment, Mandy realized she was *her* mother's daughter too.

It's why she had given into the compulsion to take Audrey's library book. As for the fact that some nut felt the urge to steal it along with her Docs—well, that was now Audrey's problem. Since she was the last person to have checked it out, she'd have to cough up the money for its disappearance.

All the more reason to ignore Tallulah's smug observation. Making Debate Team gave Mandy a great opportunity to get close to Audrey. No one was going to stand in her way—certainly not the daughter of a drugged-out rock-and-roll whore! Once she had Audrey's ear, she'd work on nudging a wedge between her and that bitch, Tallulah.

Which is why Mandy met Tallulah's jibe with a withering glower.

Tallulah dared to stare back. When she finally looked away, it was to wink and nod at Audrey.

Mandy followed Tallulah's gaze. That's when she noticed:

Why, THAT BITCH IS WEARING MY BOOTS!

To top it off, Audrey held the missing library book in her hands. When the girls' eyes met, there was no triumph in Audrey's.

Just pity.

Then Mandy remembered the photos of Egan tucked away in the book.

Damn it! Why did I have to draw a heart on it? She'll tell her little posse about it and I'll be the laughingstock of the whole school —

Unless I make a fool of her first.

"Okay everyone, we've got a lot on our plate, so go ahead and take a seat," Egan commanded.

Although Jeremy was in the middle of saying something to

Audrey, she shushed him and quickly turned away. Miffed at her snub, he shrank into his seat.

So there's still trouble in Paradise, Mandy thought.

She'd kept her ear to the ground and knew the scuttlebutt. Knowing that Jeremy was still pining after Audrey could work in Mandy's favor.

Especially if she made Debate Team captain.

She knew just how to make that happen.

EGAN OPENED WITH: "I HEREBY DUB YOU THE DEBATE EIGHT. AND, AS I mentioned on Friday, the first order of business is choosing our fearless leader."

Johnny raised his hand. "Why do we have to debate for it? Why don't we just vote on it?"

Egan shook his head. "This isn't a popularity contest. You're going to want someone who is a tent pole player. Someone who can strategize and play to each teammate's strengths. And besides, debaters are judged at the podium. That's where we'll find our team captain. So, any takers?"

Mandy and Audrey's hands rose simultaneously.

Johnny Ruiz's arm went up, as did Gemma's.

Egan nodded approvingly. "The winner of each match will face off for the prize of leading this motley crew." He held out a mug. "Who chose the first of the four possible debate questions, 'Allowing the Internet to Stay Free?'"

The hands of all four competitors went up. "Ah, well that makes life easy. We now have our first-round debate question." He walked to the blackboard. Picking up a piece of chalk, he asked, "Now, how about the question about whether statues of Confederate heroes should be taken down?"

Gemma and Johnny's hands went up.

He wrote their names on the board beside the word STATUES.

Egan eyed Audrey, then Mandy. "Make my day and tell me you two chose the topic of vice presidents."

They nodded.

"Okay, great. Now, if it turns out that either Mandy or Audrey must debate Gemma or Johnny, the topic will be the same question used Friday: about school drug policies." He nodded toward the students who'd chosen not to compete. "They will serve as your judges and use the same criteria as Friday's debates."

"You mean, you won't be judging us?" Mandy asked.

Egan nodded. "I'll fill out a score card but it'll only be used if there's a tie."

Egan had no intention of playing favorites. He'd watch as nature took its course. But he crossed his fingers that Audrey's debate skills, coupled with her popularity, would win over her voting teammates.

THEY DREW FROM A CUP HOLDING FOUR RUBBER BANDS: TWO THAT WERE blue, and two that were beige. "If your bands match, you'll debate each other. Beige bands go first."

Audrey's band was blue, as was Johnny's.

Egan put two of the bands back in the cup, one of each color. "Gemma and Mandy, you're up. Blue band argues for the Internet staying free, beige against it."

Mandy drew the beige band again. She was glad because if life experience had taught her anything, it was that nothing in life was free.

AUDREY AND JOHNNY WENT TO OPPOSITE SIDES OF THE HALL TO READ over their notes on their arguments.

That is to say, Audrey knew she should be studying them, but she was distracted at the thought of debating Mandy next.

She'd known Gemma to be a fierce competitor in all things. Then again, so was Mandy. Audrey flinched at the memory of Mandy's seething glare at the sight of her boots on Audrey's feet.

Perhaps I went too far, she thought.

But couldn't the same be said about bumping Mandy from Egan's class? Even Lavinia had chided her for doing it.

Then again, Mandy seemed bound and determined to get close to Egan, even if it meant stealing. If that weren't bad enough, the heart drawn on his photo proved she was obsessed with him.

It made Audrey sick to her stomach to think of Mandy becoming captain.

I can't let her. I have to pull it together.

By the time Egan opened the door and beckoned them in, she was ready to do battle with Johnny.

WHEN THEY ENTERED, AUDREY SAW MANDY SMILING TRIUMPHANTLY.

She'd also taken a seat next to Jeremy.

She thinks that, by doing that, she's messing with my head.

Instead, it galvanized Audrey to do her best.

Because she pulled the blue band, she'd be arguing to keep the Internet free.

When Johnny grimaced, she knew he must have felt better prepared to make her argument.

She was right.

Audrey began by pointing out that the Internet's creation was a joint venture between academia and the U.S. Government—both entities supported by its citizens' tax dollars. She then segued to its global importance, and how eliminating payment for use allowed information to be delivered freely to everyone. "A free press is the First Amendment in our Constitution," she argued.

Although Johnny was well prepared, the strength of her argument and the ease in which she made it took him off his stride. Realizing this, he overcompensated by talking too fast and stumbling over a few of his points.

No surprise: Audrey won.

It was time for her to face off with Mandy. By drawing the blue band, Audrey would argue to keep the vice presidency.

Mandy chuckled, as if she'd already won.

Audrey couldn't wait to prove her wrong.

EGAN SAW IT IMMEDIATELY: MANDY WAS QUITE THE LITTLE FLIRT.

She'd started by asking an innocent question. Her appreciation was delivered with a sultry chuckle. Her big move was the oldest one in the book, but definitely tried and true: she dropped a pen on the floor so that she could flash a bit of cleavage—something she had in abundance.

And, oh boy, Jeremy was enjoying the show.

Ain't love grand, Egan thought. Not always, but it sure as hell was fickle.

Gee, I wonder if I should toss that out as a debate question?

Despite Mandy's antics, Egan marveled at Audrey's ability to stay focused on the task at hand: winning.

Something she did quite handily.

Now for the clash of the titans.

EGAN HADN'T KNOWN WHAT TO EXPECT, BUT IT WASN'T A TIE.

Audrey's opening was eloquent. She based her proposition on the Constitution's brief three-point statement of vice presidential duties. She then explained how, throughout history, the vice president's importance had grown based on the necessities of a working democracy.

In closing, she declared: "In times of a president's impeachment, incapacitation, sudden death, or assassination, the position of vice president has allowed our government to function rationally and immediately."

Mandy's opposition began by shredding Audrey's examples of vice presidential duties, using examples of those who held the office and had ended in obscurity for not making the most of the position. "These supposed statesmen blew their chance to leave their mark on history," she argued.

And so it went on for yet two more rounds, Audrey thrusted with a point and Mandy parried with a counterpoint. Fact was fought with perception; history with observation.

And a few caustic barbs thrown in for good measure. When Mandy declared "There were several deadbeat vice presidents who should have gotten *the boot* for trying to *steal* the presidency," Audrey had countered with "Well, that's certainly one for *the books* —and quite *heart*-felt!"

Her retort left Mandy speechless, but not for long. When it came time for their final replies, Egan was wondering if they'd come to blows.

At that point he noticed the smirk on Jeremy's face. Why, that little shit is getting off on this, Egan realized.

The vote seemed to take an eternity. Before the votes were tallied, Egan had been impressed with the team's extensive albeit silent deliberations. Now, in hindsight, he wondered how much personal bias came into play—

Especially, in Jeremy's case.

Somewhat thrown by the scores, he asked the Kennedy twins to manage the recount. A few minutes later, they replied in unison, "Nothing's changed."

He asked both girls to leave the room while he conferred with the judges.

Mandy and Audrey easily guessed the problem.

And by Jeremy's sheepish face and Mandy's sly grin, Egan realized her plan had worked. Jeremy's allegiance to Audrey had disappeared–most likely to be found between Mandy's cleavage at a later date.

"You'll have to cast the deciding vote," Portia reminded him.

As a senior, Audrey deserves priority. But more to the point, Audrey would make a better leader.

It's the right thing to do.

But Egan wouldn't.

It would be tempting fate. All he had to do was gaze into her eyes to know how she felt about him.

When it's right—and if it's right—we'll know it.

With a heavy heart, he replied, "Please call them in."

HE DOESN'T WANT TO TEMPT FATE.

That was the only reason Audrey could think of for Egan choosing Mandy over her.

If he could just admit that she'd stolen his heart but that their timing was off, or that he owed Lavinia nine months of his undivided attention—at least, not divided by Audrey—she could live with that.

Instead, he said nothing.

Instead, she got the occasional placid glance or an absentminded grin.

But not a word. No indication whatsoever of what her future held.

Her future with him.

Damn! It's just not fair—

Unless it's over.

Unless he likes her better.

Yes, the thought crossed her mind. Like now, as he clapped when Mandy made her winner's speech. The roar of her misery drowned out Mandy's words, so that was one good thing.

She planned to linger after everyone else took off, but she didn't want to seem like a sore loser.

Besides, that might be Mandy's gameplay too: cling to him like some deep-sea barnacle.

No way was she going to act like Mandy! If Egan wanted to explain—or better yet, apologize—she'd let him seek her out.

Audrey gathered her things to go—

And that's when she realized the library book wasn't there.

Mandy hadn't stuck around at all.

Egan, busy at the blackboard, had his back to her as Audrey slipped out too.

CHAPTER 11

"*B*oo-*yah*, big boy!" Cornell clicked his martini glass with Egan's Scotch tumbler. "Another big win—and against University High this time! AA's Debate Eight is *on fire!*"

Egan guffawed. "So, you'll help me chaperone our trip to the State finals in LA?"

To beg Cornell—and Odette too, after school, he's taken them for drinks at Zuni Cafe.

"You bet I will!" Cornell sighed happily. "As long as there's some play time built in. The hotel is a hop, skip, and a jump from WeHo—"

"And Beverly Hills," Odette declared with a happy sigh. After taking a sip from her champagne flute, she added, "It's been ages since I broke a stiletto on a Rodeo Drive shopping spree!"

"Yeah, well, I hate to be a downer, you two, but I don't remember seeing the words 'free' and 'time' under AA's regulations for field trip chaperones."

"*Merde*," Odette muttered. "In other words, you're keeping us on a leash for the whole weekend?" She thought for a moment, then purred, "On second thought, I find that a tantalizing proposition."

Egan sighed. "Okay, yeah. Since Beverly Hills High is hosting the competition, why don't you take a few hours while our team is waiting to go onstage?"

Odette and Cornell high-fived each other. "Now, what about the sleeping arrangements?" Odette batted her eyes in anticipation of his answer.

"That's easy. There are four male and four female students. They'll bunk in pairs. We chaperones get individual rooms interspersed between those occupied by the students." Egan grimaced. "Hopefully, there won't be a lot of extracurricular activity through the night."

"Not for them or us, either, if we have to stay on guard duty all night," Cornell groused.

Egan chuckled weakly. "Taking shifts playing hall monitor may not be such a bad idea."

Odette frowned. "You're kidding! Right?"

The look on their faces told him he'd better be, or else he'd have to drum up two other saps to make the trip with him.

"I have noticed that they're a pretty tight group," Odette admitted. She raised a brow. "Who knew Debate Team could be so stimulating?"

"Yeah, who knew," Egan murmured as he swallowed the last of his drink. He motioned the bartender for another round.

Frankly, he was pleased with the past few months. They were just now in the middle of the spring semester. His classes were a success with the students, and therefore with their parents, which made Lavinia pleased to no end.

College acceptance letters had arrived last week. From the euphoria enveloping his senior students, Egan realized he'd done well in assisting them on their college essays. While he hadn't graded leniently, he'd challenged them to do their best.

They hadn't let him down.

And yet, at the end of the day, a sense of sadness overcame him. He knew why:

He already missed Audrey.

She was there, but she wasn't. Like the other seniors, Audrey's mind was focused on what lay ahead of her in the coming months. She'd gotten accepted to five universities, including her first choice: Berkeley.

Yes, she still attended his seventh period class. And her papers were exemplary. She wasn't shy in class, either.

As for Debate Team, despite having lost the leadership position to Mandy, she threw herself into every assigned task. And, by sheer personality, Audrey was usurping her rival.

Mandy knew this too.

The junior was peeved about it. Egan could tell by the way she rolled her eyes whenever Audrey got up to give an argument.

And she never failed to fume when Audrey scored higher than her, which happened often.

Like the time, during a tight match against Lowell, when Audrey's rebuttals nudged AA to a winning score by a mere two points. Egan overheard Gemma declaring, "Audrey, girl—you're on fire! How do you do it?"

It's because Audrey puts in the hard work. She makes helpful suggestions to her teammates too, unlike Mandy, who thinks nothing of deriding them with caustic quips.

The question took Audrey by surprise. "We deserve it. It's our last year, so why not pull out all the stops?"

Gemma's head shook with her raucous laughter. "You are *way* too serious about this shit. It's those boots! Admit it. They're magic! Every time you wear them, we win."

Portia nodded solemnly. "I think so too."

"You see?" Gemma insisted. "No shame in that. We all need a little mojo, right?"

Egan's eyes dropped down to Audrey's feet. It was the first time he'd noticed that she was wearing Doc Martens.

Maybe she's like every other girl her age after all.

Even thinking that made him feel disloyal to her. He knew in his heart she was anything but average.

Mandy looked down at the boots. Furiously, she stormed out.

Considering the camaraderie that had developed between

Audrey, Portia, and Gemma, Egan assumed Mandy's teammates were now regretting their choice of leader.

As for Egan? Yes, he rued the day he'd cast that tie-breaking vote.

Only Jeremy got applause from Mandy.

Grudgingly, Egan had to admit that sometimes it was deserved. Jeremy hadn't given up on impressing Audrey. Instead, he'd realized that Debate Team was the best way to win her respect. And now that football season was over, he was focusing all his energies there.

His hard work was paying off. Of the team's individual scores, he came in third behind Audrey and Portia.

Anyone can see that Mandy has Jeremy in her sites, Egan thought. Heck, the way she licks her lips whenever he's within reach, you'd think he was a pork chop.

Jeremy was clueless enough to appreciate Mandy's syrupy accolades. He always made it a point to turn to Audrey to see if she heard it too.

If Audrey did, she ignored it. To Jeremy's dismay, she ignored him too.

Egan didn't know what exactly had happened between Jeremy and Audrey that day in the locker room. He only knew that whatever it was, it had hurt Audrey.

Since then, she'd disdained her old boyfriend. But she still nursed the pain of the event. Egan wished he could comfort Audrey, with words if not with a hug.

But because he couldn't, he did the next best thing: take Mandy down a notch, whenever possible.

"Mandy, as much as we all admire your ability to think before speaking, perhaps you should consider studying the topic instead of just winging it..." he'd say. Or, "Gee Mandy, don't be so hard on yourself! I'm sure that whatever you did last night instead of working on your arguments was worth it, even if you did let your teammates down."

Thankfully, Mandy's lack of leadership skills didn't stop her teammates from working even harder. Otherwise, Ashbury Academy wouldn't be representing its district in the state finals.

Mandy is darned lucky they want to win so badly, Egan thought. *Otherwise, they'd ask that she be exiled from the team. In fact, maybe I should suggest it before I find out what ounce of flesh she covets from me.*

Egan was quite aware that Mandy's sugary compliments were leading up to something. He wished she'd just come out with whatever it was so that he could only say, "No."

He'd savor that moment.

He hoped it happened in front of Audrey so that he'd see her laugh again.

"Debate Eight: are we ready for this weekend's tournament?" Egan shouted.

"*YES, WE ARE!*" His team shouted back.

For the most part.

Although Audrey kept her mouth shut, for a second it looked as if her eyes were twinkling at his antics.

"Great!" Egan exclaimed. "There will be six rounds, total. The first two are topics we know, and therefore may prepare for, but the third round is not. Round four also allows for prep, but rounds five and six are impromptu. Here are the debate topics."

When the students had finished copying what he wrote on the board, he continued: "For the impromptu rounds, we only get an hour to prep. For those rounds, your duties are as follows." He tapped the blackboard with each point: "The Kennedy twins will pull raw data, which they will then hand off to Johnny, Gemma, and Mandy. They in turn will assess the pros and cons, then create talking points based on the data team's statistical notes, handing everything over to Portia, Jeremy, and Audrey, who will write the opening arguments."

Egan had thought long and hard about assigning Jeremy and

Audrey the final task. When it came to opening arguments, Audrey's strength was evident in her scores, which were the highest on the team. Portia's came in second. Jeremy's improvements had earned him the third highest score.

Mandy bristled.

Egan ignored the signs of an impending tantrum. He anticipated a bigger one with what he had to say next. It may not be well received, but it was for the good of the team.

"The tournament takes place at Beverly Hills High," he continued. "We leave on Friday from AA, eight o'clock sharp. Cornell and Odette are joining me as your chaperones. We'll be driving in two cars. I've rented a van for the men. The girls will caravan with us in Odette's car."

"I for one am glad for that," Gemma declared. "I've noticed that men can't control their farts during long car trips."

The Kennedy twins snickered and high-fived each other.

Egan rolled his eyes. "Continuing with more pertinent information, folks: teammates will bunk in twos. For the boys, that's the Kennedys in one room and Johnny and Jeremy in the other. For the girls, Portia and Gemma will share, as will Audrey and Mandy."

Jeremy sunk deep into his seat.

Both girls' eyes grew large. At the same time, they raised their hands and shouted, "*Excuse me?*"

Egan's way of girding for the impending battle was to honor them with a grin. "That's all for now, team. Those of you with questions are welcome to stay behind."

"No way am I sharing a room with Audrey!" Mandy's squawk could be heard all the way down the hall.

Audrey's anger came out in her hands, which were flexing.

At least they're not around Mandy's neck, Egan thought. Well, not yet, anyway.

"Why not?" Egan asked calmly.

Mandy's eyes narrowed. "No reason—other than I have it on good authority that *she snores.*"

Angered, Audrey clenched her fists tightly to her side.

She's doing her best not to blow up at the little bitch, Egan realized. Scoffing, he declared, "Mandy, that's just silly."

Mandy crossed her arms on her abdomen. "I'm serious, Egan! I mean… Well, *come on, already!*"

"I'm serious too," he retorted.

"Cut it out," she countered. When he didn't fold, she grimaced. "How dare you! Just who do you think you are?"

He snickered at her audacity. "Maybe you've forgotten I'm your teacher."

Mandy smiled sweetly. "No. Quite frankly, Mr. Gable, *you are not.*" Her gaze drifted to Audrey as if they shared some sort of secret.

But the look on Audrey's face showed that she was just as appalled by Mandy's behavior as him.

That's it. I've got to put Mandy in her place.

Coolly, he murmured, "You're right. I'm not. But I am running Debate Team. And, as of now, I view you more as a liability than an asset. So, if I were you, Mandy, I'd drop this. *The topic is closed.*" He leaned against the wall as if daring her to argue.

With a toddler's cadence, she pouted, "Well, then I wouldn't want to make 'teacher' mad. He might put me in the corner."

Egan glowered at her. *That's it, you little—*

"Okay, listen, I'm sorry. Truly, I am." Mandy shrugged. "I'm willing to bet that Audrey feels the same way. I mean—us, sharing a room? It's ludicrous! At the very least, it'll shake our confidence. At the very most, it may cost us the tournament. Am I right?"

Audrey acquiesced with an involuntary blink.

"Let me propose an easy fix," Mandy continued. "My stepfather can pay for a room of my own. So, why not let him? That way, it's not an expense for the school, and both Audrey and I get a good night's sleep before the tournament."

She's got a point. Maybe it's the best solution.

Egan nodded slowly. "Okay, sure. That works—as long as you get clearance from Lavinia."

"No problem," she purred.

She turned on her heel and went out the door, slamming it behind her.

It would be easy forging Lavinia's signature, Mandy reasoned. Hell, the woman put it on every school missive, even her personal notes to students congratulating them on their academic achievements and improvements.

Mandy's plan: to either celebrate or commiserate AA's showing with Jeremy.

Frankly, she didn't care about the results. Being the captain of a state-finalist debate team—in *her junior year, no less!*—had already catapulted her to the front of the pack.

Despite Mandy and Jeremy's numerous and robust sexploits (after the book heist in the girl's locker room, Mandy caught on quickly that it might be a perfect place for some afternoon delight), she'd noticed that Jeremy's eye was wandering again.

He certainly had a type: lithe, brunette, and big-breasted.

I'm batting one for three, she thought.

It gnawed at Mandy's ego that he refused to admit publicly that they were an item. She blamed Audrey for that.

He still thinks he can win her over, Mandy seethed. Well, I know how to kill that dream once and for all.

Just as galling was Audrey's habit of wearing Mandy's stolen boots to every match. Mandy assumed it was Audrey's way at unnerving her; to take her off her game.

And, if Mandy were to be honest with herself, she'd admit it had worked.

Yet another reason to get Jeremy to profess his love for Mandy to the whole world.

And to Audrey.

Mandy's plan was simple. On the eve of the debate, she'd wait until the rest of the students and chaperones were in bed, and then she'd sneak Jeremy into her private suite. But before they got down and dirty, they'd partake in a few recreational drugs—at a minimum some pot. Little by little, she'd stolen some primo grass from Simon's secret stash—again, in his tighty-whitey drawer. Apparently, the dude was a creature of habit.

She'd also found some hashish. When she rolled the joints, she'd be sure to sprinkle it into them before they lit up.

After Jeremy passed out, she'd pose him on top of her and take an artsy photo that would look as if they were making love. She'd already stolen Simon's new digital camera. Their house was cluttered with all the latest and greatest gadgets. She knew he'd never miss it.

If, after LA, Jeremy still refused to be seen in public with her, she'd show him the picture and threaten to tell Lavinia that he'd raped her while they were at the debate tournament. That would scare the shit out of him. Admissions letters had arrived just last week. The last thing he needed was for the six colleges that offered him a place to withdraw their offers, not to mention his football scholarships.

She'd warn Jeremy he'd have to agree to stay her boyfriend through the summer. By the fall, she'll allow him to tell others she'd kicked him to the curb. By then, her popularity would be sealed.

She could then focus on the recommendation to Berkeley from Egan.

But Mandy would have to move fast. She could see the writing on the wall. Egan was already tiring of her shenanigans. It was all too obvious in his snide observations about her toward her teammates.

Blackmail would do the trick.

Still, everyone had a weak spot. Like a wild hog hunting morels buried deep in some primordial forest, she'd rut out Egan's dirty little secrets and then threaten to expose them if he refused to give her a recommendation letter.

It would be even more fun than making Jeremy come to heel.

But nothing would top the fun of taking Audrey down.

Before the end of the school year, she'd figure some way to accomplish that too.

EGAN HADN'T EXPECTED TO BE LEFT ALONE WITH AUDREY.

With the door closed.

His heart ached to tell her what he was thinking:

That he loved her, but he knew it would be wrong to act on every impulse he had—to tease her, to kiss her, *to love her*—until one of them was gone from AA.

Until both of them were mature enough to handle their feelings.

Because he never wanted to hurt her, ever.

She was the first woman—*girl*—for whom he'd felt that way.

Which was why he kept his mouth shut.

It seemed like an eternity before Audrey finally spoke: "I have something to tell you—"

"No... don't. *Please!*" He shook his head. He couldn't bear the thought of hearing her profess her love to him.

Audrey stammered, "No.. *NO!* You don't understand what I'm going to say—"

"I do, Audrey! Believe me, I do!" Without thinking, he placed his hand on her arm.

The touch of her skin sent jolts of desire charging through him.

She stiffened as if she felt it too.

And then she pulled away. Before she hung her head, she closed her eyes, as if shamed.

No, worse: *revolted.*

What if I'm wrong, he thought. What if she's not professing her love? What if she wants to tell me she hates me?

For toying with her. And then...

Nothing.

It's true, he reasoned. Audrey has every right to hate me. For making her life so miserable.

She can't understand why it has to be this way.

He jerked his hand back. As if to stop feeling her touch—to stop all feeling for her—he shoved it in his pocket.

———

AUDREY WANTED TO TELL HIM EVERYTHING:

About how she changed Mandy's schedule so that she could take the younger girl's place in Egan's class.

How Mandy had stolen her library book; and how, in retaliation, Audrey had stolen it back, along with Mandy's shoes.

Most of all, Audrey wanted to warn him about Mandy. The heart drawn around his photo worried her. Even scarier was seeing how Mandy had treated Egan just now:

Not as a teacher, but as her equal.

Mandy had acted as if she were spatting with her boyfriend. As if she were looking forward to kissing and making up…

The thought was so revolting that Audrey shivered.

But if I tell him why Mandy hates me, he'll think I'm jealous—or worse!

He'll think I'm just as conniving as Mandy for having changed my schedule to get into his class.

Because I care about him.

But if it's true and he's fallen for her, then he doesn't still care for me.

And I'm embarrassing him…

Oh my God! Egan and…

Mandy?

Fuck it! After all this time…

After all that's happened?

Frustrated, she threw up her hands, and cried, "Why are you doing this to me?"

———

Because I care about you, Egan thought.

That was the problem: he cared too much.

Not that he could say that to her.

Not now. Not wondering if she'd already moved on.

Not if she *disdained* him.

Instead, Egan shrugged.

"Okay, right. Got it," Audrey muttered.

As she flung open the door, he flinched, anticipating the door to slam shut again.

But no. What he heard instead was the click of Audrey's heels as she walked away.

She wasn't Mandy. She had too much regard—too much *love*—for Ashbury Academy to abuse the fine old building.

Egan told himself: You did the right thing by letting her walk away.

No matter how much he wanted to believe it, he couldn't.

"*L*adies, which one of you wants to ride shotgun?" Odette's invitation was met with noncommittal mutters from Audrey, Gemma, and Portia. Urban legend had it that the breakneck speed in which Odette took the city's streets had been the reason there were stop signs on every corner of San Francisco's residential neighborhoods.

Gemma and Portia scrambled into the back seat. When Mandy attempted to follow, they blocked her. "You're the captain," Gemma pointed out. "You get the honor of sitting up front."

"And besides, we promised Audrey she could sit in the middle," Portia added.

Mandy knew it was a lie; that they didn't want to sit with her. No problem. For once she hoped the rumors about Odette's driving were true. If Audrey barfed all over the others, justice would be served.

She glanced over at Audrey, who was locked in a farewell embrace with Lavinia.

My God, you'd think we were going to the ends of the earth and never coming back, she thought. It's just LA! Get over it!

At that moment, her eye caught Lavinia's. The headmistress

smiled. She raised the hand that was stroking Audrey's hair to wave at Mandy.

Slowly, Mandy waved back.

That Audrey had Lavinia as a mom was yet one more reason for Mandy to hate her.

"I wish you all the luck in the world," Lavinia whispered.

Audrey smiled. "We're excited. I feel we're prepped. We won't let down the school."

Lavinia chuckled. "This isn't about the school. It's about you and your team. For the next seventy-two hours, you are all one and the same. You must look after each other."

Audrey looked skyward. "I wish we all felt that way."

"Let me guess. Mandy?"

Audrey nodded. "How did you know?"

"I didn't. But I suspected." Lavinia shrugged. "She just needs a large dose of kindness—and a little space."

"Well, then it's a good thing you signed off on her private room."

Lavinia pulled back, surprised. "What? I didn't…"

At that moment, she moved her gaze beyond Audrey, toward Odette's car.

Finally, she looked back at her daughter. "Whatever happens, happens. Things have a habit of sorting themselves out."

And that's how Audrey knew Mandy had lied to Egan about getting permission for a room of her own.

"Here you go: keys for seven rooms, all on the third floor." The front desk clerk at the Beverly Rexford handed Egan five bundles of keys, two for each room.

"I know we reserved seven rooms, but really, we'll need *eight*," Egan explained.

"Okay…" the desk clerk tapped her computer keyboard. Satisfied with what she saw, she turned to grab an additional key. "It's on the floor below the others. Room 204."

"That'll do," Mandy replied breezily.

"No, it won't," Egan said firmly.

He was exhausted and hungry. The drive down Interstate 5 was long and tiring—over six hours trying to keep pace with Odette, who drove like a bat out of hell. Not to mention the lunch break at some place renowned for its pea soup (not his favorite), and then the numerous bathroom stops along the way. "Perhaps you can move all of us so that we're on the same floor?"

The Debate Eight groaned. They were getting antsy. "Take the keys already," Johnny muttered in frustration.

The front desk clerk shrugged apologetically at Egan. "No, sorry, sir. The three other rooms on that floor are currently occupied. In fact, the only vacant room in the hotel is this one." She held up the key stamped 204.

Mandy snatched it out of the clerk's hand. "Thanks. The second-floor room is fine."

Egan plucked it from Mandy's fingers. "It'll go to one of the chaperones."

The clerk's mouth dropped open.

Gemma nudged Portia and mouthed, *What the Hell?*

Mandy clawed it out of Egan's fingers. Then, to make the decision final, she dropped it down the front of her sweater, into her bra. "I insist. I'm afraid of heights, so the second floor is perfect."

By now, everyone in the lobby was watching them.

Egan shook his head, resigned to this *fait-accompli*. "Okay. Fine." He turned to the front desk clerk. "I didn't bring a leash long enough, or one of those electronic ankle monitors. But I assume you have video cameras on every floor?"

She nodded.

"Good, then. Hand me an extra key for 204."

The clerk did as ordered.

Egan tossed it to Odette. She caught it with one hand but was frowning.

"Thank you." Egan turned to Mandy. "Expect a call to your room every half hour. And you'd better pick up, or Odette will barge in."

Egan's threat got an eye roll from Odette.

Mandy shrugged.

After Egan handed out the other keys, he explained: "Okay, gang, let's drop our things in our rooms, then grab a bite to eat." He glanced at his watch. "Meet back in the lobby in half an hour. Afterward, let's do a quick rehearsal on the pre-assigned topics." He turned to the clerk. "Is there a small conference room in this hotel?"

She nodded. "Yes. It's where we serve breakfast every morning. It's open until midnight, but after eight at night, it's usually empty."

"Good." He nodded to the students. "When we get back from dinner, we'll meet there."

Everyone nodded then stampeded to the elevator. But too much luggage and too many bodies meant that not everyone could ride up together.

Audrey and Egan were left behind.

Neither spoke as they waited for the elevator, and they rode up in silence too.

When the elevator came to their floor, Egan held back so that Audrey could get her luggage out first. As she made her way down the hall, he realized their rooms were adjacent.

When he entered his room, he saw that they shared an adjoining door.

He groaned.

Then he took a shower.

THE FUCKING WALLS IN THIS PLACE ARE PAPER THIN, MANDY GRUMBLED. She could hear the guy in the next room chatting—or, to her mind, practically yelling—into his phone.

Like an idiot, she'd forgotten to take her MP3 player. Mandy had no way to tune out the jerk while she laid out the items needed to make Jeremy hers, once and for all: matching black lace panties and bra, rolling papers, a plastic sandwich bag filled with Mendocino Gold, a knob of hashish…

And a square plastic tab of LSD stamped with cartoon dancing elephants.

When she found it in Simon's stash, at first she hesitated to take it. But there were several in there, so she figured he'd never miss it.

Mandy smoked pot. She knew Jeremy toked a joint every now and then too. But LSD would be a new experience for both of them.

Would that spice up their sex? Mandy hoped so. Her plans for greatness depended on her ability to hang onto Jeremy at all costs.

Mandy took out Simon's digital camera and placed it on the dresser facing the bed. She'd read the camera's manual to learn how to use its timer. As a test, she set it and then she fell onto the bed, posing erotically while it snapped away.

When she felt she'd had enough, she flipped through the shots.

Yep, that would do just fine.

She was wondering how she might slip Jeremy into her room when she heard the guy in the next room say, "Yes, tell him I'm one of the other debate judges… the one from Kansas… Thanks, I'll wait."

Mandy froze.

His next sentence included "…the impromptu debate topics? Yeah, they were given to me just before I left for the airport. I'll read them to you. Just give me a second so that I can grab my ThinkPad—"

Mandy noticed a couple of drinking glasses on the room's desk. She grabbed one, along with a hotel notepad and a pen, then ran back to the wall closest to the judge's room. There, she put the glass against the wall, then placed her ear against the glass.

"Yep, got it." The man's voice sounded more distinct. "Are you ready?"

This old spy trick really works, Mandy marveled.

"Round three impromptu topic: 'All US municipalities should install closed-circuit cameras to assist national security...'" The man's voice got louder. "Yes, closed circuit cameras... *national security*. Heard that? Good. Okay, now for round five impromptu: 'Food nutrition labeling should include added sugars and fats'... Yeah, I know, as if that'll stop kids from eating junk food, right?... Ha! Okay, and the round six impromptu: "'If a death sentence appeal is unreasonably delayed, the criminal's sentence should be commuted to life in prison.' Got it?... Okay great! Looking forward to seeing you tomorrow as well..."

Mandy almost squealed at her luck, but then realized if she could hear the judge, he could probably hear her too.

I can't wait to tell Jeremy. We can get a head start on our research and actually win this thing. We'll look like geniuses to the others—

And Jeremy will be so appreciative that he'll finally forget all about Audrey.

Finally.

$\mathcal{M}$andy made sure she was the first of their group to reach the lobby. A different desk clerk was there.

Good, Mandy thought.

She held up her key to the woman. "My roommate needs a key of her own. Room 204."

The clerk smiled and nodded. A moment later, Mandy had the additional key. She planned to give it to Jeremy.

She slipped it into her purse and made her way back to the elevator to wait for the others. And just in time too, because when the doors opened, she found herself facing Egan. She saluted him.

He seemed surprised to see her. "How long have you been waiting?"

"Just a minute or two. I didn't want you to think I was dawdling in my luxurious accommodations." She winked seductively. "Come on up and see me some time."

Egan looked at the ceiling as if the right answer were scribbled up there, somewhere. "You seem to enjoy skating on thin ice, Mandy. But a word of warning: don't push me."

Before she could retort, the elevator opened, and the rest of their team surrounded them. Audrey and Jeremy were the last to get off the elevator. Jeremy seemed to be in the middle of saying something to her. The moment they realized they weren't alone, he zipped his lip.

This has got to stop, Mandy fumed.

"We're starving, coach! So, where do we go for grub?" Johnny asked.

"How about Hamburger Hamlet on Sunset?" Mandy purred. Seeing Egan's frown, she added, "My treat! I am team captain after all. And besides, my stepdad invested in it. They'll treat us well."

Odette and Cornell slapped hands.

Egan got the message: Mandy was getting her way.

<hr>

HE ONLY HAS EYES FOR HER, AUDREY THOUGHT.

She tried to keep her focus on what Gemma was saying—something about a strategy to unnerve their opponents—but her eyes and thoughts kept shifting to Egan.

Apparently, his gaze and his thoughts were on Mandy.

It's eating at Egan that Mandy is practically climbing into Jeremy's lap, she thought miserably. That's why he's on his third Scotch.

While ordering, Egan had waved off the waiter's question as to what he might like to drink. Nodding toward the others, he replied. "Thanks, but no thanks. We're just here for a quick bite before hitting the books."

"*We* aren't hitting the books." Odette reminded him.

Egan shrugged. "Okay, sure, go for it."

She sighed, relieved. "Dirty martini! A double."

"I'll second that," Cornell added quickly as if he were afraid that Egan might change his mind.

While the other teachers were reminding Egan of his promise of free time, the waiter took the students' orders. It wasn't until the waiter popped a bottle of champagne beside their table that Egan realized it was meant for them.

"Who ordered this?" he asked the man.

The waiter nodded toward Mandy.

"Send it back," Egan commanded.

"But…" The waiter's glance pleaded with Mandy to intervene.

"Really?" she countered. "You don't want us to celebrate that AA's Debate Eight made it to the finals?"

A chorus of protests rose from the table.

"No!… Okay, well…" Egan turned to the waiter. Shrugging, he muttered, "Go ahead, leave it."

The man nodded, placing the bottle in front of Egan, who poured himself enough for a couple of sips and did the same for Odette and Cornell.

Turning to Gemma, he said, "Pass it forward, but only *this* much." He placed two fingers horizontally to indicate an inch each.

The kids groaned.

But when Egan turned his back to say something to Cornell, Mandy grabbed the bottle from Gemma and poured herself a generous portion. She then passed the bottle to Jeremy, who did the same.

In a flash the other students followed suit.

In due time, Egan reached for the champagne bottle to give Odette a refill, only to find it empty. He scowled at Mandy, but it was too late, and he knew it. He had to resign himself to the reality that the students were determined to have little fun.

Or, if Mandy was any example, *a lot* of fun.

Mandy knows flirting with Jeremy is the best way to get Egan's attention, Audrey reasoned.

At that moment, she felt sad for all three of them.

"Have you heard a word I've said?" Gemma grumbled.

"Everything," Audrey lied. "And I think you're spot on." Might as well join the club, she thought, as she took a sip of her champagne.

"Wow! Thanks!" Gemma beamed. She lifted her glass. "Well, here's to bringing home the winner's cup!"

"I'll drink to that," Audrey murmured.

It's as big a fantasy as Egan coming to his senses, but hell, why not?

She swallowed her bubbly in one gulp.

Once again, Mandy signaled the waiter to bring another bottle of champagne.

And, once again, he placed it directly in front of Egan.

―――――

By the time the meal was over, the whole table was tipsy.

Jeremy's eyelids, half-shut from drink, suddenly opened wide.

Perhaps it had something to do with Mandy's hand in his lap.

His mind was too hazy to convince the rest of him that hardening to her touch was not what he wanted. Not if he were to impress Audrey.

But it wasn't just Mandy's hand in his lap. He looked down to find a key there too.

Mandy leaned in and whispered, "I have a special surprise waiting for you in my room."

His eyes drifted to Audrey. He was surprised to see she was staring back. He knew her well enough to read her face:

Loser.

Oh, yeah? You think so?

Well then, damn it, girl! Fuck you!

Or better yet, fuck Mandy.

He patted Mandy's hand before grinding it into his crotch. "Sure. Can't wait."

Gleefully, Mandy signaled the waiter for the check.

―――――

Despite Egan's protestations, Cornell insisted he take the passenger seat. "This time, I'm driving."

The boys, loose-limbed and giggling, stumbled into the van.

Not surprisingly, Odette beat them to the hotel.

When they entered the lobby, it was empty. "I guess the girls went up to their rooms," one of the Kennedy twins deduced.

"Great, then we're off the hook for practice!" The other twin exclaimed. Snickering, he staggered into the elevator.

The others followed—

Except for Jeremy. Seemingly out of nowhere, Mandy was at his side. She shoved him out of the sightline of the elevator doors, shushing him with a kiss.

They waited for the chime that told them the elevator had started its ascent, then took the fire stairwell to the second floor.

⸻

ONLY AUDREY, GEMMA, AND PORTIA WERE SOBER ENOUGH TO SHOW UP for the strategy session in the conference room. After waiting a half hour, Portia asked, "Shouldn't we call Egan to see where he is?"

Gemma snorted. "Where do you *think* he is, silly?"

A horrible thought came to Audrey: Mandy's room?

To rid herself of that possibility, she muttered, "He's sleeping it off."

"If we're going to have half a chance of any sort of showing, maybe we should go to bed too, so that we can get up early," Portia suggested. "After a good night's sleep, the others may be sober enough to review our debate strategy."

Fat chance, Audrey thought.

She rode up in the elevator with the others but waited until they closed their room's door, pausing in front of Egan's suite.

She knocked.

No answer.

Audrey hoped Gemma was right: that he was sleeping it off. But the thought crossed her mind that he wasn't in there at all.

That maybe he was with Mandy.

CHAPTER 14

"So, what's your big surprise?" Jeremy slurred his words. The room was spinning around. He wasn't a big wine drinker. Beer was his libation of choice. He'd always assumed it had more alcohol content. If the goal was to get drunk, sooner was better, right?

He now realized that perhaps overcompensating for any perceived difference may have been the wrong thing to do.

Mandy waved the baggie of pot in front of his face. "I brought us something so that we can have a *real* party. You know, have some fun so that we're mellow and focused for the debate tomorrow. Isn't that what all you athletes do?"

Jeremy snickered. "Bang it out before a game? Nah. Just the opposite. We save all that pent-up energy for when we're on the field." He flopped down on her bed, falling on his back.

"That seems ass-backward to me." Mandy argued. "And besides, we're going to be sitting on our asses, not huffing and puffing out on the field. We want to be *ZEN*." She picked up the LSD tab. "That's what this is for."

Jeremy tried to focus his eyes. "What the hell is that?"

"It's… a sex enhancer." Mandy arched her brows. "What do you say we try some?"

He nodded uncertainly. It took very little to arouse him. A couple of perky breasts coming into view usually did the trick. But the champagne seemed to zap his mojo.

Yeah, a sex enhancer sounded just right. He'd hate for her to spread rumors that he couldn't get it up.

MANDY OPENED THE BAG OF POT. AFTER SORTING THE LEAVES FROM THE stems and seeds, she rolled it up, nice and tight.

She lit the joint with a match and took a long drag on it. She held in the hot vapors until she thought her lungs would explode before releasing it with a sigh.

Jeremy was still on his back, oblivious to her attempt to hand him the joint. Mandy looked for somewhere to put it, but since it was a non-smoking room, there wasn't an ashtray in sight. She settled for resting it on the nightstand, hanging its lit end over the edge so that the ashes would flicker to the floor.

Now for that LSD tab.

Mandy reached for it but paused before cutting it open. How much of this should we ingest, she wondered. Since there's two of us, splitting the tab should make it safer.

She didn't really know what she was doing, so she improvised. Grabbing a water glass, she emptied the tab into it, filled it with water, and then stirred it with one of the plastic spoons beside the coffee maker.

Mandy giggled. "Here I come, big boy." Humming, she began a striptease: ripping the buttons off her shirt and shimmying out of her jeans. After yanking off her panties, she threw them at Jeremy's face.

They landed on his head. He held them to his nose and sniffed. "Nice," he murmured.

"Hey, look this way! You're missing the show!" To make her point, Mandy unhooked her bra and twirled it over her head.

As far as Jeremy could tell, there were three Mandys dancing in front of him. "Which one of you should I bang first?"

As she froze, the bra went flying. It hit the wall with a soft thud.

"What do you mean, 'which one of us?'" She shoved Jeremy so hard that he almost fell off the bed. "Who do you think is here with us? Perhaps your crush, Audrey? Is that what you want, a *threesome*?"

Dazed and confused, Jeremy looked around. "Audrey—is here?"

"No, you moron! She's not!" Mandy reached down and cupped him.

He lifted his head to follow her gaze to his crotch. Noting her scowl, he muttered, "Maybe we should try that, um, sex enhancer."

"Yeah, maybe that'll get you hard—*for me*." Furious, she rose from the bed and grabbed the LSD-laced water glass. "Here, drink this."

Nodding meekly, he did as he was told.

"All of it," Mandy barked.

She shoved him back down on the mattress. Naked, she walked to the dresser and flicked on the camera, already set to click continually. It was snapping away even before she leaped onto the bed.

Jeremy's eyes were closed. Had he passed out?

If so, even better.

Mandy straddled him, then placed one of his hands on her ass and the other on her breast. Next, she lifted his head so that it looked as if they were kissing. She then rolled him over so that he was on top of her, entwining his leg with hers. She stared at the camera with a look of terror.

She was moving into different damsel-in-distress poses when Jeremy's eyes flew open. Horrified, he scrambled around the bed, knocking over everything on the nightstand before tumbling to the floor. Leaping to his feet, he shouted, "The colors... so many! And *shit! Why are there monsters?"*

"What?... What's wrong with you?" Mandy's fear was real now.

Jeremy ignored her. Frenzied, he dropped to his knees, circling the room on all fours, all the while screaming, "Don't let them eat me! *Don't let them eat me!"*

Suddenly, he came to the open balcony door. Mutely, he rose, mesmerized by the street lamp beyond.

Before Mandy knew what was happening, he rushed out the door and leaped off the balcony.

Mandy screamed as she ran after him. Petrified, she stared down at his broken body on the ground below.

Until she smelled something burning.

Jeremy had knocked the joint onto the sheet.

The bedspread was on fire.

CHAPTER 15

*E*gan groaned and covered his ears. What was that infernal ringing?

It dawned on him that it was the telephone.

He stuck out his hand, but he aimed too low because it smacked into the nightstand.

The pain, coupled with his own scream, sobered him up.

He fumbled for the phone, only to knock the receiver to the floor. At least then he could hear Mandy sobbing, "I think I killed him! And... There was a fire!"

"Killed... *who?... A fire?"*

"Yes! In my room! I managed to put it out, but the smell—"

Egan didn't answer her. Instead, he stumbled to his feet and ran out the door.

By the time he hit the stairwell, he realized he'd slept in his clothes.

At least I'm not naked, he thought.

If only the same thing could be said for Jeremy.

From Mandy's balcony, Egan stared down at the kid. Thank God he'd landed on the lawn instead of asphalt. And he was mumbling incoherently, so at least he was still alive.

Mandy was making excuses quicker than Egan could ingest them. Thank goodness she'd had the good sense to throw on a hotel robe, Egan thought.

He started for the door. "Call an ambulance—*now!*"

"But... *what if they put me in jail?*"

"They won't, but only because he's not dead! Not *yet*, anyway." Egan didn't wait for the elevator but took the fire stairwell instead.

A few minutes later, he heard the ambulance. The night manager must have heard it too because he joined Egan as he went out and explained the situation to the emergency med techs: that Jeremy had somehow gotten drunk and fallen off the balcony.

"Jeez! It's our third drunk-dropping tonight." The lead emergency med tech rolled his eyes. "By the way, we're taking him to Cedars Sinai."

"I'll be right behind you," Egan replied.

But first, he'd have to let Cornell and Odette know what was up so that they could look after the other kids.

And he'd have to call Lavinia and explain everything: how Jeremy and the other students got drunk on champagne. Worse yet, that Jeremy had ended up in Mandy's room and somehow fallen off her balcony.

And how Mandy had set her bed on fire.

Mandy hasn't the decency to ask to go with me, Egan realized. She's some piece of work.

Despite everything else, she was his first order of business.

As he walked back into the hotel, he looked up at Mandy's room. He could see her silhouetted behind the curtain, peeking out.

"THE GUY YOU'VE BEEN CHASING ALL YEAR FALLS OFF YOUR BALCONY and you can't even find it in your heart to check his pulse?"

Mandy flinched at Egan's question. "I can't stand the sight of blood!"

"He could have died," Egan retorted.

"Don't blame me," she screamed. "You're our chaperone!"

Egan looked down at Mandy's bed. He could tell where the fire had started. The veneer of the nightstand was blackened. The bedspread and sheets below it now sported a large burn hole. The remnant of a plastic bag was singed to the scorched mattress. The few twigs in it that hadn't burned up contained what was left of Mandy's stash.

He threw up his hands. "You were smoking pot too? Well, that's just dandy!"

Mandy shrugged. "So I made a little mess. Big whoop! My stepdad will pay for the damage."

"You bet he will," Egan growled. He started for the door.

"Wait a minute, you!" Mandy was nearly hysterical. "I can't sleep here tonight! This place smells like a pot house!"

"Gee, I wonder why?" Egan retorted. "Too bad. The hotel is sold out. You know that."

Mandy shook her head. "Don't start that bullshit about bunking with Audrey."

"You little pyromaniac! I wouldn't dream of putting you in the same room with her!"

"Of course you wouldn't," Mandy spat back. "You wouldn't want to lose your job because you helped me over Lavinia's *precious baby.*"

Egan flinched.

Don't show her you care.

Instead, he tossed her his room key. "Room 302. I'll be spending the night at the hospital anyway—with Jeremy."

Mandy huffed out.

Egan looked around the room. He'd have to let the hotel manager know what happened.

Later. Much later. Check-out, for sure.

He threw the bedding into the bathtub and turned on the water.

The mattress was salvageable. He'd flip it over so that the scorch mark wouldn't be seen. The sheets, though, were ruined. But it was still possible to mask the smell of pot before checkout on Sunday.

When he got back into the bedroom, he knew he should check around to see if she'd left any drugs lying around.

He went down on his hands and knees, scanning the floor around the nightstand. The culprit—a charred doobie—was under the bed.

So was the torn LSD tab.

Oh…hell.

He didn't want to touch it with his fingers, so he plucked a Kleenex from the box on the desk, folded it around the tab, and stuck it in his pocket.

A hotel memo pad sat beside the tissue box. He glanced at the notes Mandy had written on it:

Round 3 IMPROMPTU: All US municipalities should install closed-circuit cameras to assist national security.

Round 5 IMPROMPTU: Food nutrition labeling should include added sugars and fats.

Round 6 IMPROMPTU: If a death sentence appeal is unreasonably delayed, the criminal's sentence should be commuted to life in prison.

My God, he wondered. Where did she get this?

Just for a moment, the thought of using the intel from her dirty sleuthing crossed his mind, but he shrugged it away. Cheating isn't a victory, he reasoned. It's an opportunity for shame.

He went back into the bathroom, shredded the notes, and flushed them down the toilet.

When he walked back into the bedroom, he noticed the camera on the dresser. It was positioned in such a way that he deduced it had been used to take pictures of Mandy and Jeremy's sexual acrobatics.

Egan clicked through its digital photo archive. It was like fanning a picture book about Mandy's dirty deeds. This didn't shock so much as sadden him.

What was she trying to do, blackmail Jeremy?

If so, why?

One by one, he deleted the photos.

She's done enough damage to the poor kid, he reasoned. *To all of us.*

Before Egan left the room, he rummaged through Mandy's suitcase to make sure there wasn't anything else that could incriminate her, but only because he knew it would ruin the reputation of the school.

He respected Lavinia too much for that.

The ambulance's siren roused Audrey from her slumber. The chime of the elevator stymied her attempt to fall back asleep. When she heard it a second time, she was curious enough to peek out her door to see who was walking about.

Egan's room was next door. She'd seen him come out of it when they left for dinner. When she realized their rooms shared an interior door, she fantasized about leaving it unlocked just to see if he'd try the knob. If so, and if he were bold enough to open the door, she'd finally know where she stood with him.

And she'd welcome him in.

But now Mandy stood in front of his room. In a bathrobe.

Mandy didn't knock because she didn't have to. She had a key.

Silently, Audrey shut her door.

Now I know the truth.

CHAPTER 16

"Jeremy is where?" Gemma exclaimed.

The Debate Eight—now Seven—turned to stare at Mandy.

"You heard me," she sniffed blithely. "The hospital. I guess he couldn't hold his liquor."

"We shouldn't have been drinking anyway," Portia's voice trembled with anxiety. "And where's Egan?"

"He went with Jeremy," Mandy snapped. "So, we've lost our beloved coach. Big deal. Let's just keep our cool. Otherwise, we won't win this thing."

"Someone will have to take Jeremy's arguments!" Gemma pointed out.

"Duh. We can always count on you to state the obvious, can't we?" Mandy rolled her eyes. "As our captain, I say we—"

Johnny snickered. "Why should we listen to you? Seriously, Mandy, if it hadn't been for you trying to impress us—make that impress *Jeremy*—he'd be here now, and the rest of us wouldn't be nursing hangovers."

Bleary-eyed, the Kennedy twins hissed in unison, "Please! Keep your voices down!"

Exasperated, Johnny, declared, "I rest my case."

"Fine! I get it. You want me to be the scapegoat for why we're probably going to screw this up." Mandy stood up. "To hell with that! I'm taking a taxi out of this third-rate dump—"

"You'll do no such thing," Audrey said calmly. "As our captain, you have to lead us to victory…or whatever." She stood up. "We've got just two hours before we have to be at the tournament, so let's get to work." She turned to the others. "Debate rehearsal in Mandy's room, in five—"

"No!" Mandy exclaimed. "I mean…" She glared at Audrey. "You're not sharing a room with anyone either. Why don't we do it there instead?"

"Okay, whatever." Audrey shrugged. "By the way, did Egan tell you when he'd be back?"

"How would I know? You're the teacher's pet, not me," Mandy retorted. Sniffing, she added, "Okay, Audrey's room—*in five*." She stalked off.

Audrey stared after her. *I'm teacher's pet?*

For a moment, it seemed as if her world had opened up again.

At least, her heart.

Toward Egan.

***

WHERE THE HELL ARE MY NOTES?

Frantically, Mandy roamed through her room, looking for the sheet of paper with the impromptu debate topics mentioned by the loudmouth tournament judge.

Every drawer was thrown open. Every inch of the floor was searched on her hands and knees. She pulled the desk away from the wall in case it had fallen behind it.

She even upended her suitcase onto the stinky bed.

As a last resort, she looked in the bathroom.

A tiny scrap of something was floating in the toilet bowl. Tissue paper? No, it was lined note paper.

Desperate, she stuck her hand into the water and pulled it out.

Despite being smudged, she could make out one word:

IMPROMPTU

Mandy howled, *"Damn you, Egan!"*

She tried to recollect the impromptu topics: something about junk food… No, but sugar was involved…And national security… And the death penalty.

Mandy's head was hurting. She didn't particularly like champagne, and pot made her dizzy anyway. To make matters worse, whomever was next door to Egan had cried throughout the night.

So much for getting a good night's sleep before a tournament, Mandy groused. *I guess football coaches aren't so stupid after all.*

Screw it. Even if I'd mentioned the topics to the team, I'd have to lie about how I knew about them… Like, maybe say I'm psychic?

Nah. They're dweebs but they're not stupid.

She realized she'd be better off scrutinizing her room for other detrimental evidence Egan may have found.

Mandy's bedspread and sheets were soaking in the bathtub. The burn hole made her wince.

The bag of pot and the rolling papers were gone. She wasn't surprised, considering the fire. So was the torn tab that had held the LSD dose.

And the camera was in a different place on the dresser.

She grabbed it and tapped into the photo archive.

It was empty.

Damn it! Egan knows the truth about Jeremy!

Mandy didn't even try to stifle her giggles. "Touché, you son of a bitch," she crowed.

Then it occurred to her:

Before he can use it to get me tossed out of school, I've got to get something on him.

It should be easy. He's got such a big ego.

Just in case she had to make a quick getaway, she packed her things and rolled her luggage to the bag-check station.

WITH EACH OTHER'S HELP, THE TEAM HONED IN ON THE THREE PUBLICLY announced topics.

Everyone on AA's team was an orator and could think on their feet. The state winner would be chosen in the eighth round. Should the team make it through the first four rounds, everyone would have a chance to argue a pro and a con and give a rebuttal.

Throughout the practice session, Mandy kept her ego in check. No snide comments. No eye rolls. If she felt she had a stronger point than the ones offered by her colleagues, she spoke up. Otherwise, she listened and took notes.

As she suspected, Audrey filled in the leadership void.

Fine with me, Mandy thought. It's hers to lose. And if we win, I'm still officially the team's captain.

Jeremy's absence would cost them dearly. He had prepped the rebuttals for round one; and if AA were to make it into round five, he'd have been doing AA's pro argument, with Johnny on con, and Portia on rebuttal.

"Who can take his place?" Portia opined.

"Audrey," Johnny replied adamantly. "She's our strongest debater."

Like hell, Mandy thought.

But before she spoke, Audrey said, "I'm flattered. But we all have our strengths and weaknesses. Mandy seems to knock rebuttals out of the park, so she should sub for Jeremy in the first round." She met Mandy's eye. "Are you okay with that?"

Mandy shrugged. "Sure. I'll take Jeremy's place."

"And Audrey, you're our strongest in pro," Gemma pointed out. "If we make it to the fifth round, you'll replace him."

"But I just said—"

"Sure, I'll do it," Audrey declared, cutting Mandy off. Absently, she fiddled with the lace of her boot.

Mandy's boot.

Anger roiled through Mandy.

She did that to remind me how much she hates me. All the more reason I've got to win my match. Then it'll be up to Little Miss Goody Two Shoes to bring it home…

Or everyone will hate her.

Okay, yeah, that works for me.

WE'RE WINNING.

Audrey couldn't believe her team's luck.

Portia's pro argument in round one showcased her classic eloquence and Mandy's rebuttal cut the legs out from under their competitor.

In round two, Ashbury Academy pulled the con argument. Johnny pulled out all the stops, as did one of the Kennedy twins on rebuttal.

Round three's impromptu topic suggested that the country's cities should install CCTV for national security purposes. Considering that they only had an hour of prep time, the team followed Egan's plan in division of duties: the Kennedy twins pulled raw data, which was used by Mandy, Gemma, and Johnny to write first drafts of the pro, con, and rebuttal arguments, which were passed to Portia and Audrey for fine-tuning.

Audrey, assigned the pro argument, was glad to finally make it to the podium. Her statements, made clearly and elegantly, ruffled their opponents.

She was finishing up when Egan walked in. Though the house lights were dim and he stood in the back of the room, she could still make him out.

She'd know him anywhere.

This is for you, she thought.

She watched as his fist punched the air when the judges announced Ashbury Academy had won.

Egan ran up to the stage to make the group hug that enveloped her.

She reached over and took his hand.

It surprised her when he didn't pull away. In fact, he squeezed it tightly.

At that moment, Audrey's life was perfect.

"TELL US ABOUT JEREMY," PORTIA BEGGED. BECAUSE ROUND FOUR'S topic had been previously announced, she, like the others, was too curious to think about anything else.

"He's alive." Egan's bluntness made clear what he didn't want to say: If barely.

"Thank God," Audrey murmured. She turned to Johnny. "Were you asleep when it happened?'

"I guess so." Johnny paused as he tried to remember his sequence of events. "I was in the Kennedys' room for a couple of hours. They hooked up their Nintendo 64 to the TV. When I finally went into my room, I didn't even look to see if Jeremy was in his bed. I just dropped like a stone the minute my head hit the pillow."

"What does that matter?" Mandy hastily countered. "He had his own key, right?"

"Well, if he fell from our room, he must be a ghost," Johnny replied. "Our balcony door was shut."

Audrey let that sink in. Finally, she mused, "Doesn't your balcony face the parking lot? I thought he was found on the grass, which is on the other—"

"How he got there doesn't matter," Egan interjected. "I take full responsibility. This weekend, his health and safety, just like yours, was on my watch. To that end, Lavinia was informed of his injuries and I stayed with Jeremy until his parents could join him at his bedside."

Mandy smiled slyly at Egan.

She thinks I'm covering for her, Egan thought.

When she realized Audrey was watching, Mandy demurely dropped her gaze to her lap.

Egan frowned. "Round four starts in a few minutes. Let's give Gemma, Portia, and whichever Kennedy is up time for a run-through."

Audrey stood up and walked away.

AH, HELL, EGAN THOUGHT. AUDREY IS SMART ENOUGH TO PUT TWO AND two together.

But she's going to get it all wrong.

He couldn't think about that now. He owed it to the team to keep them on their winning streak.

He had no need to worry. Gemma shined in her con argument, as did the second Kennedy twin in the rebuttal.

Mandy had made it a point to sit beside him. Every time she leaned toward him, he leaned away.

She's practically in my lap, he fumed.

Egan wondered how Mandy's shenanigans looked from Audrey's perspective. He looked around, but he couldn't find Audrey anywhere.

As the judges announced Ashbury Academy as the winners, Egan stood with the rest of the team to give Gemma and Kennedy Twin Number Two a standing ovation, then waited as the judges announced round five's impromptu topic: food nutrition labeling should include added sugars and fats.

As the remaining teams broke into their workout sessions, Egan's team gathered around him. "Okay, who's up to bat?"

"Portia on con and Johnny on rebuttal. But Jeremy was to do the pro," Gemma reminded him. "Since he's not here, we all decided that Audrey would be our strongest player."

"Agreed," Egan declared. He looked around. "Where is she now?"

Portia nodded toward the door. "I think she went out for some fresh air."

"I'll look for her. Get started on the research," he commanded.

"Maybe I should come along too—in case she's throwing up in the lady's room," Mandy offered. "You know, nerves or something. If she blows it for AA, Lavinia won't be happy." She sighed as if she really gave a hoot. "In fact, maybe I should do pro instead."

"Nah," Egan countered. "You're the last person I'd choose, *ever*, to replace Audrey." Egan laughed at the thought. "Besides, you're needed here to do what you do best: rebuttal. You have this uncanny ability to find fault on any issue and make it seem important. Granted, in this case, it's only about nutrition labeling, but don't let that stop you from giving it your all."

As Mandy sputtered angrily, he strolled away.

EGAN FOUND AUDREY SITTING IN THE SCHOOL'S BLEACHERS, WATCHING a track meet.

She didn't see him until he sat down beside her.

"We won."

She nodded. "Good."

"So, you're up."

Audrey shrugged. "I'm too distracted. Maybe someone else should do it."

"You can do this, Audrey," Egan insisted.

"You don't understand." She looked away, but not quickly enough. He'd already seen the tears in her eyes. "I don't want to let… to let anyone down."

She means me, he thought.

"You could never do that." His voice cracked.

Take a deep breath.

Egan started again: "Audrey, please do it for…"

For us.

"…for Jeremy." That was what she wanted to hear, wasn't it?

Especially now.

Now, when Jeremy needs her most.

Audrey faced him. More tears had fallen. More would fall still when she nodded. "Yeah, sure. If you say so," she whispered. "For Jeremy."

She ran back to the auditorium.

THE KENNEDYS HAD DONE A GREAT JOB. THE DATA WAS ALL THERE.

By the time Audrey reached their workstation, Portia had finished the first draft for the opening argument.

Egan wasn't surprised that Mandy's rebuttal draft was half-assed at best. He could tell she wanted to sabotage the team: if not Audrey, then Johnny.

He prayed AA would win the right to present pro because Gemma pulled some excellent summation points.

And he now knew Audrey would do her best to deliver them.

ASHBURY ACADEMY WAS TO FACE OFF AGAINST BRANSON, A PRIVATE school from Marin County. As with each previous match, this one began with the two teams pulling one of two disks from a crystal bowl: one stamped PRO and the other CON.

Audrey pulled PRO.

Her argument was straightforward. It centered on the power of knowledge, and the harm done when it is withheld from the public. It segued to the science of nutrition before driving home the need for governments with open markets to protect its citizens' wellbeing with federally mandated regulations. She closed with a call to action: "A society is only really free when it has the facts to make the right decisions."

She did it, Egan thought.

For him.

IF ONLY JOHNNY HADN'T FALTERED.

The mistake came in his opening statement of his rebuttal. Whatever he read had him pausing to re-read it. Unconsciously, he mouthed, *What the fuck?*

Seeing this, students in the audience giggled.

By the time he got a grip on his argument, it was too late.

Ashbury Academy lost by six points.

Johnny stormed off the stage. Passing a trash can, he tossed his note cards into it.

Audrey was curious enough to stop and see why: When she found the card with Johnny's opening bullet points, she noticed some words had been blacked out with a Magic Marker.

Who would have done that—and why?

Audrey turned to Portia. "Who prepped Johnny's rebuttal?"

Portia thought a moment. "Mandy. Why do you ask?"

She sabotaged us, Audrey thought. Not that she could say that to Portia. She'd be angry and heartbroken, like the rest of the team. And right now, considering Jeremy's condition, they needed to hang together, no matter what Mandy threw their way.

THE DECISION TO SKIP A SECOND NIGHT AT THE HOTEL WAS UNANIMOUS.

While her teammates packed, Mandy collected her luggage at the baggage stand. When the hotel's manager presented her with a bill for the damages to her room, she tossed her credit card at his chest. "Put it on this," she muttered.

When Egan finally gathered everyone together in the lobby, he directed them to hand him their keys.

Odette handed in the two assigned to her. Nodding toward Mandy, she declared, "The second was for her room. Thank goodness I didn't have to use it."

Egan shook his head at that.

"Ooh, speaking of two keys..." Mandy reached into her purse

and pulled out a key. She held it up clearly so that Audrey could read the number:

302

She tossed it to Egan.

She laughed when she saw the look on Audrey's face.

If she blabs to Lavinia that Egan and I may have done the dirty, all the better, Mandy thought. But before he gets fired, I've got to get him to write that letter for me.

CHAPTER 17

It was past eleven at night when the Debate Team finally pulled up in front of Ashbury Academy. The ride home had been glum. Jeremy's critical condition put a damper on the team's exemplary showing.

Seeing the cars pull up, Lavinia ran out to greet them. Most of the parents were there too.

The kids shrugged off the congratulations. They were too worried about their friend.

Jeremy's parents were conspicuously absent.

When Cornell, Odette, the students, and their parents finally dispersed, Lavinia turned to Egan. "Shall we speak in my office?"

He nodded.

Audrey wished she could follow them in, but she knew better than to ask.

Despite his relationship with Mandy, Audrey hoped Egan would tell Lavinia the truth of what he knew about the incident and let the chips fall where they may.

At the very least, he owes that to Lavinia, she thought.

Audrey walked into the school to make three quick calls. She knew Tallulah, Davis, and Bliss were eager to meet up and hear about the tournament.

"No way! Egan? With…*HER?*" Bliss's screech was so loud that the late-night crowd at Tommy's Joynt—mostly cops on break—looked over curiously at her before rolling their eyes and resuming the task of tucking away their mile-high brisket platters and Hofbrau sandwiches.

"I was shocked too." Audrey shrugged. She hoped her friends missed the tremor in her voice.

"First she's all over Jeremy, and now my favorite teacher?" Bliss shuddered. "It's like playing Whack-a-Mole! Each time you smack her out of your life, she finds another hole, and *out she pops!*"

"I guess if you're going to dump Jeremy just because he had the bad luck to fall off a balcony, Egan is a considerable step up," Davis pointed out.

"More like a leap into Outer Space!" Bliss sighed. "And with her being underage and all, couldn't that get Egan into legal trouble? I mean, even if it was consensual, in California, isn't seventeen years old, like, statutory rape?"

"As it turns out, she's already eighteen," Audrey replied. "I saw it on her transcripts. Mandy was held back because her mother quote-unquote allowed her to take an 'early gap year' in the tenth grade when her stepfather's job relocated them to Singapore."

"Well, that takes Egan off the hook legally if not ethically," Davis added.

I was fooling myself. He never really loved me. It was just a flirtation.

"So, what should we do about her?" Tallulah's devious smile scared Audrey.

"Absolutely nothing! I mean that, Tal. We have no right to butt into her business with… anyone."

Tallulah shrugged. "If you say so."

Audrey nodded. "I do. We graduate in two months. Our lives are ahead of us, not behind us. In the big scheme of things, Mandy Blackwell will just be a sad footnote." Slinging her backpack over her shoulder, she added, "And frankly, that's the way I'd like it to stay. Agreed?"

Tallulah shrugged, but then finally nodded.

"Davis, agreed?" Audrey asked.

His eyes moved to Tallulah. Her slight nod took him off leash. "Yeah, sure."

"Bliss, you too," Audrey warned.

"Pinky swear," Bliss murmured through her pout. She held out her hand, pinky extended.

As the friends entwined fingers, they laughed.

"Great. Okay." Audrey forced a smile onto her lips. "We play it smart until graduation, right? Then we get on with the rest of our lives."

She'd miss AA. Because of Lavinia, it was more than just a school to her.

In a bittersweet way, Egan had made it special too. Audrey had hoped he was her future. The sad reality was that he'd soon be part of her past. She would never again walk the halls of Ashbury Academy without being haunted by the ghost of his memory.

Things will change between all of us, Audrey realized. Bliss was going to Santa Cruz, and Davis had earned a full scholarship to UCLA.

Tallulah, whose goal was to get as far away from her mother and her rotating cast of hangers-on, sycophants, and lovers as possible, had gotten accepted to Oxford. But before going, she planned on taking the whole summer to trek through Europe.

Upon hearing this, Bliss squealed, "Can I go too? Please? Pretty please?"

Tallulah rolled her eyes. "Yeah, okay." She turned to the others. "How about it, guys? A road trip?"

Davis shook his head. "Can't. I'm hitting LA the minute school is out."

Audrey understood how he felt. San Francisco was his past. UCLA was his future.

Audrey sighed. "Sorry, Tal. I've got plans this summer too.

Congressman Blanchard has agreed to let me intern for him this summer."

Audrey had known Harris Blanchard all her life. He'd been at Berkeley with Lavinia, where they coordinated the student protests that were his springboard into politics. He'd also been on AA's trustee board since the school's inception.

So, when Harris offered her the position, she readily accepted.

It's time I got on with my life.

Without Egan.

Most definitely without Mandy.

———

FINALLY ALONE WITH EGAN, LAVINIA GOT RIGHT TO THE POINT: "WHAT happened?"

"One of the kids got out of hand."

"Was it Mandy?"

Egan blinked twice. "That wasn't just a good guess, was it?"

"I've been at this for a few years. I think I know a little something about raging hormones, adolescent acting out, and questionable parenting skills." Lavinia shook her head, awed by the thought of it all. "In Mandy's case she's a triple threat. Add to that a field trip with an overnight in a hotel? My God, Egan, I'm so sorry! I blame myself for sending you into that lion's den with no one to have your back."

"I had Cornell and Odette—"

Lavinia rolled her eyes. "They're the last folks you want in that fox hole with you. I should have steered you toward Berney and his wife, Jean." She winked. "I've seen them in action. Believe me, the 'archeology' thing was a cover. They were Covert Ops at some point."

"I also had… Audrey."

The tension in Lavinia's face eased. "I'm glad to hear she was able to keep her wits about her—considering it was Jeremy."

So, she suspects Audrey still has feelings for him.

Knowing this, Egan felt his chest caving in.

"Was it Jeremy's stash?" Lavinia asked.

"Doubtful. And Lavinia, it wasn't just marijuana."

"I was a child of the sixties. I learned how to read toxicology reports as a volunteer at the Haight Ashbury Free Clinic." Lavinia shrugged. "Jeremy's attending physician says he had LSD in his system. And it would strike me that if the evening took place in Mandy's room and with Mandy's drugs, then Mandy would also have enjoyed a magic carpet ride."

"Unless..." Egan didn't want to say the obvious.

"Unless Mandy didn't tell him about it—and skipped it herself," Lavinia replied. "If so, then Jeremy was coerced into trying it." She reached for the phone. "I'll tell his parents that we are of like mind on the supposition that he didn't take it voluntarily—and that we don't feel it's worth a suspension, let alone expulsion."

In other words, Lavinia had no intention of ruining Jeremy's opportunity to accept any scholarship that still might come his way.

"Lavinia, what do you want to do about Mandy?"

There was no mirth in the headmistress's chuckle. "Wring her neck. But I'll settle for using my time with her next year to help her get over her insecurities. It's the basis of all the harm she's caused. Maybe before she graduates next year, we can help her see the bigger picture: how her deeds have a long-term effect on everyone she knows, including herself. We may yet be able to save her from herself."

Egan's guffaw was genuine. "If you say so."

Audrey is so lucky to have Lavinia in her life.

And so am I.

CHAPTER 18

"Knock, knock!" For a Monday morning, Mandy's sing-song entry knock was too cheerful by half, in Egan's opinion.

And, considering Jeremy was still in intensive care, he found her behavior outright ghoulish.

Right now, it looked as if the kid's injuries were severe enough that he might not be able to play football. Thankfully, his strong math aptitude had allowed him to apply for some academic scholarships too. Stanford had offered him one, but he'd already turned it down when USC came through with a football scholarship. Lavinia was already pulling strings to see if she could get Stanford to reconsider.

Egan beckoned for Mandy to enter.

"I have a favor to ask," she declared.

"Really?" Egan feigned shock and awe.

She shrugged. "What's got you so grumpy?"

"You mean, other than the fact that your actions sent one of my students to the hospital with an overdose, a concussion, and a few broken bones when he should have been studying for a tournament?" Egan shrugged. "Why, nothing at all." He leaned back. "So, tell me, what can I do for you?"

"Write a letter of recommendation."

Interesting. "To whom?"

"Ideally, your very best contact at Berkeley." She ran a mani-cured finger over his desk. "You graduated in Lit, am I right?"

"Aren't you the little psychic," Egan murmured.

More like "psycho"…

"And your faculty chair—Clive Cunt-Luckinbill—wasn't he that guy who won the Pulitzer?"

"It's *Munt*-Luckinbill. My, my! You have done your homework!"

"Don't tease me, Egan. I'm serious." Mandy pursed her lips into a pout. "Or trying, anyway."

"Okay, I'm now waiting with bated breath."

Mandy frowned. "For what?"

Egan chuckled. "For you to ask, my sweet! Beg. Grovel. Whatev-er." He brushed the air with his hand. "Anytime you're ready."

"I don't see why you have to make fun of me!"

"I'm not. I'm quite serious."

Anger darkened her face. "Well, for your information, I won't…" Suddenly, she smiled. "Oh, I get it. You want a little quid pro quo."

"Nope. No quid. No pro. And certainly no quo, Mandy. Because, to be honest, I can't even imagine where your quote-unquote quo has been, and I don't want to find out the hard way. You see, I'm allergic to penicillin." Despite her indignant gasp, he leaned forward. "All I want is the truth."

"The truth…about what?"

"About Jeremy's overdose. Was it accidental?"

"Jeez, Egan! Of course, it was accidental! Do you think I'd—"

"Do it on purpose?" he asked. "No. I think that you didn't realize how potent LSD can be." Egan shrugged. "And I'm glad you're willing to admit you tricked Jeremy into taking it."

"I'll admit nothing of the sort!" Mandy growled.

"A shame. Because if you were to admit the truth, then…well, just between you and me—*and I do mean just between the two of us*—the gesture would go a long way toward keeping you at the school. Rumors have a nasty way of following a student around, especially those who are encouraged to transfer elsewhere before their senior year."

He let that sink in.

"So, what you're saying is that my *admission* gets me the letter?"

"Yes. I'd feel you were somewhat contrite for your actions, and I'd have absolutely no hesitation in giving you what you want —*without* any groveling."

She smiled, relieved. "Then… yes. I brought the pot."

"And the LSD," Egan added.

"Yes, okay, that too," she declared.

You little bitch.

"And you took pictures of the two of you *in flagrante delicto.*"

"Okay! Yeah!" Mandy looked skyward as if her exasperation had fallen somewhere from above. "So, I get the letter, right?"

"I won't go back on my word. It'll be waiting for you here on my desk in the morning."

Her mouth hardened into a grimace. "Not just any letter, right?"

He kissed his fingers. "It'll be a love letter, albeit a work of fine fiction."

"Okay, then." Mandy's grin went ear to ear.

"Oh, and one more thing: your tenure with Debate Club has ended. Don't bother to try out next year."

He could tell she was seething at the slight. Still, she walked out the door with her head held high—and her middle finger straight up as well.

Egan laughed so hard he almost fell out of his chair.

Then he opened his computer and started typing Mandy's letter to Clive. After the salutation, and a few pleasantries, Egan also wrote:

I still have so many fond memories of Clementine, despite her calling me "thick." (A joke? Frankly, I concede she's right—in more ways than one!) Such a joy, sticking around that incredible woman. You are one lucky guy.

Now, for the purpose of this letter: I want to recommend a student who, I feel, fits right in with your mission for the Lit department…

From there, he made sure to include the sort of buzz words that he knew his old mentor despised: things like, "*Ms. Blackwell has a strong voice for commercial fiction,*" and "*She uses phrases steeped in the vernacular of the time, with none of the mundane adherence to classic narrative structure…*"

He also included this line, knowing it would rankle the celebrated author:

As for Miss Blackwell's drive, she will do whatever it takes to assure editors will sit up and take notice.

And, finally, Egan paraphrased the man's most cutting remarks about his thesis:

Ms. Blackwell will never hear such scoffs as 'derivative,' 'half-hearted,' pedestrian,' or 'false." No one will ever say that she has faltered in developing a unique voice. Her writing has just the right amount of gravitas.

I see so much of myself in her. I hope you do too.

In abject sincerity and regard,

Egan Gable

He then stuck it in an envelope he'd addressed to Mandy.

Egan wished he could tell Audrey about it and watch her laugh.

CHAPTER 19

"In event of a fire, an earthquake, or some other natural disaster, do not use the elevator. California State Law and City of San Francisco Emergency Safety Regulations require that evacuation of this building take place through the stairwells, or via the emergency fire escapes, which can be found attached to all classrooms on the second, third and fourth floors..."

  —*The Ashbury Academy Emergency Manual*

There was only one elevator in AA: an old Otis that, from its plaque, informed those who cared to crouch down to read it (through many decades' worth of wear and grime) that it had been installed at the dawn of the Twentieth Century.

Really, there was no need to stoop. Proof of its age came with use.

It rose at a snail's pace. Worse yet, when it went down, it jerked intermittently, moaning and groaning, like a woman in her tenth hour of labor. Those along for the ride either cursed, squealed in terror, or moved their lips in silent prayer. All of these reasons were more than the needed incentive to take the stairs.

This time, however, Audrey didn't have that option.

Tired of watching her daughter mope away the afternoons after school, Lavinia had given Audrey the task of moving some of the discarded textbooks from a fourth-floor closet to the lobby, where the janitor, who started his work at the school around eight at night, would load them onto a truck and haul them to one of the city's recycling centers.

This task meant using a cart, and that by default meant taking the elevator.

Audrey had begun two hours ago, right after school. It was May —a week until graduation. San Francisco was enjoying an unusually hot day, and the sky was a crystalline sapphire hue.

The school had emptied out quickly. San Francisco's rainy season was over, and everyone wanted to enjoy the sunshine while they could. The baseball team, which fielded balls and swung bats every afternoon in Kezar Field, wasn't around either. It was playing a school on the opposite side of the Bay Bridge. The players had carpooled over. The last of the teachers had taken off by four-thirty. Even Lavinia had somewhere else to be: she was wooing a new benefactor.

In truth, Audrey liked the peace and quiet in the building and the busy work because it got her mind off other things.

Like Egan.

That wasn't easy.

As frustrating as the year had been leading up to the debate tournament, every day since that weekend, Egan's demeanor toward her had been gracious but formal.

As if we're strangers, she realized.

It was as if the few magic moments they had shared—when they first met, and he'd teased her about Paris—had been a dream.

And then there was Mandy.

Audrey still wondered what had happened between them.

I might as well give up, she thought miserably.

She shoved the cart down the hall until she reached the elevator, and then pushed the button summoning it.

Finally, she could hear it groaning its way toward her.

Maybe Davis is right, and he's not worth all the time and effort everyone puts into pleasing him. Perhaps he's just the adult version of lame. Maybe we should just all grow up and move on—

It opened, and there was Egan.

"Oh!" Dumbfounded, Audrey stared at him, then looked away, convinced it was a dream. But no, when she glanced back, he was still there.

"I thought—I thought I was alone," she stammered.

"Sorry. Really, I didn't mean to scare you. I had to… to grade some papers." For some reason, Egan seemed ashamed to face her. As if to change the subject, he jabbed at the elevator button. "This thing throws me for a loop every time. I'm sure I pushed the down button."

"I may have pushed first, which would override your push. I'm sorry about that." She took a step back and bumped into the cart.

"Here, let me help you with that." Egan attempted to move out of the elevator. Bad move. Having a mind of its own, the doors were already closing before he had more than a leg out the door. With a hand on each door, he shoved them open again, like Superman. "Get in, quick! I don't know if I can keep this beasts' jaws open much longer."

Audrey grabbed the cart and shoved it into the elevator, running over his toe in the process.

"*Shit! Ouch!*… Oh, sorry. I guess I shouldn't have said that." He tried to hide his grin.

That made her angry. "For God's sake, I've just run over your toe! You don't have to stand at attention," she huffed. "This may surprise you, but I have heard that word before. And 'hell,' 'damn,' and 'fuck' too."

There. That should dispel any presumptions he has that I'm some goody-two-shoes just because I'm Lavinia's kid.

He glanced over, puzzled.

His stare made her blush. *Why wasn't the damn elevator moving?*

She jammed her thumb into the button, but still nothing. Frustrated, she slammed it again and again with an open fist.

Suddenly, the elevator started whining and huffing and jerking its way down to the third floor, all the while shaking back and forth frantically.

Only when it tossed them up in the air, then, again and again, did they realize that what they were feeling was an earthquake.

As the ancient lift shuddered side to side, the cart slammed into the elevator walls, flinging the books in every direction.

Audrey and Egan covered their faces best they could, but the force of the earthquake threw them up and down and into each other.

When it stopped, they were both trembling.

Audrey heard herself groan. With the electricity off, the elevator was pitch black, and she couldn't see her bruises. Instinctively she touched them with trembling fingers. The pain made her moan again.

Hearing her, Egan pulled her close and cradled her in his arms. They were warm and even more muscular than Jeremy's.

To quit from trembling, she focused on stroking his arm.

He said nothing, as if he, like she, were afraid that talking would make it happen all over again.

Would that be so bad?

No, she thought. I could stay here in his arms forever.

They sat together like that for what seemed like ages. Finally, she raised her head. In doing so, her cheek rubbed his. Its stubble felt like tiny pinpricks.

Egan lowered his head, and she felt his warm breath. That's how she knew how close his lips were to hers.

Close enough to kiss.

But they didn't. Instead, he pulled away slightly and whispered the obvious. "Jesus—an earthquake! Are you hurt?"

As she shook her head no, the top of her head scraped against his chin. She didn't want him to pull away again, so she edged into him.

She could feel his heart pounding furiously in his ribcage. She knew if she moved her hand slowly, down into his lap, she'd find him stiffened.

If he chose to move her hand there, she'd already made up her mind she wouldn't pull away.

But he didn't.

A few moments went by, and his heart slowed a bit. He nudged her up somewhat so that he was no longer holding her.

That saddened her.

For the longest time, she didn't say anything. Finally, she just came out with: "Egan, why don't you like me?"

———

EGAN DIDN'T KNOW HOW TO ANSWER THAT.

Should he tell her that he'd flipped over her, that very first time he saw her?

Or that he was rock hard that very moment?

But he knew he couldn't say that for all sorts of reasons, not the least being that he didn't need some jailbait crush to fuck up his life.

If only she were even a year older —

And it would help if her mother weren't his boss; and if he weren't also Audrey's teacher...

Instead, he opted for another version of the truth. Sort of. "Audrey, seriously, you've got it all wrong." The words stuck in his throat, like gritty grains of sand. "I do like you! I—Okay, *no.* What I mean to say is—"

He sounded like a fool, stumbling around for the right words.

Worse yet, he sounded like some lovesick schoolboy.

No, that would never do. He shook his head, knowing that she couldn't see his anguish in the dark. He had to pull himself together and fast.

He took a deep breath, then cleared his throat. "Okay, the truth? Audrey, listen, this isn't *The Dead Poets Society.* I'm—I'm just a guy looking to earn a living while I write my book."

"Oh." Audrey let that sink in. "Okay, yeah. Gotcha."

She let her hand fall into his lap.

It was there she found her answer:

Yes, he had feelings for her. His hard-on was proof of it.

She'd let that sustain her.

Audrey moved her hand quickly away to give the impression that the contact had been incidental.

They sat there for what seemed like forever.

Finally, as nonchalantly as she could, she inched away.

The silence must have been weighing on her, too, because she started chattering: about the passage from *Madame Bovary* he'd had them read the week before; about her disgust with the stupid war in Afghanistan; about the odds that the Giants would once ever win a World Series in San Francisco.

All safe topics for discussions.

They conversed politely—like a student and teacher should, for what seemed like an eternity.

Enough time for his erection to subside.

She thought she was now safe from his charms when, with heartbreaking casualness, Egan said, "I hear you got accepted to Berkeley."

She nodded.

"And Wellesley too, I'd heard. And Sarah Lawrence, USC, Bennington, Boston U, NYU..." Egan chuckled. "Did I leave any out?"

Audrey felt her cheeks heating up. "No. That pretty much covers it."

"And yet, you chose the school closest to home."

She fought off the urge to declare: *No. I chose the one closest to you. In case you ever come to your senses and realize I'm here for you.*

If he could tear himself away from Mandy.

Audrey was not surprised that Mandy had dropped Jeremy.

Around campus, he was now a figure to be pitied: someone who'd seemingly had it all one moment, only to lose it the next.

As expected, the sports scholarships had vaporized after his accident. Thankfully, with Lavinia's connections with AA benefactors who were alumni at Stanford, the private university had come through with a partial math scholarship for him.

Still, the accident had changed him, and not just physically either. Jeremy was no longer the guy whose spontaneous fun-loving attitude had made him so popular with his classmates. His smiles now quickly hardened into grimaces. There was a wariness in his stare. His spirit seemed as broken as the bones which were yet to fully heal.

Since Jeremy's return to school, Audrey made it a point to seek him out. When they were together, she slowed her pace to match that of his walker. She kept all topics upbeat, congratulating him on his acceptance to Stanford, encouraging him on his physical progress.

Most of all, she tried to ignore his jibes that she must have much better things to do than "to hang with a broken gimp like me."

The last time he made that crack, she'd finally responded, "You needed a wake-up call, Jeremy. Hey, your body may have hurt like hell, but bones mend. Hearts take a little longer."

He'd flinched, but then he reached for her hand too. "I'm so sorry we broke up, Audrey."

She chuckled. "I got over it."

It was the first time since the accident that she'd seen him laugh.

Now, she wished she could say the same about Egan: that she was over him.

She couldn't. If anything, being close to him now only heightened her longing for him.

She realized that, over time, the feelings of desire would wane.

Maybe college will change that.

Eventually, they heard Lavinia shouting Audrey's name, so they yelled back. They didn't dare beat on the door because they didn't know how well the elevator would stand up to it.

Ten minutes later they heard pounding and screeching as Lavinia edged a crowbar between the elevator doors and attempted to pry them back. It took her another half hour, and by the time she was through, the space she'd made for them was only two feet wide, but it was large enough for both to slip through, although they had to jump down a few feet since they were stuck between the third and fourth floors.

The flashlight Lavinia placed on the floor dimly lit the hall. Despite being drenched in sweat, she hugged her daughter as if she would never let her go again. The hug she then gave Egan started out clumsy and shy but ended up just as fervent. The tears of relief that followed were justified if what she was relaying about news reports of the earthquake's damages were true.

"The electricity is out in a lot of places throughout the bay! The radio says that, as a precaution they've closed the Bay Bridge and BART's Transbay Tunnel." Under the weight of worry, Lavinia's face caved in on itself. "Until the phones come back online, I won't know if the baseball team made it back over the bridge after the game, or if they're stuck in Oakland." She tried wiping away her tears, but they kept falling, fogging her glasses in the process. "Oh, Egan! I forgot that you live in Berkeley! You won't be able to make it home." She straightened up as she pulled back from him. "We've got a guest room. You must come home and spend the night with us."

"No!… No, really, that's not necessary." Egan felt the edges of his mouth waver from the weight of his shame.

Why should I feel guilty? Nothing really happened! Jesus, we could have died in that old rattrap of an elevator! I was just trying to protect the kid, and we survived, didn't we? My response was natural— adrenaline, I guess… or something like that. Besides, it was Audrey who stroked my arm. It was she who brushed her hand across my lap, not the other way around…

Even as he addressed Lavinia, he locked eyes with Audrey to gauge her response to her mother's invitation.

Her smile was polite, nothing more.

If she hated me because of Mandy, she despises me even more now, he thought sadly.

"Thanks for the invitation, really. But–well, I've still got some papers to grade, and I was going to have dinner with a friend afterward—"

"Oh!... Then, you'll be sleeping over there?" Lavinia's response was more concerned than polite.

"Yes! I'm sure that will be okay."

In truth, there was no friend. He would just have to sack out on the lumpy couch in the teachers' lounge.

And try not to dream about Audrey.

"That's good." But Lavinia seemed genuinely disappointed. She shook her head sadly. "Well, we can all say we came through it in one piece."

Egan laughed weakly. "Now, if you'll excuse me, I'll get back to my papers." He picked up his satchel and headed back toward his classroom, taking the stairs this time.

WHEN HE GOT THERE, HE REALIZED THE ELECTRICITY WAS STILL OFF. So he just sat there, watching out the window as daylight turned into twilight. Eventually, Lavinia and Audrey walked out of the old building toward their home.

Then he closed his eyes.

And cursed his fate.

She's the first girl I've ever wanted that I couldn't have, he thought miserably. In a week, she'll be gone from the school. She'll be getting on with the rest of her life.

Without me.

Fuck it—why didn't I say something?

I'm such a loser.

He must have sat there for another half hour when it hit him. Slowly he opened his satchel and took out the typewritten pages of his book.

He threw it into his metal wastepaper basket.

Then he struck a match and tossed it in too.

He stared into the basket. As the pages caught fire, he was reminded of the Shakespearean quote Audrey had used as the theme for the essay in which she compared the love of Romeo and Juliet to that of Jay Gatsby and Daisy Buchanan:

Love is a smoke made with the fumes of sighs…

It wasn't as bright as looking directly into the sun, but he knew that gazing directly into the flame was just as stupid.

The loss of his eyesight certainly wouldn't improve his writing.

As the fire brightened the room, he thought of his new novel, which was already writing itself in his head. The story would embody all the love and lust and heartache and youthful exuberance that had been missing in the other manuscript.

Its characters were right there, at Ashbury.

The quixotic Lavinia and her gently worn staff; all the sharp flirty girls and clueless horny boys.

Too handsome but too clueless Jeremy, sad little Davis, true to her name Bliss, and tough-as-nails Tallulah—even scheming, capricious Mandy—would feature prominently in his cast of characters.

But most of all, the novel would be about Audrey.

Or at least, the way he imagined her to be: the savvy, sweet, sexy heartbreaker.

At least in his fiction, she would finally be his.

THREE YEARS LATER

CHAPTER 20

"So, how's life?"

Whenever Audrey and her dearest high school friends got together, that was always the first thing asked.

This time, it was Davis who broached the question.

And, as always, it was a dare to give the most audacious answer.

"Why don't you start?" Tallulah suggested.

"I second that motion," Bliss chimed in.

"Me three," Audrey added, laughing. As antsy as Davis was, she knew he was bursting to tell them something significant. As for herself, long ago, she had resigned herself to the fact that life as a political science major at Berkeley was as mundane as it could get— at least when compared to her friends' journeys.

Granted, she was politically active and had worked on numerous causes that supported society's underdogs. As class projects for her pre-law curriculum track, she wrote white papers that sought to strengthen national health regulations.

She'd also spent the last two summers interning for Congressman Blanchard in DC. Her hard work had impressed him. She planned to do so this summer too.

At the very least, it'll give me a few interesting things to say to the gang when we meet up again in the fall, she thought.

Hopefully, the next reunion would take place then or sooner, but she wouldn't bet on it. She'd noticed that their meetups were fewer each year and further apart.

The only constant was the locale: the Magnolia Brewing Company, near the corner of Haight and Masonic.

"Okay, you twisted my arm." Taking a deep breath, Davis declared, "I've been asked to helm an action flick for Universal."

The girls squealed in surprise and then enveloped him in a hug.

"I love you guys so much," Davis murmured.

Although still a year away from graduating from UCLA's film school, Davis was already making his mark as a movie director. A few months earlier, his student film premiered at South by Southwest. Critics hailed the semi-biographical film about life in San Francisco's seamy Tenderloin district as "the ultimate statement on today's human condition," and "a haunting parable for our time."

In the meantime, he'd been invited to pitch every major film studio.

"Well, congratulations!" Audrey exclaimed. "So, which one of us gets to walk the red carpet as your date?"

"All of you, of course," he promised.

Bliss's jaunt through Europe with Tallulah ended in its sixth week. While in Paris, a professional photographer saw her on Pont Neuf, gazing at the boats drifting down the Seine. Newspapers around the world picked up the picture he took of her, clad in cut-off jeans, stiletto heels, and a gauzy midriff-cropped hand-painted blouse from her parents' shop.

Bliss was an instant celebrity. Offers from modeling agencies poured in.

Additionally, the blouse became a fashion sensation. Its sales were the catalyst for Over the Rainbow's growth into twenty other U.S. cities, with Bliss as its cover girl—just one of her many modeling contracts.

Today's news was that Bliss had just signed on as the new face for an international cosmetics line.

"Wow!" Audrey declared. "Your face will be everywhere—even bus stops!"

Bliss guffawed. "Yeah, well, that can be a curse and a blessing. That just makes it easier for pervs to defile you in public. Just ask Gisele."

Tallulah laughed. "You know, I don't think we'll ever get that opportunity."

"Sure you will," Bliss insisted. "Let's all meet up in New York during Fashion Week and I'll introduce you."

As for Tallulah, her studies at Oxford were curtailed in her sophomore year when it was discovered that Chameleon's financial manager had absconded with all of Maggie's money.

Tallulah now divulged how she'd succeeded on her vow to "chase the son-of-a-bitch to the ends of the Earth, and make him pay back every cent." But sadly, before being caught, he'd managed to punch a massive dent in the Wishart Family Trust.

Reluctantly, Maggie had agreed to give Tallulah her power of attorney. Tallulah was now in the middle of negotiating Maggie's latest contract with her record label and running her mother's next tour.

"I've also been asked to manage another band. In fact, it's the opening act on Maggie's tour. It's called Jammerhead." Tallulah's eyes sparkled with excitement. "Its lead singer and writer is…well, he's a *genius!* He's—so *deep!*"

Davis cocked a brow. "*That's* an interesting metaphor. Are you describing his lyrics or something more interesting?"

Tallulah smiled coyly. "I'd be lying if I said we haven't spent a few late nights discussing things other than the band's song list." She frowned. "I'm just hoping Maggie backs away from the idea of cutting the tour short, which always happens when she thinks she's in love."

"Who is it with this time?" Davis asked.

"Wait, let me guess," Audrey interjected. "Does he play bass guitar?"

Tallulah sighed. "Bingo! And, are you ready for this? He's half her age."

"In other words, he's our age," Bliss pointed out.

"You've been through this drill a dozen times," Davis reminded her. "What are the chances that it's really serious?"

"I'm frightened enough that I want to lock up her estate so that it's cad-proof." She glanced over at Audrey. "That new boyfriend of yours—Daniel, right? Isn't he an associate at some San Francisco law firm with six names?"

Audrey laughed. "Only four. But yes, it is a well-respected firm."

"Good! Because I like the cut of his jib. And since, from the looks of him, he's head over heels in love with you, maybe throwing some business his way will have him seeing additional advantages to wooing you besides the fact that you're the sweetest person in the world."

Audrey blushed. "Frankly, the last thing Daniel needs is more encouragement."

"Finally!" Bliss exclaimed. "If anyone deserves someone who loves them unconditionally, it's you."

Audrey, touched, toasted her friends. As their glasses met, she replied, "I have all of you, and I have Lavinia. I am already blessed."

"Oh, cut the crap!" Davis's eyes twinkled merrily. "We all say prayers that we'll find a guy who's not only a great lay but who only has eyes for us."

Audrey choked on her wine.

She had never admitted to her friends that, at twenty-one, she was still a virgin. And because the subject never came up, she let them assume otherwise.

Dating was easy for her. She was pretty enough that men flirted with her, and her openness made it easy for them to feel comfortable in her presence. But it was when they saw her kindness in action that they fell in love.

Until Daniel McKittridge, she'd never felt that she could reciprocate.

Daniel was tall and broad-shouldered, the result of making the swim team of every school he'd attended. His hair, brown but already graying, curled tightly when he missed his barber appointment, which, with his overloaded work schedule, was much too often. Audrey didn't mind because she liked it when she could brush an errant lock back behind his ear.

His brown eyes squinted naturally. His nose crooked slightly to the left, and his grin rose higher on the right, which gave the impression that this lopsidedness was his mouth's way of overcompensating for genetics' shortcomings.

All of this created the illusion of a man on the verge of handsomeness but somehow missing the mark.

Not that it mattered. His most attractive feature was his laugh, which he did often.

They'd met at the Berkeley Law Library, where she worked three nights a week. He'd come in search of a book on Costa Rican case law. He'd hoped that the antiquated tome, published in 1923, would offer a bit of arcane knowledge that might save one of his firm's pro bono clients from deportation.

She was touched that Daniel offered to climb through the library's dusty old archives with her to locate it. "Your sweater is much too nice for the amount of grime in that joint," he'd pointed out.

She looked up, surprised. "So, you've been inside the library's vault?"

He laughed. "When I was getting my JD, I practically lived in it. I was lucky to work my way through school in this building. Granted, I doubt I'll sustain my feelings of fondness if I end up dying an early death from some disease carried by dust mites."

She handed him a smock, latex gloves, surgical mask, and a shower cap. Donning the same, she followed him into the archive.

"Normally, that's not a sexy look," he murmured. "But somehow, you pull it off."

Lots of men had flirted with her. But Daniel's joke was the first time a thrill ran through her since the day she met Egan and he teasingly offered to take her to Paris.

The search for the book took an hour. By the time they'd found it, Audrey was due to clock out.

"Would you like to join me for dinner?" Daniel asked.

Now, two months later, she wondered how she'd lived her life without him.

She loved the cadence of his voice. She adored him for opening doors for women, even at Berkeley, where any sort of male patronization was disdained. When they walked through one of Berkeley's many parks, his eyes softened when they passed young mothers pushing baby carriages.

Most of all, she loved curling up in his arms at night and listening to him in the dark as he recapped his day.

But now, even after eight weeks of seeing each other every weekend, they'd yet to make love.

She knew he was a passionate man. Had she said yes, they'd have made love that very first night. Since then, on numerous occasions, their heavy petting had brought her to the edge of wanting more; of exploring her sensual side with someone so open with his adoration of her.

As her relationship with Daniel deepened, her desire for Egan seemed to fade away like a half-remembered dream. At these times, Audrey asked herself what she was holding out for.

"Speaking of someone who's come pretty far in the past three years, who'd ever think we'd see Egan Gable on the cover of *Time*?" Tallulah exclaimed.

"Not to mention *People* and *Vanity Fair*," Davis added. He reached down to grab his satchel and pulled out a copy of both magazines. "I couldn't resist buying these at the airport. Our old prof has hit the big time!"

Audrey's friends were right. Egan's face was now everywhere, thanks to his recently released novel entitled *Extracurricular*.

Audrey had only learned about it an hour before. While heading toward the Downtown Berkeley BART station on her way to meet her friends, she passed the campus bookstore. A display of Egan's novels took up the whole front window.

"Yeah, well, I was in *Vanity Fair* first," Bliss sniffed.

Davis snickered. "I said, 'the cover.'"

Bliss smacked him on the arm. "I'll get there—eventually."

The sight of Egan's face may not have been as ubiquitous as Bliss', but it was enough to chip away at Audrey's heart.

"Have any of you read *Extracurricular*?" Bliss asked.

"Not yet," Tallulah admitted. "In fact, I'm almost afraid to! From the description I read in the *Chronicle*'s review, he may have based it on Ashbury Academy."

Audrey's heart lurched in her chest. "What do you mean?"

"It takes place in a private high school in San Francisco and—" Tallulah explained

"Oh, my God! You don't think he…" Bliss's eyes opened wide. "*Did he?*"

"We've got to get a copy!" Tallulah exclaimed. "We may be in there!"

I may be in there.

Audrey felt as if she might faint. To steady herself, she took a sip of her wine. Audrey's friends had no knowledge of her history with Egan. She wanted to keep it that way.

Davis poked Audrey. "When did he leave AA?"

"Right after our senior year," she murmured.

"Well, then, hell yeah, we're in there!" Davis laughed gleefully. "Hey, if it's any good, maybe I'll option it for a movie. Of course, I'd have to pump up my character's role."

"And maybe you'll give me a role in the film," Bliss declared. "Then I will most assuredly make the cover of *Vanity Fair*. And besides, who could play *moi* better than… *moi*?" She pointed at herself with both hands.

"You're assuming too much." Despite Audrey's retort, she had an awful premonition that she was wrong.

"You mean that Bliss can actually act?" Davis teased.

Bliss socked him on the arm for that crack.

Most of AA's instructors stayed a week after the last day of school to get their classrooms ready for the following year. Knowing this, Audrey had made it a point to stay away from the school until she knew Egan had left on his summer sabbatical.

She'd been surprised when, in the first week of July, Lavinia informed her that Egan had turned in his notice.

Audrey couldn't believe her ears. "He's leaving?"

"Yes. But it's the right thing for him to do," Lavinia replied. "At some point, he realized he wasn't happy here. He's moving to New York."

Had I told him how I felt when we were stuck in the elevator, would he have stayed for me?

Now, three years later, she'd never know.

"Hey, what do you think ever happened to Audrey's library book thief?" Bliss mused. "What was her name again?"

"Mandy Blackwell," Davis shuddered. "Who knows? My guess is she'll eventually end up at some L.A. talent agency. Trust me, that piranha would fit right in." He turned to Audrey. "Did she even graduate from AA?"

Audrey nodded. "As I recall, yes. And she got into Northeastern."

Tallulah snickered. "What a joke! Let me guess: Stepdaddy Warbucks slapped his name on one of their buildings. Presto! Instant undergrad."

Audrey shrugged. "Sadly, it happens all the time."

"It may be a legal bribe, but it's unfair to the kids who aren't born with a silver spoon in their mouth," Tallulah retorted. "Audrey, you're a protector of the downtrodden. Work on that, won't you?"

"I'll drink to that," Bliss retorted.

So they did.

THE NEXT MORNING, AUDREY WENT INTO THE CAMPUS BOOKSTORE TO buy *Extracurricular*, but she couldn't find a copy on the shelves.

However, she did see a poster next to a front table. It announced:

EGAN GABLE, AUTHOR OF THE NOVEL *EXTRACURRICULAR*, WILL DO A READING FROM THE BOOK.

Supplies Are Limited. Buy Your Copy Today!

To encourage attendance, the poster included a few snippets of the novel's reviews:

"Raw, honest, and moving."—*New York Times Book* Review

"A heartbreaking parable of unrequited love." —*New Yorker*

"The must-read of our time." — *London Review of Books*

For a moment, Audrey felt as if she couldn't breathe.

Egan—*there?*

Audrey went up to the sales clerk: another student she recognized from her first-year biology class. "I'd like a copy of…" she couldn't bring herself to say the book's name. Instead, she pointed to the poster.

The clerk clicked her tongue. "*Extracurricular?* Sorry, we're already sold out of our copies." The woman leaned in. "In fact, it's sold out everywhere! Apparently, it's pretty steamy."

Audrey blanched. "What do you mean, steamy?"

The clerk cocked a brow. "You know how some books are a love story? Well, let's just say that this one's a *lust* story—and all that implies."

Lust?…

Egan didn't write about me after all. He wrote about Mandy.

Audrey didn't know if she should be relieved or disappointed.

"We still have a few reserve tickets for the event," the clerk was saying. "They come bundled with a copy of the book. If you'd like to buy one, I'd suggest you do it now. I'm sure they'll be gone by the end of the day."

"Sure, okay," Audrey heard herself mutter. "In fact, I'd… I'd like two tickets."

The clerk took Audrey's credit card and rang up the order. "Here you go! Two tickets. When you show them at the front door, the ticket taker will also hand you two books."

Audrey reasoned that she owed it to herself to see Egan one last time.

In fact, she'd take Lavinia with her.

"It's great to hear your voice—and it isn't even Sunday," Lavinia exclaimed delightedly.

"I've got a surprise…sort of." Audrey took a deep breath. "How would you like to accompany me to see Egan Gable speak on his debut novel?"

"Ah, yes! *Extracurricular*."

"You know about it?" Audrey flinched, ready for the worst.

Lavinia chuckled. "I'd have to be living on a deserted island to miss it." After a pause, she added, "Have you read it yet?"

"No. It's sold out on this side of the bridge."

"Here as well," Lavinia replied. "But I'm sure Egan will have one waiting for me when we see each other on Friday night."

"*What?* You… and *Egan*…" Audrey sat down hard.

"Yes. He's that night's speaker for City Arts and Lectures—you know, at the Herbst Theatre. He called and told me that he saved me a seat. We'll be having dinner beforehand."

"Oh…" Tears welled in Audrey's eyes. "How sweet of him. Be sure to tell him… that I said hello." Audrey covered the phone as she caught her breath.

Think of some excuse. "I've got to run, Lavinia. Class starts in a few minutes."

She hung up, hoping Lavinia hadn't caught the catch in her voice.

She knew that Egan and Lavinia had ended their professional relationship on a positive note.

If he's already reached out to her, then the novel can't be something he'd feel she'd resent, she reasoned.

It must not be about us.

About me.

Audrey felt relieved.

Then sad.

At that moment, she knew who to take to the event, instead.

Daniel.

He'd be proof positive to Egan that any schoolgirl crush she may have had was over.

Because it was.

Surely.

As for Daniel, she'd tell him the truth—sort of. Egan was her favorite teacher in high school. Going to the event was just her way of showing her support.

She was certain Daniel wouldn't mind having Egan sign his copy for Tallulah instead.

***

"Guess what we're doing Saturday," Audrey exclaimed to Daniel.

"Enjoying a picnic in the park." His answer was confident, almost cocky.

And yes, it would have been acceptable too. Certainly nicer than trying to introduce the man you'd once wanted so badly to the man who now wants *you* with all his heart.

"Um… no," she replied uneasily. "I bought tickets for a lecture by one of my former instructors."

"Oh." Daniel thought about that for a moment. "Maybe I had him too. What course does he teach?"

"He didn't teach at Berkeley—although he did get his Ph.D. from here." Had Egan ever finished his thesis? Audrey couldn't remember.

"What's his lecture about?"

"He wrote a novel. Apparently, it's a big hit: *Extracurricular.*"

"Yeah, I've heard of it." Daniel paused. She guessed he was trying to remember why. "What's it about again?"

"A prep school." *No need to go into detail.*

To change the subject, she added, "The tickets come with copies of his book."

"I know authors love signing their books. Since you're a former student, I'm sure he'll appreciate your support."

"You'll get a book too. But would you mind terribly if I gave that copy to Tallulah? She… she had a crush on him, so I know she'd appreciate it."

What a liar I am.

"Sure, no problem. If he intrigues me enough, I'll just read your copy." Daniel laughed. "Saturday, eh? What time does it start?"

"Two o'clock."

"I have to go into the office to work on a brief that has to be filed on Monday, but I should be back in plenty of time."

"Great." Audrey leaned in for a kiss.

She wondered what Egan might write in her book.

All of a sudden, she hoped Daniel would never want to read it.

By eleven o'clock on Saturday morning, Audrey hadn't heard from Lavinia. Although she was dying to hear about her mother's dinner with Egan, she fought the urge to call her and ask about it.

When the phone rang at noon, she leaped for it.

"Hi, honey." It was Daniel's voice, not Lavinia's.

Audrey stifled her disappointment with a weak giggle. "Are you on your way to campus?"

"Well, that's just it." Daniel sighed. "One of the partners walked in. For the past two hours, he's been bending my ear about one of his international cases. He'd like me to be the second chair on it."

"Wow, congratulations," Audrey replied. "Great news, right?"

"Yes and no. Audrey, I'm still stuck here, finishing the brief. You won't mind going without me, will you?"

"Not at all." *Oh. No.*

"Thanks," Daniel sounded genuinely relieved. "I'll make it up to you tomorrow. That picnic I mentioned? I'll pack it. But you're charged with bringing the wine. Noonish?"

"Sure." Audrey hoped she sounded positive.

"Hey, if you want, bring that book along. If it's funny, we can read some of the passages out loud."

As if.

The lecture auditorium was only a ten-minute walk from Audrey's apartment. The tickets included seat numbers, so Audrey had no reason to get there early.

The last thing she wanted was to seem as if she were eager to see Egan again.

She couldn't wait.

CHAPTER 21

The curtain on the left side of the auditorium's stage had been pulled back just enough that Egan could scan the crowd.

He'd agreed to a signing on the Berkeley campus for one reason: he hoped to run into Audrey.

His dinner last night with Lavinia had gone well. She'd mentioned that her daughter had purchased a ticket, which came with a copy of his novel.

Will she see herself in my heroine, Zelda?

Will the book help her realize why I kept her at arm's length, even as I longed for her? Even knowing she longed for me too?

Well, now there is nothing to stand in our way.

Unless what she reads embarrasses her.

Unless it was just a schoolgirl crush, and nothing more.

Unless—

His thoughts bolted from his consciousness when, suddenly, he felt a hand at the base of his spine.

"I've missed you, Egan."

That voice…

"Tell me you've missed me too."

It was dark enough that had one glanced at them from the

wings, one would be able to see how her hand now roamed downward—

Until Egan stopped it.

Holding tight, he lifted Clementine Munt-Luckinbill's wrist to her side.

Even in this dim light, he could see she'd aged. Granted she'd kept her figure. The paper-thin faux-leather pencil skirt stretched tightly enough to leave no doubt about it. And while most of the wear and tear on her face had been tightened and tucked away, he knew it well enough to remember when the skin under her chin didn't sag, the lines on her neck didn't crisscross her throat like railroad tracks, and the hollows under her eyes hadn't needed to be plumped with cosmetic filler.

Or maybe it was always like that but I just didn't care because she was such a great lay, he reasoned.

As if reading at least those last seconds of his thought, his surprise visitor gave a throaty chuckle. "So you have missed me!"

"Ah, Mrs. Munt-Luckinbill—what a wonderful welcome!" Egan gave Clementine a chaste kiss on her cheek. "I was wondering if Clive might release you from his ivory tower to welcome me back." Still holding her wrist, Egan twisted it so that he could kiss the back of her hand.

He'd already been on the book tour a week. Each stop had supplied him with a smorgasbord of women ready, willing, and able to follow him into his room for the night.

But the conquests had been too easy. Out of revenge for her ratting him out to Clive, Egan was curious enough to see how far Clementine was willing to go to make amends to play along.

"It's a shame about Clive's 'head cold.' I was looking forward to sharing the stage with him." In truth, Egan had almost danced a jig when he'd arrived at the auditorium only to be informed that his former mentor was to be a no-show. "Is that the code word for 'in his cups'?"

"You know him so well." Clementine shrugged. "His publisher is balking at our counter-offer to its mediocre advance for his next book. If they don't capitulate by Monday, his agent starts shopping it around."

"Let me guess. The last one never earned out."

Frankly, that was Egan's biggest fear: that *Extracurricular* would die a premature death.

As it turned out, he'd had nothing to worry about. Between the titillating title and the intriguing description, it appealed to all the right readers.

Clementine shrugged. "Prestige has its privileges. Still..."

She didn't have to finish the sentence: *a book's sales are what mattered most.*

It also didn't help that Clive was a passive-aggressive tyrant. No matter how many awards were showered on him, it was inevitable that his publisher would eventually get tired of coddling him.

The university will follow suit, Egan reasoned. One had to work hard to get kicked out of a tenured position, but it was still possible.

"We'll just tell the audience that he's got a nasty cold." She smiled. "But you're in luck! I'm his stand in."

"*You'll* be moderating?" Egan frowned. He'd hoped to avoid both Munt-Luckinbills altogether. Clementine's very visible role in tonight's event could complicate things.

"Sure, why not?" Clementine replied. "As I recall, you enjoyed our sessions of Truth and Dare tremendously."

Egan chuckled uncertainly. "But those were private, and we always ended up naked, albeit in some interesting positions."

"The day isn't over yet." Clementine smiled grandly. "Speaking of which, you arrived so close to the starting time that the university gave the key to your hotel suite to your book publicist."

"Fine, no problem." In fact, the publicist, Kimmy, had handed it to him right before he went backstage. When she mentioned she'd be visiting old friends in the area later that evening, Egan told her she could take off during the book signing.

He too hoped to be spending time with a dear old friend.

Certainly not Clementine. And he had no intention of letting her ruin his mission:

Telling Audrey he loved her.

Who knew where things would go from there?

Clementine's way of abruptly rousing him from his fantasies of all possibilities was to cup him and whisper, "Shall we?"

This is not going as planned, Egan thought.

By the time Egan reached the podium, he'd found Audrey in the crowd: fourth row, just right of center.

He had to pretend to listen to Clementine's fawning introduction. It seemed as if she gushed on about his newfound notoriety for an hour. He'd stifled the desire to tell her to shut up already.

This really wasn't about him. It was Audrey's night.

Egan had to tamp down the urge to rush through the reading so that he could finally get Audrey alone by reminding himself that, through the passage he'd chosen to read, she'd finally hear everything he'd wanted to tell her these past three years.

So he read the passage slowly, as if his life depended on her verdict.

Every now and then he'd look up from the pages and seek her out in the sea of faces dimly lit by the footlights. Since he'd known Audrey, she'd been the judge and jury over his every thought and desire.

From the look on her face, he'd finally earned his reprieve.

It was all there, in his own words.

The passage Egan had chosen took no more than six or seven minutes to read. In it, he'd told their story: the once-upon-a-time in which their paths crossed; the missteps and cross purposes that broke their hearts and changed their lives forever—

But that nothing, not even time, could stand in the way of their happily ever after.

With eloquence, he wove a tale of how he (that is, "Caleb") had fallen in love with her (in this case, "Zelda") from the first moment he'd laid eyes on her.

In just a few sentences, he relayed his dismay for how the combination of his position as her teacher and her age made the romance unthinkable.

But, despite his attempt to shove his feelings aside, he couldn't stop yearning for her.

By the time Egan had finished reading the passage, some in the audience were sobbing.

In Egan's book, Caleb and Zelda's unwitting deeds produce a tragic sequence of events before the lovers end up together.

We end up together.

But it was just a fantasy. Egan's fantasy, Audrey thought.

In real life, he was famous. Beloved.

And she was…

Still Audrey.

In real life, people change, she reasoned.

Everyone she knew—Tallulah, Bliss, and certainly Davis—had zigged and zagged off the path of the life they thought they'd lead.

When confronted with an obstacle, they overcame it. They were quick to recognize an opportunity and take advantage of it. Despite life's twists and turns and detours, her friends had still found the path to success and self-satisfaction.

Only I've stayed constant.

Constant for Egan.

Is Extracurricular *truly an homage to our love—or was it used merely as the novel's plot device?*

If I approach him tonight, will he sign my book with no more than a handshake and a polite smile, or will he finally profess his love for me?

She'd find out soon enough.

"So, tell us, Egan! I'm sure *everyone* is dying to know: who is the real Zelda?" Clementine smirked as if she already knew the answer to that question.

In your dreams, lady.

"Each of us has a Zelda in our life, don't we? An unrequited love? The one who got away?"

From the look on Clementine's face, one would have assumed Egan had broached a question as profound as how to achieve world peace. "If your Zelda is worth loving, isn't she also worth wooing again?"

Egan turned to stare out into the audience. Finding Audrey, he proclaimed. "You're right. And it's why I'm here."

He could have sworn he saw Audrey wipe away a tear.

AUDREY HAD DONE EXACTLY AS EGAN HAD HOPED: WAITED UNTIL THE last autograph was signed before finally approaching him.

And unlike the acquaintances who had shown up at his signings awed at the spectacle of it all, Audrey didn't attempt an awkward reintroduction.

Instead, true to her nature, with her unflinching gaze she simply declared, "I never knew you'd felt that way about us, Egan."

Tears glistened on her lashes.

He felt his own eyes dampening and thought it best to close them until he could smile again. Otherwise, he'd bawl like a baby.

When he opened them, he replied softly: "Now that you do, tell me, Audrey: what would you like to do about it?"

Instead of answering him, she held out her hand.

He took it, and they walked out together.

He was relieved that Clementine had disappeared immediately after the question and answer session. Apparently, she'd taken the hint that his interests lay elsewhere.

"The university is treating you like royalty!" Audrey looked around Egan's hotel suite. A sumptuous meal had been set up on a small table for two. A magnum of champagne sat in a silver ice bucket. Chocolate-covered strawberries filled a crystal cake stand. "Does this happen everywhere you go?"

Egan grabbed the champagne bottle and popped it. As the liquid rushed to its head, he put two glass flutes side by side in time to catch the fizzy libation's spillover.

Handing one of the glasses to her, he replied, "No, not quite. But now that I've hit the bestseller list, I guess Berkeley wants me to forgive and forget the Lit department's harsh words toward my thesis."

They clinked glasses. As Audrey drank from hers, Egan reached for Audrey's copies of his books. "Why the second one?"

"It's for Tallulah."

He chuckled. "Okay then. I know exactly what to write."

He scribbled with a flourish and then showed it to Audrey:

Dearest Tallulah,
You'll find yourself throughout the book, doing what you do well — creating
havoc.
Enjoy! — Egan

Audrey laughed too. "She so richly deserves that. And frankly, Egan, you've deserved all your success too."

"Coming from you, that means a lot to me." He sighed. "But the truth is, Audrey: my faculty chair was right. The stuff I wrote before I met you… Well, let's just say you were the perfect muse. In fact, I want to memorialize that fact."

He picked up the other book and wrote:

Dear Audrey,
You were the ideal fantasy.
May our reality be just as wonderful.
With all my heart, love, Egan

"Oh…" To hide her disappointment, Audrey slipped the books into her bags then turned her gaze to the window. It faced Berkeley's renowned Campanile, which was just then chiming the hour: four o'clock.

Egan walked up beside her. "You sound disappointed."

"I'd hoped…I'd hoped I was more to you than that." Audrey shook her head. "Not just fodder for your novel."

Egan stared at her, confused. "What I felt for you was very real! I just couldn't… I couldn't let us do—"

Audrey put two fingers on his lips to shush him. "I understood. I knew it then, and I know it now."

When he calmed down, she dropped her hand to her side. "I'd always wondered why you didn't feel the same about Mandy."

He frowned. "What about her? … What do you mean?"

"That you didn't view her as—you know: 'off limits.' I guess it's because she was already eighteen—"

"*What?*… I don't understand…" Confused, Egan shook his head.

"The weekend of the debate tournament I saw her going into your room—in her bathrobe. She didn't knock. She had her own key."

Egan searched his memory. "Oh… My God! You didn't know!"

"Know what?"

He shook his head, awed. "All the stunts she pulled that weekend. The whole ploy for getting her own room was so that she could blackmail Jeremy."

"*Jeremy*? Why?"

"They were screwing. But he wouldn't go public with the relationship, so she wanted to force his hand."

"Oh! Well, I guess I had *him* wrong." Bemused, Audrey sunk onto the sofa. "How is it that you knew about their relationship and I didn't?"

"Because… I was jealous. Like me, he only had eyes for you." Egan sat down beside her. "And, frankly, for a while, I thought the feeling was mutual between him and you. Or, that you were toying with him to retaliate against me for not— well, for not taking you seriously enough."

"I was upset that you were friendly with everyone but me," Audrey admitted. "So, why *did* Mandy have a key to your room?"

"Because she'd started a fire in her own room and needed somewhere to sleep the night before the tournament. I stayed at the hospital with Jeremy." Egan winced. "Really, Jeremy started the fire, when he fell out of Mandy's bed. He was on a psychotic trip. Mandy had given him LSD. It's why he leaped from her balcony."

"I had a feeling she had something to do with Jeremy's accident!" Audrey shook her head angrily. "Why didn't you tell Lavinia?"

"I did tell her! She decided to handle it in her own way—with tender loving care." Egan shrugged. "I didn't stick around to see if her theory would work. I was too busy licking my wounds over the thought that you'd gone back to Jeremy."

Audrey burst out laughing. "*Are you serious*? No way! I was too much in love with you!" Saying it out loud wiped the smile off her face.

"And all this time I thought you hated me." He took her hand. "When we were in the elevator during the earthquake, I told you I was just there to do my job—"

"And to write your novel," she reminded him.

He let loose with a mirthless chuckle. "I misread so many signals."

And that's when she kissed him.

He understood that sign well enough.

They were still locked in their kiss as he carried her into the bedroom.

CHAPTER 22

The sweetness of her lips had him craving even more of her. His fingers roamed the buttons of her blouse, undoing one after another. At the same time, his lips moved down to the cleft in her chin, a spot that had teased him for nine months, so many years ago.

In fact, the exploration of every nook and cranny of her exquisite body—every inch of skin, every dimple and pucker—was met with a groan of anticipation or a sigh of joy.

At the same time, Audrey's hands passed lightly over his chest, causing his heart to pound harder. As they floated over his abdomen, his cock, already stiffened, ached to be inside her.

By her moans, he knew she wanted him too. He parted her thighs with his hand.

When he entered her, she was so tight that his gasp was as loud as hers.

My God…I don't know if I can hold out—

Suddenly, Audrey clenched so firmly that it was all he could do to hold on; to keep from exploding.

He couldn't help himself: he came.

Egan collapsed on top of her, spent.

PAIN...

Oh my God—SUCH PAIN—

JOY.

So much joy.

Finally.

FINALLY!

He was worth the wait.

And yet...

It was over so quickly!

... Is it always like that? God, I hope not...

Suddenly she was crying. Yes, from the pain—oh, how her muscles ached down there!—and yes, from the wave of bliss washing over her.

As if reading her mind, Egan reached up to stroke her cheek.

"You're crying," he murmured. "Why?"

"Because..." Audrey sighed. "I waited so long for this."

For us.

A HAZY MEMORY ROSE IN EGAN'S CONSCIOUSNESS: JEREMY'S unsuccessful attempt to be Audrey's first lover, and Egan's own dismay that the boy may have succeeded on the day they skipped his class. But when confronted, Audrey had made it clear to Egan: she hadn't gone through with it.

Wait...

Nah. She's now a junior in college—and at BERKELEY, no less! I mean, come on. There's just no way she's still a virgin...

I mean... My God—she knew what she was doing down there...

So...

Tight.

Shit."

Egan had to ask: "Audrey... Are you...?"

How can I put this so that it doesn't seem so ludicrous: "Are you seeing someone?"

<hr />

OH, GOD! HOW DID HE KNOW?

Caught off guard, Audrey whispered, "Yes."

"Oh."

He sounds almost—relieved.

"I don't mean this very second," she said crossly.

Not until tomorrow. Noonish.

At the thought of Daniel, a volt of guilt charged through her.

I am Egan's fantasy, but I am Daniel's reality.

Egan laughed. "Of course, not. You're with me now."

What did he mean by that? Was he finally ready to make a life with her?

She'd waited so long for him to love her. And now, this was the moment—

"Yoo-hoo, darling! Sorry it took me so long to get here, but I wanted to pick up a little surprise for you…"

The bedroom alcove was positioned so that Audrey could see the woman enter through the suite's front door.

It was the woman who had interviewed Egan: Clementine something or other, hyphenated.

As Clementine stripped out of her clothes, she plucked one of the chocolate covered strawberries and ate it whole, all the while babbling about a particular sex act she'd missed with Egan. Something about his joystick…

She held up a cock ring tied in a pretty bow. "Appropriate, wouldn't you say?"

"What the hell, Clementine!" Egan sat straight up. "How did you—"

"I kept the second key, silly!" She waved it at him. "I'm sure I mentioned it to you…or your publicist." Clementine shrugged. Then, noting Audrey's presence, she exclaimed, *"Peek-a-boo!"*

Mortified, Audrey pulled the covers to her chin.

Convulsing with laughter, Clementine clucked her tongue at Egan. "Naughty boy! You started the party without me?"

Despite the pain wracking her body, Audrey scrambled out of bed.

As she scooped up her clothes, Clementine cooed, "No rush, hon." She shifted her gaze to Egan. "In fact, she can stay, if she likes. I enjoy a threesome every now and then. And if I remember, sweet Egan, it was one of your fantasies, too."

Egan's fantasy.

Apparently, he had quite a few of them.

Audrey ran to the bathroom.

Egan stood outside the door, pleading for her to ignore Clementine, to believe him that he hadn't been expecting the woman, and other things that were just as likely to be lies in the hope to convince her to stay—

And complete another of his fantasies.

As she flung open the bathroom door and rushed past him, she noticed that Clementine was already naked and in the bed.

Audrey was barely out the front door when she heard the woman exclaim, "What is this—*blood*? Since when did you start liking the rough stuff?"

AUDREY STOOD UNDER A STEAMING SHOWER FOR OVER AN HOUR. THE soreness had ebbed somewhat, but not entirely.

The condition of her heart was a different matter.

What a fool I am, she thought. All these years, I believed that I was doing the right thing: waiting for love.

Waiting for *his* love.

Instead, she got fucked.

Three years of pining after some guy whose opening line was to tease her about taking her to Paris. What a naïve dolt she was!

Three years of waiting for him to call, just to say, "I've been thinking about you. I have something to say to you. When can I see you?"

But, no. Instead, Egan's way of professing his supposed love—nope, make that *lust*—was to make her some saintly, unattainable heroine in his book!

That bastard!

The phone was ringing off the hook. Audrey's apartment was small enough that, even in the shower, she could hear the messages on the answering machine:

"Audrey, please don't freak out that I have your contact information. I had my publicist beg someone to give it to her because I... I need to apologize. I wasn't expecting Clementine to just appear like that! *I swear!* I mean, yeah, we once had a thing. But that was before I—"

Good, thought Audrey. The answering machine cut him off. But not for long:

"Listen, Audrey, before this damn thing cuts me off again: please—*I'm begging you*—please let me see you tonight. We've got to talk this out! I know you feel that way too! I'm right... *Right*? In fact, I'm standing right outside your building now. Won't you just buzz me in? *Please*? I swear, had I known you were a... well, *you* know... I wouldn't have... I think you get my drift—"

He's got my address too?
Audrey leaped out of the shower and ran to the window.
Yep, there he was: right outside her building.
Why, that cad is telling the whole world that he just broke my cherry!

Because she needed both hands to open the window, she waited until she'd wrapped her body in the drapes. Through it, she shouted, "I called the police! They are on their way! Unless you want to end up in jail, you better get lost *now*! Boy, I'll bet your publisher would *really* appreciate that!"

Audrey was sorely tempted to bean him with the signed books, but that meant giving him one more look at her naked body. He'd have to settle for watching her slam the window shut.

As for the books, they were too large for the wastebasket beside her desk, so she dumped them beside it instead.

She spent the rest of the evening sobbing her heart out.

SOMEWHERE AROUND MIDNIGHT—AFTER AUDREY'S MIND HAD RACED through all the would-haves, could-haves, should-haves, and might-haves that may have salvaged her relationship with Egan—Lavinia's words about sex came to her:

Your first time making love is a special moment. But even more important than the desire or passion you feel now is the issue of trust.

When the person you love has earned your trust, then the time will be right to share your love.

She'd never dared to assume that Egan, now a twenty-nine year-old man, had been pining for her. The assumption he'd gone the past three years without a sexual encounter would have been merely naive. Women were drawn to him like hummingbirds to nectar. His relaxed demeanor around them made his attention all the sweeter. Her attraction to him was proof of that.

Until now.

Their relationship—or, more honestly, lack of one—had given

Egan something to write about. But if a mercy fuck was his way showing his appreciation, he could go to hell.

At the very least, he could have scheduled it at a time he wasn't expecting company.

After what just happened, *I'll never be able to trust Egan again,* she realized. *Certainly not the way I trust Daniel...*

Oh, my God —

Tomorrow.

Daniel.

There was no way she could meet with Daniel. She wouldn't be able to look him in the eye.

Not tomorrow.

Maybe never again.

She couldn't lie to him about losing her head over Egan.

Or for that matter, her maidenhead.

Not that he ever pushed her on the issue. He wouldn't know to push. He just thought she wanted them to take it slow.

Now "slow" was changing status to "standstill."

Audrey dialed his number with trembling fingers. Thankfully, it went to voicemail.

She took a deep breath: "Listen, I..."

I what — lost my virginity to an old crush?

Am no longer a virgin but a fickle whore?

Am I an idiot who let a fantasy go to my head?

All of the above?

"...came down with something that has me tossing my cookies," she continued. "If it's contagious, maybe we should postpone our, um, picnic. I'd hate for you to come down with this too. I'm going to bed now. I'll call you later in the week when I feel better."

She knew she wouldn't.

I don't deserve him.

VOICE MESSAGES

Daniel McKittridge, Monday, 3:32 pm: "Hi, hon. Hadn't heard from you, and I was just wondering how you're feeling. Call me with an update. Love you."

Daniel McKittridge, Tuesday 5:46pm: "Hi, Aud. I have to say, I'm somewhat concerned that I haven't heard back from you. Whatever bug you think you've got… I hope it hasn't put you in the hospital! If you get this, can you call? If I'm in a meeting, leave a message. I love you."

Daniel McKittridge, Wednesday, 9:03am: "Audrey, just to let you know: I called University Health Services. The folks say you haven't been admitted as a patient… So, please, can you tell me what's up? Just… check in. Call my voice mail. I promise I won't pick up. I love and miss you."

IF EGAN HAD CALLED TOO, AUDREY WOULDN'T HAVE KNOWN IT because she'd asked PacTel to block his call.

AUDREY HAD SPENT THE LAST FEW DAYS SLEEPWALKING THROUGH HER classes. By midnight on Wednesday, she knew Daniel was right: she owed it to him to tell him something, even if it was that she didn't want to see him anymore.

She didn't call him at home. He was an early riser and most undoubtedly asleep. Besides, by calling his office, it would roll over to voicemail—

Only it didn't.

"Hey." Daniel was trying to sound casual, but she knew him well enough to hear the anxious tone in his voice.

"I… I thought you'd be home by now." *I thought you said you wouldn't pick up.*

"I should be," he admitted. "But I've got a case that's working me overtime."

"I'm sorry I've been so hard to get…I was feeling so ill that I slept through a couple of days of classes. I've got to play catch-up myself." *Don't lie. Tell the truth.*

"That's all I need to know—that you're alright."

Audrey felt even worse, hearing the relief in his voice. "Daniel, I think we should take a break."

"Oh?"

He's surprised. But of course, he should be. If the shoe were on the other foot, I'd feel the same way.

"I feel a bit overwhelmed at the moment," Audrey replied.

"Aw, honey, I'm sorry! I forgot. You've got exams in a couple of weeks."

"Yes. Thanks for understanding." *No! What I'm trying to say is that you deserve better than me—*

He laughed softly. "Can I help it if you're the best part of my week? But, hey, been there, done that with the cramming sessions. Call me when you feel human again. You know I'll always be here for you."

The lump in her throat made it hard for her to talk. Finally, she was able to whisper: "I know, dear friend. Goodbye."

CHAPTER 23

For four weeks the copies of *Extracurricular* sat on the floor beside the wastepaper basket—and probably would have been thrown in the dorm's recycling bin had Tallulah not called with an invitation to catch Maggie's show at San Francisco's Bill Graham Auditorium.

Audrey knew how badly Tallulah wanted to read it, so, with great trepidation, she mentioned that not only had she scored two copies of the book, Egan had autographed them too.

Tallulah giggled with glee. "Well, then, lady, get your butt over to this side of the bridge—pronto! I'll leave your name at the Bill's backstage door!"

The concert was sold out. The opening act, Jammerhead, had the crowd hyped into a frenzy.

As Tallulah read Egan's inscription to her, she snorted. "Well, he certainly had *my* number!" She looked up expectantly at her friend. "Hey, so, what did he write in yours?"

"Nothing half as cute. Basically, a one-liner." Audrey shrugged.

"Have you read the damn thing yet?" Tallulah was doing her best to shout over Jammerhead's riffing.

"No—but he read an excerpt to the audience." Audrey exhaled slowly to give herself time to choose her words carefully. Finally, she yelled back: "Davis was right. Egan sensationalized his students—and himself."

To hear over the music, Tallulah pulled Audrey into a backstage corridor. "In what way?"

"We're in there, Tallulah." *What an understatement.* "And—he has a thing for one of his students."

Tallulah's eyes opened wide. "Can you make out who it is?"

"Yes," Audrey admitted. "It's—"

"No, no—let me guess: Mandy?"

Audrey frowned. "She was certainly the obvious choice."

"You can say that again! She was one big suck-up—and all that implies."

Audrey shrugged. "Nothing is ever as it seems. That goes double in fiction."

"Quit taunting me! If I wasn't on double duty right now, I'd tear right into it."

"What do you mean, double duty?"

Tallulah smiled. "Don't you remember? I'm also managing Jammerhead. In fact"—she blushed. "I'm especially managing Mr. Jammerhead himself." Instinctively, her hand fell on her belly. "Audrey, you're the first to know. I'm going to have a baby!"

"What?" Audrey leaned against the wall, awed. It was the first time she'd noticed that Tallulah wasn't in her usual attire. Skin-tight jeans and a spaghetti-strap tank top, usually worn braless, had been replaced with a gauzy loose-fitting mini-dress. "When... and...how?"

Tallulah laughed. "I think the 'how' is obvious. As for the 'when,' I found out a few weeks ago. In fact, right after we met up at Magnolia." She blushed. "He's so sweet, and funny—and *fearless!* And most importantly, he knows my world, so he's not in awe of it —or Maggie. It's also why I felt it was so important to convince Maggie to complete the tour. I want her to get to know Jammerhead better before I break the news to her."

Audrey placed her hand on Tallulah's belly too. "Knowing

Maggie, I guess the news that she's about to become a grandmother won't go over so well."

"Yeah, you've got that right!" Tallulah shrugged. "Well, too bad. Jammerhead is just as excited as me about this little unexpected surprise."

"Will there be a wedding before the birth?"

"That little piece of paper isn't so important to me. Time will tell if we're the real deal, right? Like you, I never knew my father. Maggie was too much of a tomcat to keep track. Heck, I'm surprised she went through with the pregnancy! My guess is that just being around Lavinia while she was pregnant with you may have convinced her that bringing a life into the world might be the biggest high of them all."

"If that's so, she must thank her lucky stars every day. You're more than just a daughter to her. You're her lifesaver."

Twice, Tallulah had come home from school to find her mother overdosing.

Had she not been there, Maggie would have been yet one more rock and roll tragedy, Audrey reasoned.

Audrey hugged her friend. "I'm very happy for you."

"And I'm happy for you too," Tallulah winked knowingly.

Does she mean Egan? How does she know?

Audrey felt her cheeks grow hot. "I don't know what you mean."

"I meant about you and Daniel!" Tallulah threw up her hands. "Do you know how long I've been waiting for you to get over Jeremy?"

"*Jeremy*?" Audrey couldn't believe her ears. "All this time, you thought I was pining for Jeremy?"

Tallulah rolled her eyes. "Well, who else could it have been— especially after he started screwing that little slut, Mandy."

I guess I really was the last person to know about them, Audrey reasoned, but only because I couldn't care less.

"By the way, how is lover boy?"

Audrey winced at Tallulah's coy reference to Daniel. "I... I haven't seen him for a while. Exams and all." She hesitated. "In fact, I suggested we take a break. Frankly… I don't deserve him."

Tallulah went nose to nose with her. "Audrey, don't be a fool. Trust me, there are a lot of jerks out there. Daniel McKittridge is smart, funny, kind, and head over heels in love with you. Think hard now: do you really want to let him go?"

She's right. Daniel loves me unconditionally.

"Thank you." Audrey kissed her friend on the cheek.

Surprised, Tallulah laughed. "For what?"

"For putting everything in perspective," Audrey shouted as she ran down the hall.

SHE'D ONLY BEEN TO DANIEL'S PLACE A COUPLE OF TIMES. HE HAD A one-bedroom apartment on Russian Hill. It was small and on the fourth floor of an old Edwardian, but it had an awe-inspiring view of Angel and Alcatraz Islands. And, after the fog burned off, the Berkeley Campanile could be spotted across the bay from his windows.

Because it was after nine at night, she took the risk that he was home from the office.

She wouldn't be able to find out immediately because Daniel's building had a closed garage. He always left a light on in the apartment's front window, so that wasn't a telltale sign either. She knocked twice on his door. Then twice again, harder.

No answer.

She was about to leave when she realized Daniel was walking up the stairwell. He was carrying a bag from a local Thai restaurant. When she was here last, he'd taken her there: just a little hole-in-the-wall place, down the hill, on Polk Street. There, they'd tucked into a feast: spring rolls, shrimp pad Thai, rainbow beef curry, and tofu basil.

The sack of food in his hand was much smaller than what they'd brought back as leftovers. He'd ordered for one.

His eyes opened wide. "Gee, what a pleasant surprise! In fact, I was just thinking about you."

"Were you? What about?"

Instead of telling Audrey, he showed her with his kiss.

She'd missed Daniel's mouth: the way it skimmed hers first before finding its place against her lips, then parting them.

She loved the way his eyes closed sleepily as if the most important thing in the world was the task at hand: proving the depth of his love.

His hard, strong arms drew her in closer.

When her fingers grazed his chest, she felt him harden against her.

"Perhaps we should go inside," she whispered.

She didn't have to ask twice.

ON SO MANY LEVELS, SHE KNEW IT WAS WRONG TO COMPARE HER second experience with the first one.

Sex with Egan—achingly longed for and fervently anticipated—had been a hot, raw frenzy of lust.

Sex with Daniel was more encompassing. His actions made it clear that he wanted to savor every moment with her; to treat her like a precious treasure.

As for Audrey, she strove to capture every second in her mind's eye in the hope that it would erase that tortured afternoon with Egan.

She marveled how Daniel took his time undressing her: gently slipping her shirt over her head, then unsnapping her bra before his hands caressed her breasts.

Once naked, Audrey followed his lead: slowly loosening his tie before pulling it off, flicking each button on his shirt free, and unbuckling his belt, allowing his pants to fall to the floor.

It was harder to pull off Daniel's boxer briefs, what with his erection in the way. Audrey tried not to stare at it. She had no desire to compare it with Egan's.

She saw immediately that his goal was to explore with her a new and deeper sensual intimacy, something they had yet to experience but both desired passionately.

When Daniel entered her, she flinched in apprehension. She was pleasantly surprised at how her body opened to him, to find pleasure in gripping him, in hearing his contented groans.

Every surge was a rollercoaster of bliss. Each stroke thrummed her to her core. When the moment came in which he exploded with ecstasy, her joy was just as intense.

She fell asleep in his arms wishing she could stay there forever.

A SHAFT OF SUNLIGHT SOMEHOW SLIPPED BETWEEN THE CURTAINS, warming her face and awakening her.

Audrey opened one eye to see Daniel propped up on one elbow, grinning down at her.

"Marry me," he whispered.

"We haven't known each other all that long," she whispered back.

"I think that works in our favor. We can spend the rest of our lives discovering all the great things we love about each other."

"And what about the bad things?" she countered.

"Okay, you start," he challenged. "Name one thing you think will make me hate you."

Audrey teared up. "I can't."

Because I'll ruin us forever.

"I knew it. You're perfect."

She shook her head. "No, that's not true *at all*."

Tenderly, Daniel traced her nose with his finger. "Don't assume I think you're perfect. I don't. If you need proof, I've found a small pimple." He tapped the side of her face. "Right here."

"Thanks for pointing that out," she retorted.

"I'm sure you'll do the same for me, over the course of time. Hopefully, a very long time." He took her hand in his. "But first things first. You have to say yes."

"And what if I refuse?" she teased.

"You won't. Because you know in your heart no man will ever love you as I do."

When their eyes met, she realized he was right.

"Yes, then. I'll marry you."

They celebrated by making love again.

Afterward, sore but content, Audrey fell asleep, thinking: *Egan may have been my first love, but Daniel will be my last.*

AUDREY SPENT THE WHOLE WEEKEND WITH DANIEL IN THE CITY. ON Sunday morning, they paid a surprise visit to Lavinia.

Audrey's mother had heard her mention Daniel, but had not pressed to meet him. She knew her daughter well enough that, should he prove right for Audrey, that time would come soon enough. So, when Lavinia opened the door, she looked Daniel over, then said, "It's about time."

Puzzled, Daniel exclaimed, "You know then—about our engagement?"

Surprised and delighted, Lavinia laughed. "I guess that gives us two things to celebrate! A beautiful day and a happily ever after."

AS AUDREY SUSPECTED, IN THE COURSE OF THE AFTERNOON, HER mother and fiancé developed a mutual admiration.

While Lavinia puttered around the garden, Audrey and Daniel made themselves at home in the lounge chairs. Daniel, curious about Ashbury Academy, asked Lavinia about her goals for the school. In turn, Lavinia quizzed him about his legal cases.

They found common ground by trading arcane observations

about Audrey that had each other laughing and invariably embarrassing Audrey.

Especially when Lavinia asked, "By the way, were you able to connect with Egan when he was in town?"

Audrey's attempt at a nonchalant nod was a bit wobbly. "Yes. He autographed books for Tallulah and me."

"So, you did find someone for your second ticket after all," Lavinia exclaimed. "I'm so glad."

"Me too, since I couldn't make it either," Daniel chimed in.

Audrey felt uncomfortable for allowing them to think that Tallulah had gone with her, but it was better than admitting she saw Egan alone.

In his hotel room—

Where Clementine What's-Her-Name barged in.

"Audrey, have you finished the book yet?" Daniel asked.

Audrey shrugged. "To tell you the truth, I haven't even started it." *At least that's truthful.*

"I have," Lavinia said.

Audrey felt a sudden chill. "Oh? What do you think of it?"

Lavinia lowered her sunglasses in order to look at her daughter. "Well, let's just say he certainly has an active imagination."

Daniel laughed. "Now you've got *me* curious. I've got a business trip coming up. Maybe I should borrow it so that I can read it on the plane."

Audrey realized the first thing she'd have to do when she got home to her apartment was to hide that damn book.

WHILE BACK AT SCHOOL ON MONDAY, AUDREY TOOK HER LONGEST break between classes to visit the university's health clinic.

The sex she'd had with Egan had been unprotected. Now, just over four weeks later, Audrey felt relieved she'd dodged a bullet. But with her relationship with Daniel moving into an intimate phase, she couldn't take the risk of a pregnancy.

At some point, she and Daniel would want children. But that would happen much later: after she'd attained her undergrad degree, completed law school, worked for a firm—

Much later. Right now, other things in life were ahead of her.

Them.

"I'd like birth control, please," she told the clinic's nurse.

The woman nodded and handed her a clipboard holding a form. "Fill this out, completely."

A history of her sexual activity? *Well, that was easy enough. Twice only: once, four weeks ago. And once, three days ago.*

The date of her last menstruation? *Hmmm. Shouldn't it be any day now?*

She looked at the clinic's wall calendar and started counting backward on the number of weeks…

Oh, no.

She walked to the nurse's desk. "Excuse me, may I have a home pregnancy test?"

The nurse nodded. She went down the hallway behind her and was back a moment later with the requested item. Pointing to a door marked WOMEN, she said, "You can use this in there."

It took a minute to pee on the stick.

The results took a few minutes longer.

She spent the next half hour staring down at the stick and cursing the fact, in the past seventy-two hours, she'd felt both the happiest and saddest she'd ever been in her life.

IF DEBATE CLUB HAD TAUGHT HER ANYTHING, IT WAS TO LOOK AT THE pros and cons of every situation.

CON: I'm pregnant before I wanted to be.

PRO: I could abort, or put up the child for adoption.

> *CON: I'd never do either of these things. Not to some soul who is my flesh and blood.*
>
> *PRO: I'll have the baby.*
>
> *CON: I'll lose Daniel because the child isn't his.*
>
> *CON: I'll put my college on hold or else spend it being pregnant.*
>
> *CON: I'll raise the child by myself.*

From every angle, there were no more pros, just a long line of cons.

———

UNLIKE HER GUILT OVER HAVING SEX WITH EGAN, AUDREY FELT SHE should tell Daniel immediately about her situation, and that she would not hold him to his promise of marriage.

She felt she should tell him in person. The sooner the better. She picked up the phone and dialed his number.

"Hi, beautiful," he said. "Miss me already?"

"Yes, terribly." Audrey wasn't kidding. "When can I see you?"

"A week from Saturday, unfortunately. That trip I mentioned when we were at Lavinia's? It means I fly to Japan tonight, for that new case I'd mentioned a while back. A big international merger with a lot of moving parts."

"Oh!..." Audrey was dismayed. By the time he got back, she'd be almost six weeks along.

"I know. It's driving me crazy that we can't be together."

For the rest of our lives.

"Look, Audrey, I've got to go into a deposition. I'll call you tonight, okay?"

"No... no, don't, Daniel. Just... have a safe journey. We'll talk when you get back."

PRO: Daniel will make a wonderful father.

PRO: My child won't grow up fatherless.

PRO: My child will have two parents who love him or her.

PRO: I can spend the rest of my life with Daniel.

CON: He'd hate me if he ever found out that I'd lied about my child being his.

THE NEXT TWO WEEKS WENT BY TOO QUICKLY FOR A WOMAN WITH Audrey's honest nature, but not fast enough for a woman in love.

She was there to meet Daniel when his return flight arrived at SFO.

They took a taxi back to his place. He couldn't stop kissing her.

The taxi driver seemed to enjoy playing voyeur. But when he had to swerve to avoid the car in front of them, Audrey shook her finger at Daniel. He got the message.

When they arrived at his place, she tried to stop him from taking her to bed. But then she realized that perhaps the rumors about break-up sex were true, and since it was probably the last sex she'd ever have (probably the rumors about single mothers' love lives were also true) she decided she should take advantage of the opportunity being offered.

All was great until their mutual climax was interrupted by her first bout of morning sickness.

"Audrey… are you… ill again?" He stood at the door to the bathroom while she heaved into the toilet.

"I'm… pregnant," she admitted between heaves.

There. Now he knew.

What she couldn't understand was why he was hugging her. And kissing her. And proclaiming that he was the happiest man on earth.

And that he'd be fine if she wanted to move up their wedding before her graduation.

"But... but..." Audrey was speechless.

I have to tell him the truth.

PRO: He's happy about being a father.

CON: Egan wouldn't be. He'd feel resentful.

PRO: Daniel makes me happy.

CON: Egan doesn't.

PRO: My child deserves a father who loves his or her mother.

CON: I was infatuated with Egan.

PRO: I need a husband I can trust.

PRO: I love Daniel.

PRO: I am marrying Daniel.

Daniel hugged her. "I've never been happier in my whole life."

"Me too," Audrey whispered.

RIGHT NOW

CHAPTER 24

"The twins will laugh if they see you crying."

Daniel was right, of course. Charlene and Charles—Charly and Chuck to their friends and family—were in the stage of their young lives where they covered their own embarrassment by snickering at the foibles of others.

In other words, they were typical teenagers.

"Crying about the first day of their senior year in high school is silly, I know." Audrey's attempt to blot both tears and trepidation from her lashes without smearing her mascara was futile.

The kitchen had no mirrors for her to scrutinize any cosmetic damage. She pulled a hand mirror from the satchel.

She shuddered at what she saw. Besides the muddy puddles in the hollows above her cheeks, mascara had seeped into the tiny web of lines around her eyes, making her look even older than she felt that day.

I wonder if this year will change their lives, as it did mine. If so, here's hoping that any transformations are for the best.

"Honey, you'd better hurry or you'll make them late for school." Daniel wrapped his arms around her waist. As his lips nuzzled her neck, he breathed deeply, enjoying the scent of her hair.

She resisted the urge to lay her head on his broad chest and sob away her silly melancholy.

Or, more honestly, her guilty regrets.

He wants to comfort me, but there is no way he can.

Instead she put on her sunglasses. They were wide enough to hide her smudges until she could fix her face in AA's parents lounge, where she was due to meet the two parents who would replace her this year as Ashbury Academy's PTA chair.

Now that the twins were in their senior year, Audrey wanted to leave the *sturm* and *drang* of the school's politics behind her. It had been a constant in her life since the Ashbury Academy's inception.

She was handing the reins to two of her dearest friends who also happened to be alumnae: Tallulah and Bliss.

Bliss' career as a fashion model had put her in front of the man who swept her off her feet and was now her husband: the celebrated Italian couturier, Raffaele Belluci. These days Bliss only stepped onto a runway to promote her husband's line of clothes or for a favored charity.

Their daughter, Sienna, was now a junior in the school. The girl, blessed with her mother's willowy figure and stunning face, was already following in her mother's footsteps. Through Snapchat and Instagram, she was building an army of avid followers, and she'd signed with a modeling agency. However, her father insisted that her photo shoots take place during weekends or school breaks, or the summer months.

"He's always telling Sienna, 'You're not just a model. You're the heir to a dynasty!'" Bliss fretted. "I wish he'd just let her do her thing."

As for Tallulah, she and her common-law husband, Jammerhead, had a son in the school. Quest was a senior, just like Chuck and Charly. The kid, sweet but clueless, had one love: music. Even as a toddler, it was his first and only interest.

This, plus the fact that he sang like an angel, had convinced his grandmother, "Mimi Maggie," to get off the drugs that had haunted her since the early days of her success.

Her belief—that a family who toured together stayed together— was the impetus for the annual summer tour of both Chameleon and Jammerhead. Quest had grown up on the road. Now seventeen, he felt he had to live up to his musical legacy. To his parents' dismay, his studies suffered because of it.

"Hey, why don't I drive the twins to school today?" Daniel's question was proffered with studied nonchalance.

"You're hiding out from Lavinia, remember? If she sees you, she'll twist your arm until you commit to joining the school's trustee board."

"Maybe it's time I said yes," Daniel countered. "It's Chuck and Charly's last year of school, and you've had all the fun up until now."

Audrey laughed. "Your plate is already full, my love. You're the managing partner of your law firm, remember?"

"And you're Congressman Blanchard's speech writer," Daniel countered. "He makes over a hundred speeches a year, and tosses out at least three times that in the sound bites you write that make him the darling of his district. He owes every reelection to your eloquence. So, isn't it time that I tend to this home fire?"

Audrey sighed. "Daniel, trust me. Sitting on the school's board won't be a cakewalk. As the parent liaison, I know it firsthand. All those humongous egos in one place, jockeying for a chance to mark their children's school with their Grade-A liquid gold piss–"

Daniel guffawed. "I doubt Lavinia would appreciate your urinal metaphor for her school."

"Don't be so sure," Audrey countered. "She's seen them all at their worst! Remember, since the board's inception, she's had to play referee; tamp down all their ludicrous expectations for what they think the school should do and be." She sighed. "Lavinia has singlehandedly turned AA into the most desirable private school in the San Francisco Bay Area. Why don't they just leave her alone to do what she does best?" She hesitated, then added: "Frankly, Daniel, I think it's finally wearing her down. She seems so tired lately."

Daniel nodded. "I've noticed that too. But 'retirement' is not in Lavinia's vocabulary. In this case, the school wouldn't be the same without her. She's been its heart and soul since Day One. This is, what, its twenty-fifth anniversary?"

"Silver, yes. And to celebrate, AA's PTA is pulling out all stops with the annual spring fundraising gala. In fact, it's taking place over the whole weekend. Not only will it include the parent gala, there will be a carnival brought in on Saturday for the students too —*and* a concert with big-name headliners."

"Let me guess: Tallulah has somehow convinced Maggie to come out of retirement."

"Yep. And Jammerhead will also be on the bill. As will a slew of other acts."

Awed, Daniel shook his head. "Just between those two names, there are two dozen platinum albums, not to mention Maggie is in the Rock and Roll Hall of Fame."

"And there's talk of Jammerhead being inducted this year," Audrey pointed out.

"Well, the alumni are certainly pulling their weight!"

"I wish I could say the same for the Titans." Audrey rolled her eyes. "Titan" was the nickname the alumni used for wealthiest parents whose children made up the school's second generation. "The stuff Lavinia's done to appease them is mind boggling. Frankly, I think it's doing more harm than good to the school's reputation. Why, just the other day, I overheard two Town School moms at Whole Foods, comparing notes on private high schools for their eighth graders. One of them called AA 'the Crystal Cruise Line of San Francisco prep schools!'"

Daniel laughed. "But it's true, isn't it? What other high school has a Michelin-rated chef and hot tubs all over campus to relax the kids?"

"The chef is an alumnus himself, remember? And by the way: he approached Lavinia," Audrey argued. "He insisted he'd never been happier than when he was at AA, and he wants to find that bliss again. It's a win-win for him *and* the school."

"Okay, I'll concede that—but only because he makes some of the best grub in the city. Still, Audrey, I mean come on! Just last summer, the whole junior class went on a field trip to Antarctica!"

"The best way to learn about the history of a time or place is to experience it in person," Audrey countered. "They went to Ernest Shackleton's expedition site—"

"Yeah, okay, sure." Daniel looked at the ceiling so as not to laugh out loud. "Then tell me this: what other school's 'Family Fun Fridays' feature fireworks and Cirque de Soleil? Admit it, babe: Ashbury Academy is no longer the little hippy school run out of a dilapidated Victorian."

Audrey frowned. When she was a student at the school, the Friday night gatherings were merely potlucks initiated by the students' parents. To offset this fond remembrance, she shrugged. "Perks like that come with the territory. The parents who pay full freight at the school have…well, I guess you could call it a sense of entitlement."

"That's putting it mildly," Daniel muttered. "Heck, my old high school had an ancient gym. We studied off photocopied pages from the few school books allotted to each class, and I came out alright."

"You've always been the exception to the rule," Audrey teased.

"Believe me, Daniel: *I hear you.* When it comes to bells and whistles, AA is practically in a class by itself. But its real selling points are an average class size of only seventeen students, and a teacher-to-student ratio of one-to-eight; and the thirty-one Advanced Placement courses it offers its students. And the best part of all: Ashbury Academy has an eighty-three percent college acceptance rate to its graduates' first-choice schools."

She reached for her keys. "It's why those parents who pay the full freight of $51,000 are here in the first place."

"And why those parents—as you call them, the 'Titans'— resent the fact that half of AA's students pay nothing at all, or, based on a sliding scale of their household family income, no more than five thousand dollars."

A quilt embroidered with Ashbury Academy's mission statement, created by the school's first graduating class, was now encased in the glass frame that hung over the school's reception hall. It stated:

We, the students, teachers, staff, administrators, and parents of Ashbury Academy, vow to uphold our mission of individual honesty and institutional integrity. Students seeking intellectual engagement and a pure pursuit of knowledge will be welcomed with open arms, despite any social or economic barriers they must overcome.

"In the meantime, if the Titans are slowly taking over the trustee board, Lavinia's vision may not stand for long." Daniel continued.

Deep down in her heart, Audrey knew he was right.

"From what Lavinia told me, this year's board president, the fund manager Seamus McCoppin, doesn't seem to have an altruistic bone in his body," Daniel added. "Did you know he actually suggested that the school should quote-unquote 'quit footing the bill for some deadbeats' kids'? And that most of the board would prefer that their fees and donations go toward, say, a grander gymnasium designed by a renowned architect, or maybe hiring

Lady Gaga to sing at the junior-senior dance?" He shook his head in disgust.

"The alumni won't let that happen," Audrey insisted. "For some of them, it's the only way their children will have a chance to have the same sort of education they had."

"Audrey, why do you think Lavinia wants me on the board?" Daniel put his arms around her neck. "Honey, with your resignation, she's lost her majority. I'm serious when I say I'd love to do this for Lavinia. It would only be a one-year commitment. The trustee board has just one meeting a month. I'll be taking part in votes and giving legal counsel on pertinent paperwork. That wouldn't be so bad."

Audrey sighed. "For the past three years, our lives have revolved around that school. And it starts all over again next year, when Noah enters as a freshman."

To his credit, the youngest McKittridge favored Daniel—not just in looks but in demeanor. He was sweet and kind; funny, but soft-spoken. And like Charly if not Chuck, he took his studies seriously.

"I for one am ready to give it a break," Audrey insisted. "Seriously Daniel, take my word for it: run fast and far."

He nodded forlornly. "Okay—but only because you're so adamant about it." He looked at the kitchen clock. "We'd both better get going. But I'll drop Noah at Town School while you take the twins to AA." He smiled slyly. "Oh, and while you're there, break the news to Lavinia that you've forbidden me to join her board."

Audrey's frown warned him that she wanted to slap that knowing grin off his face.

But, instead, she kissed him—*hard.*

"*Gross,* Mom! Quit pretending you guys still know how to get it on and let's move it. Otherwise, we're going to be late for school."

Chuck's voice, coming from behind Audrey, roused her from the safest place she knew: her husband's arms.

"Is your sister still upstairs?" she asked.

Chuck rolled his eyes. "Are you kidding? She's queen of the

nerds and it's the first day of school. She's already in the car." He plucked the car keys from Audrey's hand. "I'll drive, okay?"

Before Audrey could protest, he added, "Otherwise, that's two things I'll have to bring up with my shrink: the vision of you sexing up Dad, and the fact you're a helicopter mom."

Audrey punched her oldest son's arm as a warning that he was about to go too far.

But she didn't take away the keys.

Despite Audrey's insistence that all three of her children were her favorites, Daniel teased her that Chuck—the kid who knew no barriers, broke all the rules, and could talk his way out of any situation—had his mother wrapped around his little finger.

She'd never admit he was right.

Or why, for that matter.

CHAPTER 25

*E*xcept for one time that Chuck forgot to stop at a crosswalk and when he rushed through a yellow caution light in front of a police car, the ride to school was uneventful.

"You drive like you eat—as if the house is on fire," Audrey scolded.

Charly giggled. "Yeah, well from what I hear, that's not all he does fast."

Chuck eyed her through the rearview mirror. "Oh, yeah? What's that supposed to mean?"

"If you must know, the scuttlebutt in the senior girls' lounge is that you're a bit quick on the draw—"

Audrey's head whipped around to stare at her daughter. "Are you telling me that my son has loose morals?"

"Let me put it this way," Charly retorted. "If 'his morals,' as you call them, were any looser, they'd be hanging down to his knees."

"Hey, watch it," Chuck growled.

"No, *you* watch it," Audrey exclaimed. "You almost hit that motorcycle in front of us!"

"Charly's distracting me, Mom," Chuck grumbled.

"No, it's *Fawn McCoppin* who's distracting you," Charly replied.

Oh, now, that's just great, thought Audrey.

Since the twins' earliest years, one of Audrey's greatest fascinations in life was listening to the patter that Charly and Chuck had developed between them.

But by the time the gibberish they shared as toddlers gave way to actual words, Audrey responded with awe, laughter, or concern.

At four, they processed their curiosity in the world around them in very different ways. Chuck took everything at face value. Charly questioned everything.

By seven, while Charly was journaling her observations in her diary, Chuck reveled in being an enthusiastic participant in the world around him. He was active in soccer, baseball, and most enthusiastically, basketball.

This led to a pattern that held to this day. Whereas Charly saw trouble as an iceberg to avoid, Chuck threw caution to the wind, consequences be damned.

As they grew into their teens, like her mother at her age, Charly's circle of friends was small, but choice. They shared quick wits and a love of learning. Charly studied hard and was dependable.

And, like the man who sired him, Chuck was a fun-loving bon vivant: widely admired by guys, and strongly desired by girls.

Charly's taunt was proof of that.

As Chuck pulled into one of the school's guest parking spaces, Audrey tapped his arm. "Chuck, I raised you to be a gentleman at all times. Please remember that."

"I'll try, Mom! But it ain't easy when the girls are practically throwing themselves at you."

"Give it a go. Just... *pace yourself.*"

Chuck rolled his eyes. "It's not like back in your day—you know, when everyone stayed a virgin until they were married."

"This may come as a surprise to you but I wasn't born in the Victorian era," Audrey retorted.

Chuck grinned viciously. "Next you're going to tell me that Charly and I weren't immaculate conceptions either!" He nodded toward Charly. Seeing his mother's shocked look, he added, "Hey,

Miss Brainiac there did the math, so we know better." Chuck kissed his perplexed mother's cheek then leaped out of the car.

Charly was about to follow when Audrey stopped her. "What did he mean by that?"

"Oh, Mom, please! We've known since we were twelve." Charly raised a brow. "We were born less than nine months from your wedding day."

"Twins are known to come early!" Audrey protested.

Charly guffawed. "Mom… *really*? Not *that* early!"

Oh, God…

Audrey stammered, "Honey… I would hope that if you were… you know. I mean, if you were inclined to—"

Charly patted her mother's shoulder. "Mom, *please*! Seriously, do you think I'm stupid enough to let some idiot man-boy take advantage of me? When I do 'it,' it'll be with someone who's mature enough to love and respect me—like you did with Dad."

"Yes, but…" Audrey stuttered, "We were in college—"

"People can be stupid in college too," Charly pointed out. "It's not when, it's with whom, isn't it? You don't have to worry about me. Whoever my 'he' is, I know for a fact I won't find him while I'm at AA!" With a quick kiss, Charly was out of the car too.

―――――――

Audrey was making her way to the parent lounge when Clare, Lavinia's assistant, called out to her from the reception desk. "Do you have a moment to meet with Lavinia?"

"Of course," Audrey replied. She detoured to her mother's office.

The door was shut, so Audrey knocked.

My mother looks so tired, Audrey thought.

Slowly and cautiously, Lavinia raised from her chair to greet her daughter, but Audrey waved her to sit again.

Kissing her mother's cheek, she pulled up the closest chair. "Happy first day of school!"

"Same to you!" Lavinia smiled. "Are Charly and Chuck excited to be back?"

"Charly, for sure. Chuck—well, he's ready for basketball season to begin."

Both women laughed.

"You and Daniel will bring the children over on Sunday?"

"Of course. Family tradition, right? We wouldn't miss it."

Since the children were toddlers, everyone—children and adults alike—spent Sundays helping out in Lavinia's garden. At first the children learned to pick out the weeds. Next they were taught when to pluck tomatoes or strawberries or any other task for which they could better appreciate the garden's delicious bounty.

"Good." Lavinia nodded absently. "I've been lax in my gardening lately." She shrugged. "It was one of the things I wanted to talk to you about."

"If you need help, we can always hire a gardener to pitch in," Audrey suggested.

"Eventually..." Lavinia's smile faded. "Audrey love: I've been diagnosed with breast cancer. Stage Four."

For a moment, Audrey felt as if the world had stopped spinning.

No, no, no...

God, no.

"Your doctor... Is she suggesting surgery? Chemo? What does she—?"

"Surgery is an option, yes. But I won't lie to you. She isn't hopeful. As for radiation or chemo at my stage of life..." Lavinia leaned forward. "I'm sorry, my love. I've made you cry."

Audrey blinked away her tears.

I should be thinking of her, not the other way around. I have to be strong...

"Eventually, I'll be stepping down as Head of School. I'll give the board enough notice that it can conduct a search for my replacement." Lavinia took a deep breath. "As for the board, a couple of members are already pushing to alter the school's core mission, especially as it pertains to our fifty percent scholarship mandate."

"You expect a fight," Audrey murmured.

"Unfortunately, yes. Seamus McCoppin in particular has made no bones about it. I'm sure he spent the summer rallying some of the others to his side." Lavinia's face hardened with resolve. "Before I leave this world, I will prove him wrong. Besides you and the beautiful family you've created, Ashbury Academy is all I leave behind."

Sadness surged through Audrey.

"I respect your decision to stay off the board," Lavinia continued. "But I hope you'll reconsider your reticence about Daniel joining in your stead. It would be a great comfort to me."

"Of course. No problem!" Audrey heard herself say the words, but she didn't remember opening her mouth. "If you want, Lavinia, I'll stay on the board too."

Her mother shook her head. "Unfortunately, by state law, the number of trustees who can be family members is dictated by the board's size. In this case, we're allotted only two seats. As a lawyer, Daniel will hold his own against Seamus. And with both Tallulah and Bliss taking your place as PTA co-chairs, they'll also vote to hold steady on the mission. We'll have Harris' support too. Unfortunately, the rest of the board is a toss-up, but between all of you, I know you'll keep AA safe." Lavinia sighed. "Audrey, at this point, only you know of my condition, and I want it to stay that way."

"But shouldn't we let Daniel know too?"

"Daniel in particular should not be made aware of it. Otherwise, he'll have a fiduciary responsibility to tell the board. I'd prefer to wait for a final prognosis. In the meantime, I'll be interviewing for a Dean of School in the hope that this person can step in quickly should I"—Lavinia took a deep breath—"should I become incapacitated."

Audrey nodded. "Okay, I'll keep it a secret for now. But you'll let me know when the time is right to tell Daniel."

"Thank you, darling." Lavinia hesitated. But before she could continue, her phone buzzed. She picked it up. "Yes?... Oh yes!... Audrey is leaving now, so do send her in."

Reluctantly, Audrey got up. "I'll check in with you after school."

"Not to worry, dear. I'll be leaving for a meeting with one of our benefactors—"

She was interrupted by a knock on the door.

A woman peeked in. She was stately, blond, and dressed in an exquisite belted sheath. "Lavinia, may I enter?"

"Yes, Miranda, please come in!" Lavinia rose. "My daughter, Audrey—"

"Ah, yes—but of course!" The woman's tall heels clicked loudly as she made her way across the floor to shake Audrey's hand. "So good to see you!"

"Thank you, my pleasure as well." Audrey did her best to muster a smile.

"Miranda D'Arcy is now AA's new college admissions consultant," Lavinia explained. "She comes highly recommended. Quite an impressive track record in private school administration! And of course, her biggest asset is that she's also an AA alumna."

"Always a plus. Well, I'll leave you two to talk business." Audrey was too stunned for niceties. Right now she wanted to go home and curl up in her bed, and cry. It didn't help that she still had to meet with Tallulah and Bliss.

I have to keep Lavinia's secret from them too, she realized miserably.

She steeled herself to put on a good act.

CHAPTER 26

s the door closed behind Audrey, Miranda winked at Lavinia. "I don't think she remembered me."

"Perhaps not. Then again, it's been, what, two decades or more?" Absently, Lavinia waved away the years. "And we all change, don't we, Mandy? You, for example. I'm so proud of you! What a success you've made of yourself! And in the field of academia, no less!"

"Thank you for that," her guest purred. "But Lavinia, I don't go by Mandy anymore. It's a childish name. And to be honest, I never really liked it." She shrugged. "It was my stepfather's name for me."

"I understand." Lavinia nodded. "I've noticed you changed your surname too."

Miranda shrugged. "A marriage that didn't work out. At least I got a pretty name out of it."

"Then, Miranda D'Arcy it is." Lavinia turned to the credenza and picked up a sheaf of papers before turning back to her guest. "I've got your contract right here. I must say, I'm surprised you'd rather consult than go on staff full time. I know the fee works out to be the same, but the school does have marvelous benefits."

"Trust me, it works out best this way. You, your students, and their families get my full attention during school hours. At the same time, the few client families who still count on my services for the siblings of children I've already successfully placed in their first-choice colleges won't be left in the lurch. It's a win-win for everyone."

"Agreed." Her question answered, Lavinia signed the contract, then handed it back. "As you know, we have one hundred and twenty-five seniors and the same number of juniors. This first semester, of course seniors must take precedent. But don't be surprised if some of the juniors and their parents are anxious to get into your good graces."

Miranda chuckled. "That's always the case, isn't it? Rest assured I don't play favorites."

"I appreciate that," Lavinia replied.

"In fact, Audrey's children—you previously mentioned that they're seniors this year." Miranda closed her eyes as if the memory of their names escaped her. "They are twins, right? Charlene and Charles?"

"Yes," Lavinia confirmed. "With Charly, you'll have no problem. She's a dream student." Lavinia's smile dimmed. "Chuck will be more of a challenge."

Miranda laughed. "I do love a challenge! And considering that private schools live and die by their Ivy League acceptance rates, I'll make him my pet project."

"That's kind of you, but remember: no playing favorites."

Miranda nodded contritely. We'll see about that, she thought.

"And, do remember one of AA's longstanding tenets: that each student must devise his or her own path beyond high school, which may or may not include immediate college admission—or, for that matter, college at all."

Miranda shrugged. "Yes, I remember it well. I just thought…you know, with tuition fee increases and all—doesn't the thought of their children skipping college worry AA's parents?"

"Initially, yes. Still, this philosophy has had great success. Those students who are ready to continue their academic journey are encouraged to analyze their options based on their life goals. Ninety-two percent of our graduates are college bound. Of these, eighty-three percent end up at their first-choice school. But not all our graduates see college as the best path to their happiness or professional success. For those who go without, I assure you: their successes in their chosen fields are almost one hundred percent."

Miranda grinned and nodded, all the while thinking, *Well, that will change once I take charge.*

Out loud, she replied. "For the college-bound, I'll make it my goal to best the current record."

"I love your enthusiasm. Miranda, with all my heart, I'm glad you came home to us."

Miranda tried not to snicker out loud at that.

"Clare will show you to your office while I move on to my next task." Lavinia sighed. "We've just learned that our literature teacher must take an emergency leave. Poor dear Mercy's pregnancy has been more difficult than she anticipated. And after two miscarriages…well, she feels it best to take the year off. I'd like you to head up the interview process for her replacement."

Miranda smiled. "On it. I'll go through the usual channels." She paused, as if a thought had come to her. "In fact, have you considered reaching out to Egan Gable?"

"Egan?" Caught by surprise, Lavinia blinked. "Considering his literary success, why would this position appeal to him?"

Miranda shrugged. "From what I've heard, sadly, his subsequent novels never caught fire like the first. And there was a recent blurb in Leah Garchik's *San Francisco Chronicle* column that he's now back in the Bay Area. His father recently passed and his mother, poor thing, is in a care facility. Egan is taking care of his parents' estate."

"So sad about his loss." Lavinia shook her head sadly. "And I know he had high hopes for his writing. At least he had one huge success."

"Yes, it certainly put him on the map," Miranda murmured. "For a short time, anyway." *Son of a bitch.*

His fictional depiction of her was galling. Even if the character had been a truer rendition, Miranda would never admit it because she found the character's name appalling: *Fanny.*

"You're right. It's a good idea to reach out to Egan. Thank you for following up," Lavinia exclaimed. "Heaven knows, in the brief time he was here he was popular with the students."

"Yes, we found him charming." Miranda smiled. "I'll see if I can find a telephone number and reach out to him."

OF COURSE, HE'LL DO IT, MIRANDA REASONED.

He's a failure. A loser. An egotistical louse who lives to impress those who don't know better. Like clueless teens and their wannabe parents who consider has-beens the next best thing to actual celebrities.

AA is perfect for Egan.

She reveled at the opportunity to make the call. To play his savior.

And more to the point, to get back at him for screwing her over with her Berkeley application.

It wasn't until she became a college admissions counselor that she discovered the truth about his dirty trick. As part of her job, she made annual pilgrimages to all the top-tier schools, Berkeley included. Over drinks with one of the school's recruitment specialists, she'd casually asked what was the *worst* thing an otherwise perfect undergraduate candidate could do in the admissions process.

"You mean, besides getting arrested for a felony?" He chuckled. "Well, let me think…" Suddenly, his eyes opened wide. "Ha! We once had a letter of recommendation from a former Ph.D. candidate—he'd also been a teaching assistant in the department." The man took a gulp of his beer and then stifled a burp. "Anyway, this guy had the audacity to write a letter recommending an admissions candidate to his faculty chair, whose wife he'd been caught boinking!" He winked at Miranda. "Here's the real irony: when the chair found out, he'd fired the guy. No way would he take the Lothario's recommendation!" He shook his head in disbelief. "In fact, the letter was written as if Lover Boy *knew* he'd be screwing over the poor kid who asked him for the recommendation."

"That's disgusting," Miranda muttered.

And now, years later, Miranda knew just how to get back at Egan.

He's down on his luck. His last six books flopped. His editor has retired. His agent dumped him.

I'll bet he's low on money. Why else would he be living in his parents' old house?

Egan's cell number wouldn't be easy to find, but his parents' phone number was easily Googled.

EGAN PICKED UP THE PHONE ON THE FIFTH RING. "YEAH, WHAT IS IT?"

He knew he should be polite—especially if the family's lawyer was on the other end of the phone line. The old coot was claiming it would take at least six months to settle his parents' estate. Until then, Egan wasn't allowed to sell their house, let alone salvage what was left of his father's savings for his mother's nursing care.

This realization had eviscerated whatever pride he'd had.

I can't support myself, let alone Mom.

If he sounded rude, so be it. Six scotches on an empty stomach made him ornery.

Sleeping in his old bedroom didn't help his mood either.

"Egan?"

"Yeah, speaking."

The voice sounded familiar. Maybe it belonged to one of his parents' friends. Those who were still alive had been calling all week, expressing their condolences. A few had even stopped by with casseroles and asked after his mom, not that they'd get off their duffs to visit what was left of her in the geriatric facility a mere two miles away.

In some cases, they brought copies of *Extracurricular* for him to sign.

A few times he'd noticed a bookseller had stamped REMAINDER on it. When that happened, he longed to throw the book at the culprit and shout, *Fuck you! Oh, and seriously? Do you think anyone will actually give you a dime for it on eBay?*

But by now he'd learned his lesson about keeping his cool. All it took was being tossed in jail for cold-cocking an off-duty cop in some New York Upper West Side bar for eyeing some woman's ass so longingly.

The woman was Egan's date.

Well, almost. He'd been in the middle of making his move.

Popping the cop in the jaw may have seen chivalrous at the time, but it had cost him too much, and not just the woman. It led to his publisher deeming him more of a liability than an asset.

Other publishers took that at face value.

The money went fast.

Fame was just as fleeting. These days, pick-ups occurred less frequently.

He prayed the call wasn't from some old bat with yet another casserole.

"Egan, I'm calling on behalf of Lavinia Thorpe of Ashbury Academy…"

Lavinia…

Audrey.

He hadn't thought of either of them in years.

Not in a conscious state, anyway. But with the amount of liquor he drank these days, those hours were fewer and far between.

Egan stammered, "Lavinia?… How is she?"

How is Audrey?

"You know our fearless leader—indomitable as always." The woman chuckled softly. "She would have called herself, but she is stepping into a meeting and asked me to do so in her stead. You see, an emergency has left the school without a literature teacher. She'd heard of your loss, and she sends her condolences, of course. It had her wondering if perhaps you'd be available to step into the position."

"Would I teach again at AA?" Emotions surged through him: curiosity, nostalgia, excitement, anxiety, hope—

Desire—

Shame.

Finally, he muttered, "I don't think that's a good idea."

The Miranda woman sighed longingly. "You were Lavinia's last hope. But she knew it was a long shot. And it would be quite an honor for the school, to have a *New York Times* best-selling author on the academic staff. That would mean a lot to parents! They seem to give more generously when underwriting chairs for prestigious instructors—"

The money.

If he were to get a cut of it above and beyond a teaching salary…

But I'm Egan Gable, damn it! I can teach at any university—

Okay, maybe not after the assault and battery charges…

"You know, I'd hate to let Lavinia down. Tell her I look forward to it."

"Wonderful! We'll look forward to seeing you tomorrow! Perhaps you can come in an hour early? You know. Get the lay of the land, as it were. At AA, some things never change, but a lot has too." The woman giggled at her poor attempt at a joke.

God, what a horrible laugh.

"Yeah, well, it'll be good to see some of the old crew—if they haven't all retired." He hesitated. "And, I guess Lavinia's daughter, Audrey, still lives in the area?"

"Oh, yes. In fact, she just retired from the board. But she shows up on campus intermittently. Who can stay away from the place that gave us the best years of our lives?"

"True." For once, he wasn't being sarcastic.

We're sure to run into each other.

Does she still hate me?

No, it's not possible. Otherwise, Lavinia would never have reached out to me…

Having convinced himself of that, he exclaimed, "Tell Lavinia I'll get there by seven to give myself time to settle in."

"Splendid!" Miranda Whomever gave a sigh of relief. "Oh! I forgot to add: the position entails heading up Debate Team as well. Lavinia hopes you won't consider it too much of an imposition since you already know the ropes. It'll be just like old times, right?"

"*Debate?*" Egan flinched at the thought.

His desperation for money stiffened his back again.

"Sure," he murmured. "Just like old times."

CHAPTER 27

The tip line to the FBI's San Francisco office rang incessantly before the only person in the bullpen, Lionel Porter Polk III, finally picked it up.

It was very early in the morning—just after six o'clock. Lionel had been reviewing the final summary of a case he and his partner, SallyAnne Jagger, had recently closed. It involved a stockbroker who had been making fraudulent trades to cover up his client's losses while he lived *la vida loca*.

SallyAnne had stayed until one in the morning, typing it up before leaving it on his desk. Despite her late night, Lionel had no doubt she'd be back in her cubicle at eight sharp. Her dedication was one of the things he found most endearing about her.

Well, that, and the fact she had no qualms speaking her mind, sometimes sprinkling in a few salty phrases that left him admirably slack-jawed along with anyone who might be the object of her ire, be it a suspect or their boss.

He'd often wondered if she also talked dirty in bed.

As much as he'd like to find out personally, he respected Sally-Anne too much to jeopardize their three-year professional partnership. Instead, he settled for admiring her from the mere few feet between their adjacent cubicles. Or even better, as they sat side by side in a stakeout vehicle. It was an imperfect compromise for a man married to his job and afraid of rejection.

The tipster refused to identify herself. No issues there. All calls to the bureau were instantly traced. Her ID came up as a Los Angeles area code. If her lead panned out, he'd have a way to follow up.

"I'm not sure, but I think what I have to report is illegal," the woman insisted. "You see, my husband sits on the trustee board of a private prep school. The trustees recently discovered that an administrative employee—the college counselor—was guaranteeing admissions placement into top Ivy League schools."

Lionel's ears perked up at that. "Which prep school?"

"I can't tell you that! My husband swore me to secrecy. I shouldn't be talking about it at all! But I'm just so angry—as are several other parents—at the increase in our tuition fees because of this debacle!"

Whether the counselor could or couldn't deliver, the situation had the distinct odor of fraud. "Were the fee increases tied to the counselor's success?" Lionel asked.

"If only!" The woman sighed longingly. "What parent *wouldn't* pay to have that sort of guarantee?"

Lionel was tempted to answer "A smart one," but he'd learned long ago to keep his mouth shut and let the informant rattle on.

"No," the woman admitted. "I mean, yes, she delivered, alright! For a pretty penny, I might add. But, as one of the board members informed the others, there actually is no way to ensure acceptance unless"—here, the informant lowered her voice to a whisper —"bribes were somehow offered to the colleges."

"And, if so, fraud has been committed," Lionel replied.

The informant sighed mightily. "That's why I called you! But to save the school from embarrassment, the trustees offered her a severance package to keep her lips zipped and go away quietly. The severance was five times her annual salary!"

Her. So the alleged suspect was a woman.

"And here's the kicker: they even gave her a letter of recommendation before she went on her merry way!" The tipster's voice shook with anger.

"You're right. It's B.S." Lionel words were strong, and his tone was fervent. Yes, he felt her pain. "I'll need the names of the parents who used the counselor's services in the past and got the college acceptances they'd anticipated."

The woman gasped. "I really don't want to name parents whose kids go to school with mine!"

"Ma'am, it's the only way we can build a case against the alleged suspect. And since your tip is anonymous, the parents will never know our source." This woman is lucky that SallyAnne didn't pick up the phone, Lionel thought.

Had the informant balked to SallyAnne, she would have threatened to charge the woman as an accessory after the fact. Lionel's technique was more velvet glove and less hammer, albeit Sally-Anne's hard-nosed tactics never failed to get results.

The tipster was silent for so long that Lionel wondered if she'd hung up. Finally, she whispered, "Okay, then. I guess we should meet."

Heck, yeah, we'll meet, Lionel thought. "Ma'am, to get this moving, I'll need the college counselor's name. And do you know if the counselor got a job at another school?"

"It's Miranda D'Arcy," the informant declared. She even spelled it for him. "I heard our Head of School mention she's now in San Francisco. The school is Ashbury Academy."

Lionel scribbled that down. He couldn't wait for SallyAnne to get back into the office.

Their next case had just fallen into his lap.

udrey's worst nightmares are coming true:

Despite being gravely ill, her mother does not want to give up her position of Head of Ashbury Academy, the school she created and nurtured into a success. Doing so means watching the status-conscious leaders of the school's trustee board change it core mission: keeping AA affordable, or free, for children who weren't born into wealthy families.

Not only that, Egan's return to the school puts Audrey's dark secret in jeopardy, especially now that twins Chuck and Charly are enthralled by him.

To make matters worse, Miranda's quest to burnish her reputation as the region's premier college admissions consultant includes some questionable practices that could put the school's reputation in jeopardy and entangle Egan in her plan of deceit.

OTHER BOOKS BY JOSIE BROWN

The Totlandia Series (8 Books)

Books 1 - 4 (The Onesies: Fall, Winter, Spring, Summer)

Books 5 - 8 (The Twosies: Fall, Winter, Spring, Summer)

The Housewife Assassin Series

The Housewife Assassin's Handbook (Book 1)

The Housewife Assassin's Guide to Gracious Killing (Book 2)

The Housewife Assassin's Killer Christmas Tips (Book 3)

The Housewife Assassin's Relationship Survival Guide (Book 4)

The Housewife Assassin's Vacation to Die For (Book 5)

The Housewife Assassin's Recipes for Disaster (Book 6)

The Housewife Assassin's Hollywood Scream Play (Book 7)

The Housewife Assassin's Killer App (Book 8)

The Housewife Assassin's Hostage Hosting Tips (Book 9)

The Housewife Assassin's Garden of Deadly Delights (Book 10)

The Housewife Assassin's Tips for Weddings, Weapons, and Warfare (Book 11)

The Housewife Assassin's Husband Hunting Hints (Book 12)

The Housewife Assassin's Ghost Protocol (Book 13)

The Housewife Assassin's Terrorist TV Guide (Book 14)

The Housewife Assassin's Deadly Dossier (Book 15: The Series Prequel)

The Housewife Assassin's Greatest Hits (Book 16)

The Housewife Assassin's Fourth Estate Sale (Book 17)

The Housewife Assassin's Horrorscope (Book 18)

More Josie Brown Novels

Secret Lives of Husbands and Wives

The Baby Planner

The Candidate

Hollywood Hunk (True Hollywood Lies series)

Hollywood Whore (True Hollywood Lies series)

HOW TO REACH JOSIE

To write Josie, go to:
mailfromjosie@gmail.com

To find out more about Josie, or to get on her eLetter list for book
launch announcements, go to her website:
www.JosieBrown.com

You can also find her at:

www.AuthorProvocateur.com

twitter.com / JosieBrownCA

facebook.com / josiebrownauthor

pinterest.com / josiebrownca

instagram.com / josiebrownnovels